Poisoned Ivy

M.D. LAKE

To Jenny,
Thanks for having me
here. I hope you enjoy
this !

md lake

AVON BOOKS ◆ NEW YORK

POISONED IVY is an original publication of Avon Books. This work has never before appeared in book form. This work is a novel. Any similarity to actual persons or events is purely coincidental.

AVON BOOKS
A division of
The Hearst Corporation
1350 Avenue of the Americas
New York, New York 10019

Copyright © 1992 by J. A. Simpson
Published by arrangement with the author
Library of Congress Catalog Card Number: 91-93011
ISBN: 0-380-76573-X

First Avon Books Printing: March 1992

AVON TRADEMARK REG. U.S. PAT. OFF. AND IN OTHER COUNTRIES, MARCA REGISTRADA, HECHO EN U.S.A.

Printed in the U.S.A.

RA 10 9 8 7 6 5 4 3 2 1

For my son Greg and his wife Monta
And Reed Allen, my grandson,
And my daughter Kaia and her husband Carey
And my wife Jo
With love

Many thanks to Dr. Garry Peterson, the Hennepin County (Minnesota) Medical Examiner, who cheerfully answered all my questions about cyanide except how it tastes: "How the hell should I know?" was his answer to that one. And Torild Homstad who put me on to her husband Keith, a man with practical experience in the use of cyanide.

One

It had been a dreary, early spring day, rain mixed with snow or the other way around, and the night wasn't any better. I was late, so I hitched a ride with Jesse Porter, who had the squad car. The campus police used to have three cars, but when the University fell on hard times, we had to get rid of two. In order to maintain themselves in the style to which they've grown accustomed, the administrators have cut back on such non-essentials as teaching and police protection.

Jesse drove slowly past Adamson Hall so we could take a look at the demonstrators huddled under umbrellas across the street. They were a small and dispirited-looking bunch. A half dozen campus cops, their rainslicks glittering in the light reflected from Adamson's windows, faced the group from the entrance to the building. They looked cold, too.

"Their hearts aren't in it," I said to Jesse. "It's not like the '60s."

"What do you remember about the '60s?" Jesse asked.

I tried to think. "Rocky and Bullwinkle," I said, finally. "Ringo and Mick Jagger. But my parents watched the six o'clock news, so I know a campus protest when I see one, and I don't see one here. Besides, what's the fuss all about? A dean's getting an honor he doesn't deserve.

Who's going to get tear-gassed, or clobbered with a riot stick over old news like that?"

"What's new," Jesse reminded me, "is that someone threatened to kill this dean."

He stopped the squad car at the curb next to the Administration Building, and I got out and dashed for the side door. Jesse called after me, "Save lives!"

I went down the stairs to the basement and pulled open the entrance door to the tunnel system that connects most of the buildings on the Old Campus. We use the tunnels in blizzards, heavy rain, and when the temperature plunges below zero, which it often does in the winter.

A couple, a woman and a man, were standing just inside the door as I came through it. She was short and blonde. Her head was tilted back so she could look up at him. "It was your idea in the first place, Bert," she was saying, "so why're you chickening out now, just when the fun's about to start? And let go of my arms."

"It's a dumb idea, Donna," he said, not letting go. He was tall, about six foot, and dressed in a yellow T-shirt with the sleeves ripped out, and baggy, bright green trousers. He must have been cold, since the tunnels aren't heated. His blond hair looked as if it had been cut with kitchen shears and his arms were long and sinewy. "Let's go somewhere," he said, "let's talk. Please."

"Let her go," I told him, roughening my voice a little. "I'm a cop."

He spun and stared at me. Since I wasn't in uniform, I took my shield out of my purse and showed it to him.

The startled look on his face faded, replaced by something like defeat or sadness. "Oh, shit!" he said. He let go of the woman and looked from me to her and back again. He swore one more time and then pushed past me, leaving the tunnel the way I'd come in. He looked as if he were going to cry.

"What was that about?" I asked her. I had to walk fast to keep up.

"Campus cop or city cop?" she asked, ignoring my question.

"Campus."

"You look like you could do better than that."

"I like what I'm doing," I told her.

"Why?"

"I think I can make a difference."

She turned to look at me. "As a woman?" she asked. She had a pale face that reminded me of every blonde child I've ever known who played the flute.

"That, too," I replied.

"Haven't you just plugged into the patriarchal system? Aren't you just a man in drag?"

She made statements into questions, the way people do who lack the courage of their convictions.

"No," I said.

She decided to leave it at that, since I didn't react and she probably didn't know where to go with it anyway. "You're on your way to the banquet, right? To try to keep the honored guest alive?"

"That's right."

"Those death threats were just somebody's idea of a joke," she said. "There are better ways of dealing with a man like Jeremiah Strauss than killing him. Don't you think?" She turned to look at me again, and this time gave me an ugly smile that marred the sweetness of her face.

Before I could ask her to give me some examples, we came to the flight of stairs that leads up into Adamson Hall. To my surprise, she started up them. She wasn't dressed for a banquet.

At the top of the stairs, a passage next to the kitchen leads into the dining room. As I hurried up behind her, I saw a tall figure in a powder-blue suit, his back to me, examining the invitation she'd extended to him. It was Lawrence Fitzpatrick, our best-looking cop. He handed back the invitation, and she continued down the corridor to the dining room. From there, she turned to look back at me.

She didn't say anything, just smiled that smile that defaced her prettiness.

Meanwhile, Lawrence was staring at something in the kitchen. I came up behind him and peered around him to see what it was.

It was Paula Henderson, another campus cop, and I could understand why Lawrence was staring. She was in the kitchen, talking to one of the cooks, who was sliding a tray into an oven. I'd seen Paula dressed up before, but never anything like this. She looked transformed, like Cinderella after a particularly inspired wave of the good fairy's wand. She was wearing an emerald-green dress that fitted her tall, lean body like a sheath, just enough off the shoulders to display her collarbone and the long neck I envied.

I whistled a low whistle. Lawrence jumped and spun around as if I'd goosed him. Paula glanced over at us.

"Who was she," I asked him, "the woman who just came through here?"

"Donna something," he replied. It was clear the question didn't interest him.

I went over to Paula. She looked me up and down. "You really spared no effort, did you?" she said, grinning.

"I don't know what you're talking about," I replied, pleased with myself and knowing exactly what she was talking about. "At least I'm able to carry my gun and walkie-talkie. You're not." It didn't look like there was any room in her tiny purse, much less on her body anywhere, for police equipment, except possibly a pair of handcuffs.

"Bixler didn't say anything about coming armed," she retorted, "he just said dressy. Besides, I've got *tae kwon do*. If the party gets rough, I'm prepared to kick an assassin through a window with an ancient grace that's in perfect harmony with the music of the spheres. What're you staring at?" she hollered over to Lawrence.

"You," he said honestly.

Although they were close friends during working

hours—they usually got to work early and played word games while waiting for roll call—Lawrence had obviously never seen Paula dressed up, or even looked at her closely before. It was having a devastating effect on him.

"What are you two doing out here in the kitchen?"

Lt. Melvin Bixler, our boss, was standing in the swinging doors that led to the dining room, his little stoat's eyes moving from Paula to me. Without waiting for an answer, he turned to Lawrence. "And what do you call that outfit you're wearing?" he asked him.

"I was wondering the same thing," Paula said to me under her breath. Lawrence had complemented his three-piece, powder-blue suit with ivory loafers with tassels. He made me think of a bowler dressed up for a TV awards banquet.

He looked down at himself, not knowing how to answer.

"And you, O'Neill," Bixler barked, swinging his gaze to me. "Couldn't you have done better than that?"

" 'There's lint on that skirt, girl,' " I chanted softly, " 'and that's not a crisp white blouse!' "

"Huh?"

"Nothing." I'd quoted a Chief I worked for once, in the Navy, a lifer, a lone woman hoping to pass for one of the guys among the other Chiefs. Bixler reminded me of her. "I'm waiting for a raise," I told him, "before I buy any fancy duds."

"Hey," Paula said to Bixler, "what about me? You haven't said anything about me."

Reluctantly Bixler looked at her. "You're fine," he said.

"Thanks, Lieutenant," she replied, and gave him her most gracious smile. It should have knocked him off his feet, but he was immune to the charms of black women. "And you look quite dashing yourself," she added.

Bixler had encased his body in evening dress, with a tartan cummerbund that strained to hold in a couple of decades of beer and chips with dip. He looked at Paula closely, searching for any trace of sarcasm on her face, and then he hustled us out of the kitchen and into the dining room. Lawrence was left in the kitchen, to guard the tunnel entrance against trespassers and check the invitations of any guests who came to the banquet that way.

The dining room was empty except for a waiter who was moving among the tables, putting down silverware. "Go check out the upstairs," Bixler ordered us. "Nobody's supposed to be up there tonight."

We were at the head table. Each place was marked with a name card.

"What's this?" Bixler stopped abruptly in front of a card that read "Jeremiah Strauss." Strauss was the guest of honor.

There was a thin manuscript next to his place setting, and on top of it a large red apple, brightly polished, just about the only color in the dining room.

"Waiter!" Bixler hollered. "What's this for?"

The waiter came over and said that Dean Strauss had come into the dining room a few minutes before and left the manuscript there, and the apple, too.

"Maybe it's a part of some diet he's on," Paula said.

"He's going to use it in his speech," the waiter said. "It's a prop. That's what he told me."

Bixler, who'd been holding the apple, examining it suspiciously, finally put it back where he'd found it. "Beat it," he said to us.

Paula and I went out into the foyer. A lot of guests had already arrived and were milling about, sipping wine and nibbling cheese and looking one another up and down surreptitiously—why, I couldn't imagine, since they all seemed to be dressed alike. I recognized the University president, Wolf, and the guest of honor, Strauss, talking together in a corner. Strauss loomed over the president. He loomed over everyone.

I looked for the woman I'd met in the tunnel. She was standing next to a man who looked like he might be her father. The woman was staring at Wolf and Strauss, her teeth bared in that ugly grin I'd seen before.

Paula and I went upstairs.

Two

Adamson was the University's conference center, built around the turn of the century. It was a beautiful old building, but the University had long since outgrown it and was forced to use hotels off-campus for large conferences. A new, much larger center was being built near the New Campus across the river. The University planned to tear Adamson down and put something modern and monstrous in its place among the ancient, ivy-covered buildings on the Old Campus. I'd seen a computer-generated photograph of the planned building. It was going to be mostly opaque glass that would reflect the surfaces of the more interesting buildings around it. A bizarre notion of creativity. Someday there'll only be buildings like that, and what will they reflect?

Paula and I stood on the mezzanine, looking down over the balustrade at the guests. I looked Paula up and down, grinned, and said, "You're not exactly unobtrusive, you know that?"

"That's right," she said. "I figured you'd be unobtrusive enough for both of us."

"What's the dress made out of?"

"Angora."

"You've been taking bribes, haven't you?" I accused her. "A cop gone bad. By the way, I do like how you've accessorized your outfit."

"Me, too," she replied, ignoring my snottiness. "My sister, Renee, owns a boutique. She loaned me the dress. The accessories, however, are mine." She flicked a complex arrangement of copper and glass dangling from an ear and then looked me up and down. "You, on the other hand, are dressed for your high school graduation picture."

I was wearing a dark skirt and an inexpensive white blouse. My one concession to the occasion was that I'd replaced the blouse's buttons with fancier ones. I'd read in a magazine in my dentist's office about how doing that would make a cheap blouse look more expensive. It apparently wasn't fooling Paula.

"Don't you even have patent leather pumps?" she asked.

"I've never felt comfortable wearing patent leather."

"Why not?"

I felt myself turning pink. "It's like a mirror, boys can see up your skirt," I said.

"Where'd you hear that?"

"Junior high. The nuns," I said.

"Don't Catholic girls wear panties?" Paula asked. Then she saw something below us that interested her more than hearing my response. "Look," she said, "there's Bixler, rubbing bellies with Dean Strauss."

Bixler was in the act of explaining something to Strauss, perhaps the security arrangements that night that were designed to keep him alive. Strauss seemed uninterested. He was scanning the room as if Bixler weren't there, something we all do after we've known him a while.

Although he was in his early sixties, Jeremiah Strauss had a full head of hair, a dirty-looking, reddish-gray mane that flowed around the sides of his head. I'd seen his smile a couple of times on television. It reminded me of a picture I'd seen of a crack in a sidewalk caused by an earthquake that had killed a lot of people. There was a child's shoe next to the crack, perhaps to give it moral scale.

Strauss was about six and a half feet tall, and probably weighed close to three hundred pounds. If one of the guests planned to kill him that night using a gun, Strauss would be a hard target to miss. Without knowing why, I glanced over to where the woman I'd met in the tunnel, Donna something, had been standing. She was no longer there.

We have an institution at the University called the University Scholars. It's made up of twelve distinguished professors, and once you're a Scholar, you're a Scholar until you retire, accept an offer from a rival university, or die, whichever comes first.

One of the Scholars—Emily Cauldwell, a professor of Genetics—died last winter and, after a selection process so secret that nobody seems to know for sure how it works or who the committee members are, a new Scholar was chosen to fill the gap. The new Scholar was Jeremiah Strauss, the Dean of the Graduate School.

The news surprised the entire campus. Strauss had been an administrator for so long that few people even knew that he'd once been a teacher and scholar. An editorial in the student newspaper wondered why somebody with such an outdated scholarly record had been selected for the honor over a number of active and excellent scholars, which included African-Americans, Native Americans, Hispanics, and women.

After the initial shock wore off, most of the faculty accepted the appointment with a shrug and a roll of the eyes. Most students didn't know or care what a University Scholar was anyway. Some of the women and minorities among the faculty and students, however, were outraged, and demanded an explanation from President Wolf. Wolf, of course, was unavailable for comment, but he sent one of his vice presidents, Bennett Hightower, to listen to the complaints and kiss them better. Hightower gave the protesters his solemn promise to look into the matter and that's where it seemed to end. Known as "The Black Hole," nothing that lands on or near Hightower's desk is ever heard from again.

The protestors went away, the fuss died down, and Wolf

set about arranging a banquet to honor the new University Scholar.

Then the threats began arriving.

The first arrived on April 1 and the last on the day of the banquet, two weeks later. There were four of them in all. The police didn't release the letters for publication but simply summarized them. They all said much the same thing: Strauss didn't deserve to be a Scholar; as Dean of the Graduate School, he'd crippled or ruined the careers of many fine scholars over the years; he'd probably engineered his own appointment to the ranks of the University Scholars; and he was occupying a place among the Scholars that should rightfully have gone to a woman or minority faculty member. All the letters concluded with the promise that Strauss wouldn't live long enough to enjoy the annual stipend that accompanied the honor.

Even though the first of the letters arrived on April Fool's Day, they were taken seriously. The campus police found that all of them had been typed on a single rental typewriter in the basement of the University library, probably at the same time. They were typed on good-quality bond paper with the University watermark, available to anyone who had access to a campus office.

The city police advised the University to postpone the banquet for a while. Jeremiah Strauss, however, refused to take the death threats seriously, and rejected the advice. It was rumored that those weren't the first he'd received in his fifteen years as dean. President Wolf, citing a university's moral obligation not to bend its collective knee to terrorists, supported Strauss, and went ahead and scheduled the banquet for Friday night of the second week in April.

"The dean looks like he could eat the Rooster, doesn't he?" Paula said, staring down fondly at Strauss and Bixler, as if she'd created them and was pleased with her work. "I wonder what's going on outside."

We went over to one of the recessed windows. The weather hadn't improved much. Sleet blurred the yellow light of the street lamp. The protesters were still clustered around it. Beneath us, around Adamson Hall's front entrance, the campus cops, cold and wet, were facing them. I was glad I'd drawn an indoor assignment that night.

I was about to turn away when I spotted the man I'd seen in the tunnel arguing with the young woman. He was standing off to one side, alone, holding an umbrella over his head, but still wearing the same inadequate clothing as before. He seemed to be staring straight up at us.

I pointed him out to Paula and told her about our meeting in the tunnel.

"I've seen him before," she said. "He's a juggler. He's been out on the Mall every day it hasn't rained or snowed since the end of winter. He's good."

At the moment, he looked like a clown at a circus funeral.

Three

By the time we got back downstairs, the guests were filing into the dining room. We waited until they'd all gone in, then followed them. Heads turned at the sight of Paula.

We stood up against a wall as far from the head table as we could get, Paula, Lawrence, and I, watching people maneuver for seating. Except at the head table, placed at a right angle to the other tables, there were no assigned seats. People just sat where they wanted to, or where they could find an empty seat.

"Break it up," Bixler said, coming up behind us. "Spread out. This *soiree* isn't for you." Bixler gets the same satisfaction from expressing the obvious that other people get from having a good bowel movement.

"Soiree," Paula corrected him.

"What'd you say?"

"It's pronounced *soiree,"* she said.

"What is?"

"Forget it."

"You lock the back door?" he asked Lawrence. Lawrence said he had. The look on his face as he moved reluctantly away from Paula was heart-rending. He was obviously smitten.

I heard someone call my name. I looked around until I spotted her, waving to me. It was Edith Silberman, a Humanities professor. She'd been my adviser on my senior

12

thesis, almost three years before. I'd chosen her because I'd taken several courses from her and liked the way she taught. I was lucky: Many students have trouble finding their advisers, even during their office hours, and get little time with them when they do. Edith Silberman wasn't like that. She loved literature and loved to discuss it with her students. I didn't have many teachers like her.

She was a short, wiry woman with dark, cropped hair threaded with gray and a burst of white hair at her left temple. Everything about her looked sturdy and comfortable.

"Hi, Edith," I said. "May I join you?" We'd been on a first name basis since she'd discovered that not only was she going to be my adviser but she was going to enjoy the experience. After I graduated, I continued to drop by her office for a while. I hadn't seen her recently; when her husband died about a year ago, I'd sent her a card.

"Here on business, are you?" she asked me as I sat down. "Going to keep our beloved Dean Strauss alive and well?"

I told her I was going to try.

"Well, stay alert," she said. "Those miserable cops outside are wasting their time and risking catching their death of cold to no purpose. If anything's going to happen to Jeremiah Strauss, it'll be one of us in here who'll do it."

"Us? You, too?"

"Of course," she said.

"You feel that strongly about him becoming a University Scholar?"

She laughed angrily. "Who'd want to kill Jerry Strauss for that? Besides, very few women commit political murder."

"What's he done to you?" I asked her.

"Always on duty, aren't you, Officer O'Neill?" she said, and changed the subject.

The entree was put down in front of us. Chicken Kiev, peas, a slice of apple stained with red food dye, the kind I always assume they've banned because it's poison.

"I hate Chicken Kiev," Edith muttered.

"Me, too," I said.

We stuck the sides of our forks into it simultaneously and watched as the butter oozed out of the wound and spread slowly around our plates.

I asked Edith why, if she disliked Strauss so much, she'd come to the banquet, and why she'd been invited in the first place.

"He had to invite me," she answered, "since he invited the rest of the Humanities department. Before he became dean, you know, he was a member of my department. I wasn't planning to come at first, but then I decided it might be fun. To remind him of what's in store for him when he returns to the department. Maybe torment him a little."

I asked her what was in store for him when he returned to teaching.

"Me," she answered.

We ate in silence for a while. The young woman I'd seen in the tunnel earlier, Donna, was sitting at the head table, down near the end, next to the man I'd thought looked as though he might be her father. He was short and sturdy, as she was, with sandy hair and puffy white sideburns. Even from where I was sitting, I could see that his face had once been handsome, and it was handsome still—at least from a distance—but largely through the effort of will that heavy drinkers are able to sustain for a time.

I pointed him out to Edith and asked her if she knew who he was.

"Don't stare," she said.

I looked back down at the melted butter congealing on my plate. The edges of the puddle were red, as if the chicken were bleeding.

"He's the University's chief attorney, and the young woman next to him is his daughter. He's a close personal friend of Jerry Strauss's. Wolf wants to get rid of him and, without Strauss to stand up for him, he probably will. Ru-

mor has it that that's Vice President Hightower's most
pressing assignment at the moment—finding a way to
dump Donald Francis Trask without creating a fuss."

"I think his daughter's name is Donna," I told her.

"It is. She's an only child."

"I'll bet her middle name is Frances, too," I said, "as in
Donna Frances Trask. But with an *e.*"

"Close, Peggy, but you've underestimated the man's
vanity. It's Francis, all right, but with an *i.* I know," she
said, raising a hand to stop me. "I know the feminine form
of Francis is spelled with an *e.* Tell that to Donald Trask,
but don't expect him to care."

"Did he want an heir or a mirror?" I asked. Edith just
shrugged and, using her fork, drew a pretty pattern in her
butter with the red stain from the apple slice. "How do
you know all this about her?" I asked.

"She was my advisee for a while," Edith said. "She also
took one of my courses—one of the same ones you took
from me."

I looked up again at Donna Trask and, as I did, her eyes
came up, too, seemed to meet mine, and then switched to
Edith. She stared at her for a long time before turning to
her father to whisper something in his ear. He didn't look
up from his plate, his expression of concentration never
wavering.

Edith made finishing our Chicken Kiev more bearable
with her commentary on some of the guests, in a voice she
didn't lower.

"See that gorgeously clad fellow sitting at the table next
to the head table," she asked me, pointing shamelessly
with her fork, "the man with the face that looks like it was
designed by a committee? That's Strauss's assistant dean,
Hudson Bates. He never manages to make it all the way to
the head table—not in any sense of the word—and never
will, but he always sits as close to it as he can. I'd keep
an eye on him, if I were you," Edith went on. "Over the
years, he's run a lot of sleazy errands for Strauss. Rumor
has it Jerry's paying off debts left and right, but leaving

poor Bates with nothing but the thing administrators dread most—having to return to teaching. Although I doubt he'd have the guts to murder anybody, writing anonymous death threats would be right up his alley."

Dessert arrived. It didn't sweeten Edith's mood. "All those women up there," she said, "with the blank eyes and bitter mouths, are the wives, aging Brünnhildes, still trying to dress like Gigi."

"Who's the woman sitting next to Strauss?" I asked her. He'd been a widower for years.

She shrugged. "An assistant to a vice president, I think, a glorified secretary. Probably ordered to sit with him so there'd be an equal number of men and women at the head table."

"Where's Trask's wife?"

"Donald Trask no longer has wives, and the kind of women he keeps company with now wouldn't be appropriate for a banquet like this. Donna often fills in as his consort, I've heard."

There was a stir of activity at the head table. I looked over in time to see President Wolf wipe his mouth with his napkin and say something to Strauss next to him. As Wolf rose from his chair, a loud scraping noise made me turn back to where Donna Trask was sitting. She'd shoved her chair away from the table and was getting up, too.

She looked down at her father and said something, then turned and walked quickly to the end of the table. President Wolf hesitated, puzzled, as she passed him. Her father started to get up, but fell back into his chair and stared after her as if frozen in place.

I looked to see if Paula, Lawrence, or Bixler were close enough to stop her, in case she pulled out a gun or knife. They weren't. We hadn't been told what to do if a dinner guest got up unexpectedly and made for Strauss, especially if the guest was the daughter of the University's chief attorney.

She stopped behind Strauss. He twisted to look back at her. As he did, she quickly reached over his other shoulder and snatched the apple from beside his plate. A few people laughed nervously in the sudden stillness of the room, maybe thinking this was a part of the festivities.

Donna walked to the small platform a little way from the head table and went behind the podium from which the dignitaries were going to speak. I noticed for the first time that she was even less appropriately dressed than I: a long white wool skirt, a white blouse with a high collar buttoned at the throat, and a navy blue blazer. It looked like an old-fashioned nurse's uniform.

She tapped the microphone with a finger. When nothing happened, she reached down and fiddled with a switch. The mike came on with a hollow, eerie noise.

From across the room, Paula was looking at me. Her eyebrows were raised. I shrugged. We weren't there to prevent Donna Trask from making a speech.

Donna smiled out at all of us, a smile of mean pleasure, of triumph—I couldn't describe it, then or ever. President Wolf had sat down again, trying to conceal an expression of outrage on his face; he didn't like public surprises. The look he gave Donna's father would have killed him if he'd seen it. But Donald Trask didn't see it. He was staring hard at his plate, as if hypnotized by something on it.

Donna Trask reached into her blazer pocket as she opened her mouth to speak. Suddenly, Jeremiah Strauss pushed back his chair and heaved himself out of it. Donna turned and looked at him. Then she held up the apple so we could all see it, turned it this way and that so it glittered in the room's soft lighting. Strauss was bearing down on her. Unhurried and in a loud, resonant voice, she said: "Eve's only mistake was in sharing this with Adam." She held the apple out to Strauss, now almost within reach of her, then put it to her mouth and took a huge bite out of it, and swallowed it as if enjoying the taste enormously. A flashbulb exploded from somewhere in the room.

Then her face contorted, first with terror and then with pain. Both her hands went to her mouth and she tried to scream, started to gag. As if struck in the stomach, she bent over so suddenly that she hit her head on the podium. The sound echoed through the microphone as she fell to her knees and out of sight.

People were rising from their seats all over the room, some of them crowding toward the podium. I had my walkie-talkie out of my purse and was calling the cops outside the building, telling them to detain anybody who tried to leave. Next I called the dispatcher at campus police headquarters and told him to send a doctor and an ambulance. I may not have been dressed for a banquet, but I was equipped for whatever this was. I glanced up and saw Bixler throwing people out of his way, trying to get through to the podium. I saw Donald Trask toss a drunken punch at Paula, who fended him off easily. At some point, a blur of powder-blue told me Lawrence was on his way to close off the exit through the kitchen.

None of this was any help to Donna Trask. She went into a coma almost immediately, and fifteen minutes later she was dead.

Four

It was a media circus, of course, and a feast for ghouls, for it had everything but sex: the University, the state's most hallowed institution; a female student murdered by mistake; a banquet in honor of the intended victim; distinguished scholars from all over the country. And the murder weapon, of course, a poisoned apple. It made prime-time television and the front pages of some of the bigger newspapers all over the country.

A color photograph of Donna Trask's last moments, taken by a University photographer who hadn't known her actions weren't part of the program, took up a third of the front page the morning after the banquet, and was shown on television repeatedly. In it, Donna was holding the apple a few inches away from her face, swallowing the piece that was about to kill her. Her eyes were on Dean Strauss. They seemed to be mocking him.

I couldn't keep my eyes off the photo. Finally, I crumpled it and burned it in my fireplace.

The speech Dean Strauss had intended to give at the banquet—his inaugural speech as a University Scholar—was entitled "Women in Academia: Past Achievements, Future Promise." According to the newspaper accounts, he'd been inordinately pleased with it and made no secret of what it was about among his friends and colleagues. He boasted that he planned to end it with a retelling of the story of Adam and Eve, arguing that, without Eve's rebellion against God, mankind (his word) would still be living among the animals in an enclosed garden somewhere. "All the progress we've made," he would conclude "our restless discontent . . . our striving . . . the unremitting rebellion against the status quo so characteristic of mankind (his word again), is thanks to Eve for having used her feminine wiles, her womanly charms, to lure Adam into taking a bite from the forbidden fruit, to seduce him into rebellion against God."

The closest he ever got to giving that speech was the excerpts printed in the newspaper several days after Donna Trask's death. When I read the account, I didn't find it difficult at all to imagine that somebody might want to poison him. I might have considered doing it myself.

Several days later, my friend Buck Hansen, a city Homicide lieutenant, and I were drinking after-dinner coffee and looking out the window at the lights of downtown to the left—his world—and the University to the right—mine—and the dark river running through both like a scar. It was a beautiful spring night, clear and cold outside, but with the promise of summer, not winter. Buck owns a condo that's high up and all curves, and the only reason I can enjoy being in it is because it's not mine. It feels like the inside of a spaceship to me, and I've never wanted to spend time in a spaceship, since it's a place in which you have minimal control over your own life.

"Okay, Buck," I said, "who did it? What're you holding back from the media?"

We hadn't discussed the case over dinner. Buck's a good cook—possibly a great cook, I wouldn't know. He expects his guests to appreciate what he's done, or at least not distract him from his appreciation of what he's done. I never go to Buck's hungry, but I sometimes leave that way.

"We're not holding anything back, Peggy. It's a nasty case. Unless we get lucky, we're not going to solve it very soon. Strauss had a lot of enemies, and you wouldn't have had to be present at the banquet to poison that apple."

I asked him why not.

"Because the damned thing sat on Strauss's desk for a good six hours before he left for Adamson Hall. His secretary bought it for him on her lunch break and gave it to him when she returned to the office. Anyone could have gone in and exchanged it for a poisoned one, either after she'd left for the night or during the day. Both she and Strauss were in and out a lot all day long. However," he added, "it's just as likely that somebody brought the poisoned apple to the banquet and exchanged it with Strauss's there."

As the waiter had told Bixler, Strauss had put an apple and a copy of his speech by his plate. Then he'd gone out to the foyer for wine and cheese and to be fawned over by the other guests as they arrived. Anybody able to enter the dining room unobserved could have switched apples.

Lawrence Fitzpatrick, who'd been assigned to check the invitations of people arriving through the tunnel, guessed that about a dozen people, singly and in groups, had come that way. Homicide investigators asked him if he thought he'd be able to identify any of them if he saw them again. Lawrence remembered that President Wolf had come that way, alone, and so had the victim herself, Donna Trask, although I had to remind him about her. He didn't recall anybody carrying anything suspicious—not that it wouldn't be easy to hide an apple in a raincoat or overcoat, which most people were wearing that night.

The poison that killed Donna Trask was cyanide. It had been injected into the apple in several places, the holes covered with wax, and the apple polished.

"She didn't stand a chance," Buck said. "Cyanide's got a pleasant smell, like almonds, for those who can smell it. Forty percent of the population can't. I'm one of them."

"How'd you find that out?"

"A couple of years ago, a fellow who worked in an electro-plating shop used cyanide to commit suicide," he replied. "Cyanide's used in electro-plating. I was called in because at first they thought it might be murder. I couldn't smell a thing, whereas the medical examiner couldn't smell anything else." He took a sip of coffee. "If Donna Trask smelled it at all, it didn't stop her from taking a huge bite out of the apple and gulping it down in her eagerness to make some dramatic point."

"Cyanide can't be all that easy to get hold of, can it?" I asked him.

"No, it's not. Besides its use in electro-plating, it's used as a fumigant and as a cleaning agent for some metals. Research hospitals, including the U's, stock it, too."

"What about Strauss's family?" I asked him. "From what I've heard, he's supposed to have quite a lot of money. A dissolute brother-in-law with a thin dark moustache, whose wife stands to inherit? A ne'er-do-well son or daughter?"

"He's a widower," Buck answered. "No kids, a few relatives scattered around the country, none close enough to have been invited to the banquet. He says he's leaving his money to a scholarship fund at the U in his name." Buck paused for a second. "I suppose the apple could've been poisoned before the secretary bought it—the random act of a sicko in a supermarket with a hypodermic."

"But you don't believe that."

"No, too much of a coincidence. The only people who ever seem to die that way are people who've never harmed anyone. Strauss has at least as many enemies as any administrator on campus. He's been Dean of the Graduate School a long time, and stepping on people is apparently the only exercise he gets."

"How did Donna Trask know what was in Strauss's speech?"

"Through her father. Strauss has a small group of colleagues he lunches with regularly at a restaurant near campus. A couple of professors, the deans of one or two other colleges, a tame regent or two, even Vice President

Hightower, and Donald Trask. Trask told his daughter about it. She decided to build her revenge on that."

"But revenge for what?" I asked. "Did she feel that strongly about him becoming a University Scholar?"

"Probably not," Buck said. "But she'd tried to get into graduate school. When she was turned down—her grades weren't good enough—she expected Strauss to intervene on her behalf. He wouldn't, or couldn't. Both of her parents agree that she was stubborn and hot-tempered, especially when she didn't get her way."

"Stubborn and hot-tempered, and in the wrong place at the wrong time," I said. "If she hadn't eaten the apple and died—if Strauss had, instead, she'd be a suspect, wouldn't she? She had a motive, knew about the apple, and passed through the dining room alone, after Strauss put the apple at his place." I held out my empty cup to Buck.

"A little more of the cheesecake, too?" he asked hopefully.

"No, thanks. One piece of cheesecake with shiitake mushrooms on it's enough for me."

"Not shiitake mushrooms," he said. "Kiwi fruit."

"Whatever." Buck seemed blissfully unaware that this nouvelle cuisine had gone the way of the yuppie some time ago. I wasn't about to break the news to him. He'd just find exotic new ingredients, and I was starting to get used to some of the old ones.

"I wonder what Donna planned to say before Dean Strauss got up and tried to stop her?" I said.

"Don't you think what she *did* say was enough? 'Eve's only mistake was in sharing this with Adam.' That's a pretty good speech in anybody's book."

"It was an exit line," I said, "but I don't think she meant it to be her entire performance. I think she meant to make a speech first, but didn't have time."

"What makes you think so?"

"Because she was reaching into her jacket pocket for something when Strauss got up. I saw it. I thought it would be a speech of some sort—or maybe notes for a speech."

"She didn't need notes," Buck said. "That single short sentence undercut Strauss's speech completely. He wouldn't have dared go on and give it, after that."

"I suppose so," I said, doubtfully.

"Maybe what you saw her reaching for in her pocket was a paper napkin, Peggy. Maybe she'd taken one with her to the podium to wipe apple juice off her chin."

"Was Donna angry about Strauss's becoming a University Scholar?"

"We haven't talked to anybody who thought she was a feminist. But we haven't been able to find many people who knew her well, either."

"What about that guy I told you about, Bert something?"

"Coombs. An odd one, a part-time student. Earns money for school by juggling—at least, that's what he claims. I'm not sure that's the whole story. He says he was Donna Trask's boyfriend. We talked to him, and he said all you overheard was a lovers' quarrel. But to be on the safe side, we got a search warrant and searched his place—a little dope, no cyanide. He's been busted for drugs before. We're investigating his background."

"He was begging her not to go to the banquet," I said.

Buck shrugged. "He admitted he didn't want her to go. He says he wanted her to spend the evening with him instead."

There was more to it than that, I thought.

I remembered what Edith Silberman had told me at the banquet, that Strauss and Donna's father had been friends. I asked Buck about that.

"That's right," he said, "they go back a long way. And Strauss blames himself for Donna's death. He thinks that if he'd taken the death threats more seriously, he'd have canceled the banquet, and Donna'd still be alive. He's taking the threats seriously now."

I knew that. A campus cop was stationed outside

Strauss's office during working hours. Strauss himself was armed too, although he didn't believe he had to worry about a direct attack, and neither did the police. Whoever had wanted him dead appeared to also want to remain alive and free to enjoy a Strauss-less world.

"You're not focusing on women and minority faculty members," I asked, "the ones who might have been angry enough to want to assassinate him?"

"No," Buck said. "But of course it's possible that one of them felt strongly enough about his being made a University Scholar that he or she sent the death threats, and then tried to kill him when the banquet went on in spite of them."

"I suppose you're getting a lot of pressure to solve this one fast."

"This is the first night I've taken off since Friday, Peggy, and I feel guilty about it. It's not just Strauss who's demanding action. Wolf is, too. I've been told that even the Governor's called, wanting to know how soon we'll find the killer."

"It's only been four days," I said.

"It doesn't usually take that long. Donna Trask's funeral's on Friday. Maybe the murderer will attend, and be so overcome with remorse for having killed the wrong person that he'll stand up and confess. Or she will."

"You going?"

"Of course. There'll be quite a lot of police there, in fact. After all, Jeremiah Strauss'll be there, too."

I looked at my watch, got up, stretched. It was almost ten o'clock, getting close to when I'd have to leave for work. I always work the dog watch, from eleven P.M. to seven A.M.

"How's Al?" Buck asked.

"Fine, I guess."

"You guess?"

"He's got his son living with him now."

"Really? I thought his kids only came here on holidays, or he went there—Nevada?"

"Arizona. That was then," I told him, "this is now. Looks like his son's here for good. He was driving both parents nuts, wanting to live with his dad. So Al asked his ex if he could have him, the way people do these days, and she finally agreed."

"Nice," Buck said. "For Al."

I said "For Al" at the same time he did, and we both laughed. We stood there another few moments looking at each other and smiling—his smile is beautiful—and then I asked him how his fellow cops were doing in their efforts to fix him up with their sisters, daughters, ex-wives, friends' ex-wives, and their neighbors.

"They must be losing heart," he said. "I haven't had to turn down a blind date in several months."

He got my coat and held it out for me, and I turned and stuck my arms into the sleeves. I do that for him, too. He followed me out to the elevators.

"When was the last time you saw him?" Buck asked.

"Al? Right after that last big snowfall in early March. We took his kid skiing at the zoo." Buck's elevator is slow.

"Family fun," he said, watching the digital dial above the elevator. "How old's the lad?"

"Fourteen, and he needs a mother. At least, Al thinks he does."

"You managing to fill the void?" Buck asked.

"Some of it," I admitted.

"Something'll come along," he said, "or someone."

The elevator arrived and the door opened. I stepped up to Buck and kissed him, not putting much more into it than some parents do with their kids, but a little more than a French politician bussing a rival.

The elevator took me back to earth safe and sound.

Five

I called Edith Silberman the next day and asked her if she'd have lunch with me some day soon. She said she'd be delighted. We compared schedules, couldn't find a suitable time, so I asked her if we could meet that afternoon in her office, after her last class, and maybe go someplace where we could talk.

She wanted to know what the rush was. I told her that, after sitting with her at the banquet, I remembered how much I enjoyed her company and how long it had been since we'd last gotten together. She sounded skeptical but agreed to meet me at her office at four.

She was right, of course, to be skeptical. Although I probably would have called her about getting together someday soon, it wasn't the pleasure of her company I wanted now. She was the only person I knew who'd had anything to do with Donna Trask—she'd been Donna's adviser, too.

More than the actual memory, the photograph of Donna in the last happy—or triumphant, at least—moment of her life haunted me. I wanted to know more about her, and about what had led her to that moment and to that particular death. I don't believe that people die only because they happen to be in the wrong place at the wrong time. It's even less believable if I've known them, and I'd known Donna Trask, however briefly.

I biked to police headquarters that afternoon, chained my bike to a rack, and strolled down College Avenue to the Old Campus, heading in the direction of the Humanities Building, where Edith had her office. I was early, had a good hour to kill among the students in rolled-up shirtsleeves taking advantage of the day, which was unusually warm for the middle of April. The good weather wouldn't last.

A small crowd of people and some colorful movement on the Mall in front of the Campanile caught my eye. When I got closer, I saw that it was Bert Coombs, Donna's so-called boyfriend. He was wearing the same outfit he'd been wearing in the tunnel, bright green pants and a yellow sleeveless shirt, and juggling three balls in front of him: red, yellow, and green. I went over and stood at the edge of the crowd watching him.

There was a tattered suitcase open on the steps behind him, and occasionally he'd turn and dig into it and come up with something new to juggle: hoops, bowling pins, fruit, vegetables, even knives that glittered dangerously in the sun. The onlookers, mostly students, would sometimes come up and drop a coin or bill into a tattered blue cap at his feet and then drift off, but more often they departed without making any contribution at all. It seemed a hard way to make a living.

His eyes kept darting to his audience as he juggled, and eventually they landed on me. A puzzled kind of recognition appeared on his face. "Hey, I know you from somewhere," he called.

"We met one night last week in Old Adamson," I called back.

He didn't say anything for a while, continued to juggle, glancing over at me every now and then. "I remember," he said, light finally dawning, "you're a campus cop." He flashed a grin. "Hey, come up here, cop, you can be my assistant. You can empty my cap for me. It's gettin' so full that there's no room for all these people to put their money in. Just dump it in my suitcase, okay?"

I did as he asked, then sat down on the marble steps next to him and watched him work. Paula had told me he was good, and she was right. He began juggling what looked like brightly colored bowling pins. A sudden breeze came up and one got away from him. It landed at my feet with a hollow thump, then bounced into my lap. I picked it up and held it out to him. It was a plastic bottle of some kind, which he'd wrapped with colored tape. He tossed the other two bottles high in the air, snatched the one I was holding out of my hand, and continued juggling all three. There was a smattering of applause, as if we'd rehearsed it.

"What color's your hair?" he asked me, not looking down. "There a name for it?"

"Red," I answered.

"Sure! And the sky's blue, grass is green, and snow is always white, ain't it?" He winked broadly out at the crowd, grinning. "Man," he added, "if I had an assistant like you, I bet I could double my take."

"You'd lose on the deal," I said. "I don't come cheap."

In spite of our banter, or maybe because of it, Bert's audience thinned out and, after a few more minutes, he gathered in the hoops he was now juggling, as if harvesting the sky, tossed them into his suitcase, and sat down next to me. Close up, his face seemed to be as stringily muscled as his thin, white arms. When he wasn't performing, he looked old.

"You're really a cop, huh?"

"Really. Your name's Bert, isn't it? My name's Peggy O'Neill."

"Yeah, Bert," he said. "You got a good memory." He hummed a snatch of the song I'd been named after, grinned slyly at me. "Catchy old tune." His face suddenly turned hard. "You fingered me to the cops," he said, "the real cops, I mean. Told them about me and Donna arguing in the tunnel."

"That's what cops do," I said, "even campus cops.

Somebody dies violently, you tell the cops—the real cops—everything you know."

"Her death was an accident," he said. "What they wanted from me was to know how come she got up there at the banquet and did what she did. Like they thought I was part of it."

"You were," I told him.

"I wasn't!"

"I was there, Bert, in the tunnel. Remember? I heard you talking. You begged her not to go through with it—even though it was your idea, she said."

"We were talkin' about something else," he said, his eyes meeting and holding mine without blinking, "something else entirely."

"What?"

"That's none of your business."

I knew he was lying and he knew I knew it, and we both also knew there wasn't a thing I could do. He was pleased about that; it seemed to relax him. He leaned back, resting against the cold granite base of the Campanile, looking up at a passing cloud.

"But what she did was stupid, too," he went on. "I mean, so she didn't get into grad school. So what? She could've gone to law school. That's what her old man wanted her to do, and then go into practice with him. What was she so mad at Strauss for that she wanted to get up in front of all those people and ruin the banquet for him?"

"And what was in the speech she intended to give?" I asked him.

He turned and stared at me. "What speech? She gave a speech, didn't she? A great one, too—nice and short!" He grinned crookedly, his eyes looking me over fast, not pausing anywhere long. "And if she hadn't died, it would've probably been the happiest moment of her life."

"I don't think she meant the speech to be that short," I told him.

"What makes you think that?" He folded his arms across his chest. "Is that what the cops think, too?"

"I was watching her pretty closely," I said. "I saw her reach into her pocket for something."

"You must have gotten that wrong," he said, shaking his head. "She didn't need to read what she said. She had it memorized. She did exactly what she told me she was gonna do. There wasn't nothin' else, believe me."

Sure. "She was your girlfriend," I said. "How'd that happen?"

"You mean, how come a guy like me was the boyfriend of the daughter of the University's top ambulance chaser?" He laughed, suddenly a little angry. "I don't know, maybe she liked slummin'. I never asked."

"I mean, how did you meet?" I said.

"We took a class together last year, and hit it off. We both griped a lot about all the work we had to do and complained about the teacher and all."

I had half an hour before I was due at Edith Silberman's office. I picked up one of the bowling-pin-like things he'd been juggling, tossed it in the air, and caught it by its neck.

"What do you call these things?" I asked him. "I thought they were bowling pins at first."

"Clubs. Why're you interested in Donna Trask?" he asked me, taking the club out of my hand and holding it in his lap.

"I'm just curious about her, about what made her mad enough to want to ruin the banquet for Strauss."

"She expected the son of a bitch to get her into grad school over the objection of the Humanities department. He didn't. That's all it took."

I said, "You knew Donna from a course you took together, you said. She was a Humanities major, wasn't she? Are you?"

"Not me," he said. "Where's the future in that? Bus. Ad., when I can afford it."

I waited for him to say something else, but he didn't.

He tossed the club into the air, caught it, and, reaching behind his back, returned it to the case.

"What course did you take together?" I asked him.

"A Humanities course. Business students got to take one of them, you know. We're supposed to get a well-rounded education." He didn't sound like he subscribed to the theory of the well-rounded education.

"I took a Humanities course once, too," I told him. "Spent a fortune on books. Taught by some woman— Silverman, I think her name was."

"Silberman, not Silverman. Jewish lady. Yeah, that's the course we took, too, Donna and me."

"She could really be opinionated," I said, shaking my head in disgust at a teacher who had opinions and let them show.

"That's your word," he said. "Mine's intolerant. She wouldn't accept any ideas but her own, just wanted to hear all the old ideas and didn't give a shit what her students thought. A real arrogant bitch."

"I take it you didn't exactly ace the course," I said.

"I got a D," he said with a shrug. "But that wasn't so bad, 'cause a D's okay in Bus. Ad., as long as it's not in somethin' important. But boy, did it piss Donna off!"

"That you got a D? Why?"

"Because she liked the paper," he told me, giving me another sly look out of the corner of his eye. "She thought it was pretty good."

He reached into his suitcase and picked up an apple among the things he juggled, and brought it out and put it in his lap. He reached back again and found one of his juggling knives. Then he starting peeling the apple in one long spiral.

"Lunch," he said.

"What did Donna get for the course?" I asked him.

"Her paper was better than mine, I guess, though it was pretty much the same. She ended up with a C. That pissed her off, too, naturally, but what really got her was the comment Silberman wrote on her paper: 'Read this again in five years and see what you think.' "

It was true that Edith was a little short with people she thought were fools.

"Y'know," Bert went on, "I think it was right then Donna decided she was going to get into the graduate program in the Humanities department. I don't think she'd have done it, if it hadn't been for the way Silberman treated our term papers."

"But she didn't get in."

"Nah, her grades weren't good enough. At least, that's what they said. Donna thought Silberman was behind it. So she went to Strauss for help—she'd known him since she was a little kid, you know—but he wouldn't do nothing. Claimed he couldn't." Bert laughed suddenly, and held a piece of apple in front of my mouth with his grimy fingers. When I shook my head, he put it into his own mouth instead. I waited for him to die. "I bet he regrets that now," he said.

"Sorry I'm late, Bert. I'm ready, anytime you are."

I looked up. A man was standing at the bottom of the steps, his eyes going from Bert to me and back again. He looked about twenty-one or twenty-two, tall, heavy, with long, dark-brown hair and a pleasant face, wide-set eyes just the opposite of Bert's. He was wearing old jeans, an even older Army shirt with the traces of a private's insignia on the rolled-up sleeves, and carrying a guitar case.

"My roomie," Bert said to me, getting to his feet. He wiped apple juice from his lips with the back of his hand, and the back of his hand on his baggy trousers. "Omaha. That's your real name—right, Omaha?" He grinned his tight grin, using lots of small muscles around his mouth.

"Yeah." Omaha grinned, too. His grin was slow and easy. He didn't look as if he did anything that required a lot of work, especially with his head.

He climbed up to us, put his guitar case down next to Bert's equipment case, and knelt to open it. It contained juggling stuff, too.

I said, "So Donna got the idea to ruin the banquet for Strauss because he wouldn't use his influence to get her into the Humanities graduate program?"

Bert picked up his daggers and set them in motion, catching them by the handles. He was standing too close to me. But when someone juggles daggers that deftly, how far away is far enough? "Yeah, right," he said. "She just decided to play a little practical joke on the guy, you know? That's all it was supposed to be."

He suddenly tossed a knife in a high arc over my head. I turned to look behind me. Omaha was there, caught it by the handle and returned it the way it had come. I didn't want to be part of the act, so I moved aside. Bert laughed as the two men passed the knives back and forth. Light danced in his eyes, as if now he were really living.

"She was kinda nuts, you see—Donna was," he went on, grimacing with concentration, showing his irregular, yellow teeth. He threw out a long arm to catch a wayward knife from Omaha. "She thought Strauss'd tricked her into thinkin' he'd get her into the Humanities program. People were always 'tricking' Donna, you know. That was just about her favorite expression. What the fuck you been smokin', Omaha?"

Omaha had dropped one of the knives. He caught the other two, and held them while he retrieved the one on the ground.

"She was really lookin' forward to the banquet, to doin' what she did, you know?" Bert went on, grinning through his concentration. "And she did it, too, didn't she? She must have died happy." His brow furrowed suddenly. "Though, in another way," he said, "she saved the son of a bitch's life by taking a bite out of that apple. I mean, she died for Strauss, like in the Bible! She probably wouldn't like knowing that. I'm not sure the joke would have been worth it—not even to her." He laughed wildly, turned to Omaha. "C'mon, Omaha, toss 'em?" To me he said, "So long, Peggy O'Neill, see you around!"

Six

A student was coming out of Edith's office when I got there. "I'll try," she called back through the door. She was struggling to look brave.

"That's all it'll take, I'm sure," Edith answered gruffly. "You've got a good mind, but it wants a will determined to put it to some use."

The student hesitated, as if not able to understand that thought and walk simultaneously. Then she smiled inanely at me and took off down the hall.

I peeked into the office. "Is it safe to come in?"

Edith was putting some papers in a desk drawer. "I need a drink, Peggy. I've taught a two-hour graduate seminar this afternoon, and just finished spending another two hours with a bunch of undergraduates whose most burning question was how long their term papers are supposed to be. How about we walk over to Frazier's—it's close to where I live. Do you know it?"

"No, sorry," I said.

"You've spent the last what?—five, six years?—on this campus and you don't know Frazier's? You must prefer the noisier bars, full of students and rock 'n roll. Frazier's is quiet, with neither video games nor big-screen television, and the jukebox's been out of order since 1956."

I smiled instead of saying that I preferred no bar at all. We didn't talk much as we walked across campus; Edith

35

looked like she needed time to shift out of teacher mode. I could see Bert and Omaha, doing some kind of tumbling tricks in the lengthening shadow of the Campanile to a thin crowd of onlookers.

We were about to cross College Avenue at Frye Hall when the University patrol car pulled up, and Lawrence, in the passenger seat, leaned out and waved.

"Friends of mine, Edith," I said, and went over to say hello. I expected her to follow me, but instead she continued on across the street. She called back, "I've got to pick up a book I ordered before the bookstore closes." She had to shout the last words at me, as she disappeared into the bookstore on the other side of College Avenue.

I asked Paula and Lawrence what they were up to, since we usually patrol alone, not in pairs. Lawrence turned pink and said nothing, while Paula leaned across him and explained. He'd been patrolling on foot that afternoon. As she'd passed him in the squad car, he spotted her and threw himself suicidally in front of it. So she'd been forced to stop and pick him up, and now they were on their way over to one of the fast food places for a quick dinner before resuming their patrols. Lawrence sat there beside her and nodded, apparently staring at nothing. I assumed he was tongue-tied with love, thanks to the unseasonably warm spring weather.

They drove off, and I crossed College and went into the bookstore after Edith. When she'd paid for her book, we continued on our way to Frazier's Bar and Grill.

When I was a kid, if I was lucky, my dad would pay my way into a matinee at the movie theater next to his favorite bar. If I wasn't so lucky, I'd have to sit with him in the bar, gradually forgetting that outside the sun was shining as he outlined his future plans and past triumphs to his drinking buddies. That's one of the reasons I don't like bars, especially when it's still light outside, and why I don't ever go to matinees.

The cocktail waitress was there as soon as we sat down. Edith asked me what I was drinking.

"Whatever kind of sparkling water you've got," I told the waitress. "I'm not particular."

Edith gave me a raised eyebrow sort of look. "It's soda water from the hose," the waitress said, speaking to me through tilted nostrils, as if they were tiny loudspeakers. "You pay the same if there's booze in it or not, okay?"

"Okay," I echoed, giving her an agreeable smile. I wondered what she'd do if I'd said it wasn't okay. Douse herself with kerosene, probably, and set herself on fire. "Luckily, I don't go to bars much," I said to Edith after the waitress had gone away. "I don't think I could stand paying three bucks for sparkling water more than a couple of times a year."

I half expected her to get defensive, say that she didn't go to bars much, either, and I was glad when she didn't. Instead, she looked at me as if to make sure I was okay with this and, satisfied, leaned back against the dark green plastic of the booth and waited for the drinks to arrive. When they did, she took a big swallow of her Scotch.

"I needed that," she said, a smile of perfect happiness on her face. "Teaching can still be the greatest pleasure there is—even greater than sex, I think. At least I think so now—having been a widow for over a year." She ran fingers through her thick hair, the smile of contentment still on her lips. In the gloom of the bar, I couldn't see the gray threads I'd noticed at the banquet, just the burst of white at the temple.

I said I assumed her seminar had gone well.

"It did! I can still attract good graduate students, and today they really came through. I spent most of the time just trying to keep up with them."

"Still?" I repeated. "You think you're getting too old to attract good students?" She couldn't be more than fifty-five, I thought.

"I don't think so, but some of the younger members of the department do. Not too old exactly, either, just too old-fashioned in my views. I'm one of the old guard, you see.

I still believe it's possible to find meaning in a text. And that doesn't make me very popular in my department."

"What do the others believe?"

"That there's no discoverable truth in anything, including life."

"But isn't that a truth?" I asked.

"You always were a quick study, Peggy. Of course it is. But it's okay for them to possess that one truth, because they've managed somehow to avoid all the lies that people like me are caught up in. They're privileged, you see. Now, why'd you all of a sudden want to have lunch with me? Just the fortuitous meeting at the fatal banquet for Jeremiah Strauss?"

"That, too," I said, deciding to tell her the truth. "But the real reason is that I'm interested in Donna Trask."

"Why?"

"I bumped into her in the tunnel on my way to Adamson, just before the banquet. She was quarreling with her boyfriend, a guy named Bert Coombs. I'm interested in knowing more about her. You told me you were her adviser."

"Only for a short time. She switched to one of the younger faculty members after I tore apart the paper she wrote for my class—and the paper she wrote for Bert Coombs, too, by the way."

"I kind of gathered she'd written his paper for him," I told her.

She leaned across the table at me, elbowing her drink aside. "Peggy," she said, "those papers were so bad that I can't believe she expected they'd get away with them. I'm convinced that, on some level, Donna wanted to do badly in my class, didn't want to get into our graduate program. I think she even used Bert Coombs and wrote that paper for him as a kind of joke she was forcing me to take seriously, at least long enough to read the paper."

"Why do you think she didn't really want to get into your program?"

"How should I know? I gave up trying to figure students out a long time ago! I'm just a teacher, not a psychiatrist or chaplain. But almost from the first week of class, I believed that Donna's behavior was a cry for help. All semester long, every piece of work she turned in was full of resentment, as if she were deliberately holding back whatever creativity she had, or making a joke out of it. I confronted her about it once. I called her into my office and told her that's what I thought she was doing. She just laughed in my face, said I didn't like her and was out to get her. After that, I left her alone. She had a shameful smirk, Peggy. And she died with that smirk on her face, too."

Edith finished her drink and waved her glass at the waitress, who brought her another one. I sucked ice. Edith took a slug of her new drink, then put it down with a bang. "Then came the term papers," she continued. "I knew I hated—no, that's too strong a word—I knew I was biased against Donna, and I was afraid I wouldn't be able to grade her paper objectively. But that was one concern I didn't need to have. It was easy to give her a C for her paper and just as easy to give Bert an F. And yet I was so spooked by her that I hesitated. I seriously considered giving her paper a B—maybe even an A—just to get her out of my life with a minimum of trouble. With a C, I knew she'd come stomping into my office and start screaming, which is exactly what she did. And when that didn't work, she applied to our graduate program. And when she got rejected there, she marched over to Jerry Strauss's office and, I guess, demanded that he use his influence to get her into the program."

"But he couldn't get her in," I said.

"No. That SOB's got a lot of power, but not even he can force a student on a department that doesn't want her. Luckily for me, Donna had done poorly in other courses, and her overall GPA wasn't that great either. It wasn't just me who stood in her way although, as chairman of the graduate selection committee, I did cast the tie-breaking vote. I thought briefly of abstaining, because I disliked her so much—trying to be 'fair,' you know! Maybe she'd still be alive if I'd let her in."

I noticed that Edith didn't look at all guilty about Donna's death. She finished off her drink in a gulp, then looked at her watch. "I've got a dinner date at eight, and I have to go home and get cleaned up. I hope I've given you what you wanted, and you can let it rest now."

"No," I told her, "I can't. I want to know more about Donna Trask. I want to know what kind of rage would compel a person like her to get up in front of all those people—the University's movers and shakers—and ruin a banquet for a man? I want to know what created that smile that made her so goddamned ugly. You say it was a shameful smirk. Maybe so. But whatever it was, it reminded me of when I was in kindergarten. There was a girl who made the prettiest pictures of any of us, but when she was finished with them, she'd take a black crayon and cancel them out with angry slashes. Donna Trask's smile was like those crayon slashes."

"What became of her—the girl in kindergarten?" Edith asked.

"One day she wasn't there anymore," I answered. "I never found out what became of her. I want to know what became of Donna Trask."

Edith got up suddenly and squeezed out of the booth, dropping money on the table to pay for both of us. "She died," she said harshly. "Leave it at that, Peggy. There was something compulsively destructive about her," she added as we walked to the door, "as if she wanted to destroy herself, but didn't quite have the guts. So she tried to destroy other things in the meantime, as a kind of stop-gap measure. That's what I think. But all I really know is that I'm glad she's out of my life. I'll be able to forget her. I hope you will, too."

"Not just yet," I said.

Seven

The next day, the newspaper reported that the police, after six days, had nothing new to share with its readership concerning the death of Donna Trask. The University president, Wolf, was quoted as saying his confidence in the abilities of the police was still largely unshaken. Jeremiah Strauss, the dean of the Graduate School, wasn't as generous. After all, as the newspaper reminded us, Strauss had been a longtime friend of Donna Trask and her family, and his own life was still at risk as long as the killer remained at large. Donald Trask, the victim's father, was quoted as saying he hoped the killer, having destroyed an innocent life, would show remorse and come forth and confess.

I dusted my apartment for the first time in a month, in preparation for possibly vacuuming it sometime in the next week or so, and then biked over to the campus, arriving at police headquarters a little before two. I had a three o'clock racquetball date, but first I wanted to talk to Ginny Raines, my oldest friend among the campus cops.

The University Police Department is housed in a wooden two-story building on the edge of the Old Campus. Built in a hurry at the end of the Second World War, it was meant to last just long enough to provide extra classroom space for GIs returning to school. It was supposed to be torn down when they graduated and the area returned to pre-war normal: grass for the students, stone benches for the faculty, and a statue or two of a long-departed administrator for the birds. But then the baby boomers came along—the kids the GIs made before, between, and after classes—and by the time they graduated, there was no one left who remembered what pre-war normal had been, or that the old temporary building hadn't always been there, so it never occurred to anyone to tear it down. Winter as well as summer it was like an oven, and when the faculty finally refused to teach in it anymore, the building was given to the campus cops.

Ginny was the first woman hired and she managed to cut through the discrimination to become a lieutenant. She's thirty-five, short and dark, and looks almost as tough as she is. Spending most of her time at a desk now has her convinced that she's getting fat.

She was tapping computer keys with one finger while reading the results into a phone. When she saw me, she gave me a smile and a wave. I sat down and eavesdropped. She was talking to somebody on the city police's fraud squad about a student's unauthorized use of University invoices to furnish his and several of his friend's apartments with the advanced electronics necessary for a successful academic career these days.

I'd left the door open. Paula stopped as she passed by in the hall to say hello. Lawrence stuck his head in over her shoulder, grinning fatuously. Paula looked disgusted. Both of them were in uniform. We exchanged small talk, and then Lawrence told Paula it was time for them to head out on patrol.

"I'll walk out with you," he told her.

"Will you carry my gun for me, too, sir?" she simpered.

He didn't answer, just turned a shade pinker than he already was. She laughed at him and, hand in hand, they walked down the hall together.

"No wonder you work nights," Ginny said to me, putting the phone down. "You're spared scenes like that."

"How long has it been going on?" I asked her.

"Since Adamson Hall, I guess. Lawrence hasn't been

the same since. He walks around as if somebody'd just dropped a plate of hot spaghetti in his lap."

"That was the first time he'd ever seen Paula all dolled up," I told her. "It took him by surprise."

"It did a lot more than that to him."

"How's Paula taking it?"

"I don't know. I think she thought it was funny at first. Now I think she's wondering what God hath wrought and what the harvest might be."

"I don't think it was God," I said. "Spring can be a dangerous time of year for all living creatures. I only hope he doesn't get hurt. He's a nice guy. They're both nice."

When we'd exhausted that topic, I asked Ginny if she knew anything about Donald Trask, the University's chief attorney.

"Why?" She looked at me suspiciously.

"His daughter got murdered."

"I know that. Why?"

"I was there when it happened."

"That's right. How could I forget?" she taunted me. "You might have been able to prevent it, if you'd been more on your toes. You actually had the murder weapon in your hand, didn't you, and you could have eaten it, instead of her. You could have made the supreme sacrifice."

"Actually," I said, "it was Bixler who had the apple in his hand."

"Too bad he wasn't ravenously hungry at the time," she said.

She told me that she'd had to deal with Trask a few times in criminal cases. The most recent ones involved a custodian and a professor in the Medical School.

"We had 'em both cold," she said, "and for felonies just as serious: Misusing University funds. Trask took the evidence I gave him against the custodian and used it to pressure the guy into quitting. In the case of the Med School professor, he glanced through the evidence, thanked me for my hard work, and, with me standing there, dropped it in his wastebasket. He told me he'd talk to the man, but the case was closed. I was angry, but you don't want to show it to a man like Trask. I said he'd better not leave the evidence in the wastebasket because one of the other custodians might find it when he emptied it, and give it to Clemsen, the guy who'd been fired for the same thing. Trask's face was even more red than usual, but he kept his cool and just thanked me for my concern. I bet he retrieved the evidence from the wastebasket and put it in his shredder before I was out of the building."

She brooded for a moment, then looked at me. "That's the only personal experience I've had of him. There's a rumor, though, that he's been on Wolf's hit list for a long time and in danger of losing his job. Somehow he manages to hold onto it year after year."

"Why? Because he knows how to bend the laws?"

"That's a *sine qua* for a university attorney, of course," Ginny said with a shrug. "No. So far, he's been protected by Jeremiah Strauss, his old friend."

"Strauss's influence reaches that high?" I asked her.

"You bet. When Strauss speaks, the president listens."

"Why? What power does a dean have, anyway?"

"Depends on the dean. Strauss is dean of the Graduate School, which means he controls a lot of research money for equipment, labs, paid leaves of absence, travel—you name it. And he's got contacts with every major grant-giving foundation in the country. You get on Jeremiah Strauss's hit list, and all of a sudden you can't afford to buy paper clips, much less take trips to study the elimination habits of mollusks in the Yapp Islands, or whatever it is you do around here to get advancement and salary increases. You'd better just cut your losses and look for another job."

Ginny reached behind her, opened her refrigerator door, pulled out a Diet Coke, and offered me one. I shook my head as I watched her pop the top and take a slug.

"But Trask's drinking and womanizing habits are starting to become an embarrassment—even around here," Ginny went on, "and Strauss is losing patience with his old friend. That's bad news for Trask, if true. Out in the private sector, he'd have to chase ambulances, and I seriously doubt that he could catch enough of them, in his present condition, to feed his needs." Ginny emitted a whispery cola belch. "Now c'mon, Peggy, what's your interest in Trask and his daughter?"

"Pure curiosity," I assured her, "from watching her die at what looked like one of the happiest moments in her life—or most triumphant, anyway. And I talked to her, too, for a moment—"

"Right," Ginny interrupted, "you told me that. The two of you had a deep, meaningful relationship, didn't you?" She studied me over her pop can for a long moment without speaking. Then she said: "I think you're in danger of becoming a ghoul, Peggy, a kind of psychological coroner, you know? You don't know that was the happiest moment in her life."

"Don't be so literal," I said. "Of course I don't. But if it wasn't the happiest moment, it was one of them."

"So what? She's dead," Ginny said. "I don't know what her problem was. However, I do know there are a lot of people out there who're unhappy, not because they feel sorry for her, but because she intercepted a death meant for Strauss."

"You investigated the death threats against Strauss, didn't you?" I asked her. "What'd you find out?"

"Well, I can rattle off the names of a dozen people whose hearts would beat as happily as clowns on pogo sticks, if they heard Strauss was dead."

"Who else, besides the people upset because he's occupying a place among the University Scholars that ought to go to a woman or a minority faculty member?"

"One of my favorite candidates is Myles Kruger, an associate professor in History, who thinks he'd be a full professor now if it weren't for Strauss."

"How did Strauss derail his plans for advancement?"

"Kruger cheated on his wife. Strauss found out about it. Apparently Strauss has set himself up as the University's morals' cop—or sexual behavior cop, which isn't exactly the same thing."

"That's kind of spooky," I said.

"Yeah, and it gets a little spookier. Kruger's wife discovered what her husband was up to, too, and she filed for divorce. Kruger asked her to give him another chance and she agreed. They went to counseling together, and everything was starting to look rosy again. And then Kruger applied to the Graduate School for a travel and research grant for a book he was working on. Strauss turned him down. Kruger thinks it was because he—Strauss—didn't like Kruger's morals."

"What business is it of Strauss," I asked, "the private lives of the faculty?"

"We've got to keep up the standards, you know," Ginny said, "for the youth of today, tomorrow's adults. Which really means that Strauss doesn't like people he suspects are having more fun than he is."

"How does he pick up all this dirt?"

"Who knows?" she said with a shrug. "Maybe he's got spies everywhere."

"If Strauss has done a lot of this sort of thing," I said, "why is Myles Kruger your favorite candidate for Strauss's attempted murder?"

"*One* of my favorite candidates." She took a sip of her Coke. "Because Kruger freaked out. According to some of his colleagues, he thought that it was Jeremiah Strauss who tipped off his wife about the affair in the first place. He started making anonymous phone calls to Strauss, late at night. Strauss had a tap put on his phone, and the police caught Kruger. In order to avoid prosecution, and losing his job, he had to agree to get psychiatric help, which he's still doing. Apparently, his marriage is back on the rocks—a 'trial' separation."

"That's an ugly story," I said. "Not a redeeming social value in it anywhere. You have more like it? Who're some of your other favorite suspects?"

"Over the years there've been a number of former fac-

ulty members here—men and women alike—who've
gone away mad, for one reason or another. Some of them
have been indiscreet enough to send Strauss nasty letters. Strauss saved all those letters, being a canny,
forward-looking man. But next to Myles Kruger,
my personal favorite is a woman in the Humanities
Department—Strauss's department, too, you know, before he became a dean."

I sat up straight. "Who?"

"Edith Silberman. You probably took classes from her."

"She was my adviser," I said. "I also sat next to her at
the banquet for Strauss. And I talked to her about the case
yesterday afternoon."

Ginny got all professional suddenly. "What'd she say?"

"Why's she so high up on your suspect list?" I count-
ered.

"She went to Strauss's office in January and, in front of
witnesses, threatened to kill him."

My lips felt strange as I asked Ginny what she'd done
that for.

"She thinks he's had a vendetta against her for years,"
Ginny replied. "Fifteen years ago, before he became dean
of the Graduate School, Strauss was chairman of the Humanities Department. Silberman was up for promotion to
full professor. The rest of the Humanities faculty supported her, but Strauss said he didn't think she was
ready—she hadn't published enough. So he voted against
it, which meant the University turned her down. The same
thing happened the next year. She finally did win promotion, but only after the affirmative action regulations became tighter and there was a good chance she could have
won a discrimination suit against the University."

"But that was a long time ago," I said. "What's Strauss
done to her recently?"

"Withheld a teaching award from her, apparently. Her
graduate students put her up for it. It's quite a prestigious
thing, and carries a nice monetary prize, too. It's awarded

by a big local corporation—on the recommendation of the dean of the Graduate School."

"Damn," I said. "Edith's a wonderful teacher." I watched my knuckles turn white on Ginny's scarred old desk. "It just proves what I've always said. Murderers always kill the wrong person!"

Ginny laughed. "Then, if Strauss had died instead of Donna Trask, he would've been the wrong person, too."

"What's your point?" I demanded. Not waiting for an answer, I asked her what Edith had said to Strauss that sounded like a threat.

Ginny got a file out of one of the boxes on her desk and thumbed through it. "It was quite memorable, just the sort of thing you'd appreciate, Peggy—unfortunately. Both witnesses agree with Strauss that she said the only reason she didn't kill him was because she couldn't think of a way to do it safely. Sticking him with a knife would put her in danger of the escaping sewer gas, and a bullet might cause him to explode, endangering the lives of innocent bystanders." Ginny paused, looked up at me, and then added: "According to the witnesses, Professor Silberman came up with a third possibility. Can you guess what it was?"

"I think so," I said, my heart down around my ankles. "Poison."

"Yeah." Ginny closed the file and put it back where she found it. "She said that someday, at feeding time, she was going to put poison in his slop."

Eight

I gave Ginny the gist of what Edith had told me at the bar the evening before. It didn't interest her much, since there wasn't anything about her relationship to Strauss, only about Donna Trask. Then I had to hurry off to my racquetball date.

My opponent that afternoon was an associate professor of psychology, a tall, angular woman who'd been moving steadily up the racquetball ladder as if her career depended on it, and now she was knocking for admission to my rung. I don't think she thought it appropriate that a mere campus cop should be standing in her way to the top.

I was so preoccupied with what Ginny had told me about Edith that I almost lost the match, making my opponent look better than she was. As we were standing under the showers afterward, she told me she'd been working day and night on an article "of some importance"—those were her words—and she apologized for her game being off. She gave me a strange look as I left the shower trying not to giggle.

I only giggle when I'm feeling frustrated, stressed, or worried, and I was worried about Edith. Threatening Jeremiah Strauss hadn't been the most judicious act of her life, but I could understand it, especially if she had no intention of carrying out her threat. I knew she was hot-tempered and impulsive.

I'd noticed that she sometimes called him "Jerry" and then corrected it to "Jeremiah," or "Strauss." I wondered what had happened between them to provoke Strauss's vendetta against her—if, in fact, that's what it was.

Buck Hansen had told me that Donna Trask's funeral would be the next day, a week after Donna's death, at Valhalla Cemetery at two o'clock. I decided to attend.

I threw on the same outfit I'd worn at the banquet and drove to the cemetery in my Volkswagen Rabbit. I keep promising myself I'm going to get rid of it and buy something new, swift, low-to-the-ground, and sexy, but I never get around to doing it. The Rabbit runs, after all, which is why I bought it in the first place. It's blue and losing the battle with time and winter's chemicals.

I arrived half an hour early, but not before Buck, who was standing outside the chapel door. It's an odd looking chapel, brown, with rough stone walls that rise to a rounded dome of cream-colored marble. It looks like a giant ice cream cone.

"We can't go on meeting here like this," Buck said. The funereal darkness of his suit and sunglasses contrasted dramatically with his hair, a light blond that looks silver in bright light.

"I know," I replied. "People are going to start talking." Buck and I had met here once before, at the funeral of a University Scholar last summer.

We stood at the door, watching people arrive. I saw Jeremiah Strauss walking up the path between tombstones. He was looking even more solemn than usual, as well he should, considering that this could have been his funeral. He was accompanied by Donald Trask. Or rather, he seemed to be supporting Donald Trask. Trask was overcome either by emotion or something else—I couldn't tell which without going up and smelling his breath. His sandy hair looked as if it had been caught in a high wind, but there was no wind that day, just fluffy clouds scattered

around in a blue sky. It was slightly chilly. Jeremiah
Strauss was looking grim and, I thought, angry.

"Where's Donna's mother?" I asked Buck.

"Not here yet. My guess is, she'll wait to see where
Trask sits, then sit as far away from him as possible.
They've been divorced a long time. When I talked to her
yesterday, after she arrived in town, she made it plain that
the divorce wasn't an amicable one, and nothing's changed
between them since then."

I'd read in Donna's obituary that her mother lived in
New Mexico. Her name was Theresa Durr now.

"Here she comes," Buck said, "with President Wolf."

She was about five-seven or eight, and obviously got a
lot of sun, for her complexion contrasted dramatically with
everyone else's, still pale from the long winter. Her hair
was dark and pulled back into a loose bun. Considering
that her daughter had been twenty-one when she died,
Theresa Durr was probably in her early forties. She
walked with the easy grace of someone who enjoys exercise and thinks well of herself, and she had no trouble
keeping up with Wolf, who always walks as if the fate of
the planet depends on him getting to where he's going as
soon as possible. Dogs walk that way, too. She didn't look
radiantly happy, but she didn't seem to be overdoing the
mourning, either. She was wearing a full navy skirt that
swung around her legs as she walked, and a matching
jacket. Silver glittered at her throat, on her wrists, and at
her ears. She looked like the sort of person I might like.

The funeral service didn't take long, and there weren't
many people present since the date and place had been
kept out of the newspaper to thwart the curious. A minister
who admitted frankly that he hadn't known the deceased
did the honors, lamenting the untimely passing of a loved
daughter, etc. The last time I was here, President Wolf had
given a eulogy for the dearly departed, but happily he
didn't do that this time.

We sang "I Walk in the Garden Alone" and then filed
out of the chapel and milled about, waiting for the hearse

with the coffin to appear so we could walk behind it to the gravesite.

"I'm going over to talk to Hudson Bates," Buck told me.

"Who?" I asked. When he nodded in the direction of a man standing with Strauss, Trask, and some others, I remembered where I'd heard the name before. Edith had pointed him out to me at the banquet as Strauss's associate dean. "A suspect?" I asked Buck.

"You bet. Somebody said they saw him step on the poisoned apple, in the confusion after Donna dropped it. He admits it, but says it was an accident." Buck drifted over toward Bates, who, when he saw him coming, seemed to try to crowd even more closely into the group around Jeremiah Strauss. Edith had said that he looked like a clothing store dummy. It was an apt description, if dummies ever had fear in their eyes.

Because Donna's mother didn't look particularly bereaved, I approached her, on an impulse I couldn't explain to anybody's satisfaction but my own, and told her who I was and what I did for a living. She responded with a half-smile. Glancing over my shoulder to make sure Buck wasn't within earshot, I said I was helping the police with their investigation into her daughter's death, and I'd like to take a few minutes of her time to discuss Donna with her.

She seemed startled. She started to say something and changed her mind. She looked over at Buck, whom she'd talked to the day before, and then back at me. "All right," she agreed.

She was staying with friends in town, she told me, gesturing to a small group of people waiting for her near the front of the funeral procession. We agreed to meet after the service was over and go somewhere nearby for a drink or coffee.

"He confess?" I asked Buck when I rejoined him at the rear of the procession.

He ignored the comment. "What were you talking to Mrs. Durr about?"

"Condolences," I said, looking for his eyes behind his sunglasses and seeing only myself and some tombstones behind me.

"It looked to me like you were arranging something—maybe to meet her after the service. You didn't tell her you were working for me, did you?"

"No," I said, "I didn't." Strictly speaking, that was true.

He started to ask me another question, but luckily for me his attention focused suddenly on something behind me. "Look!" he said.

Off to our right, on a hill piled with the kind of old gravestones they allowed before space became a problem, there was color and movement. It was Bert Coombs, the juggler. He was wearing his usual green and yellow outfit and standing on an elaborate monument to someone whose survivors had paid a lot of money to have something heavy put on top of him. Bert was juggling red, yellow, and green balls, tossing them high against the sky. The procession slowed to a halt as the mourners stopped to stare. A tall, elderly man in front of me looked down at his wife and said, "Desecration! Where are the police when you need them?"

I could see Donald Trask, shielding his eyes to look, ask Jeremiah Strauss something. Strauss gestured an answer and they hurried forward to catch up with the slow-moving hearse. Buck had reached for his walkie-talkie, but relaxed when he saw two men emerge behind Bert, one on each side. Bert disappeared from view. A yellow ball rolled down the hill toward us until it was stopped by a small grave marker.

The procession continued on its slow way, mocked by the cheerfulness of the day and the swelling buds on the shrubs and trees that lined the path, until we arrived at the freshly dug grave. I stayed close to Buck during the rest of the service, counting the number of plainclothesmen strategically placed near Jeremiah Strauss. They were easily identified by their striking resemblance to the Secret Service men you always see around the president on TV.

Donald Trask seemed almost to fall, or jump, into the grave when the time came for him to throw dirt into it. Strauss, moving quickly for so heavy a man, shot out an arm and pulled him back. He said something to Trask that I couldn't hear. Trask pulled his arm away and said something to Strauss that was no doubt inappropriate at a funeral. Trask's ex-wife stood on the other side of the grave and watched the spectacle without any expression on her face, just as she'd observed the service before it, as if none of this were any of her concern. She sprinkled dirt on the coffin, too, stood looking down at it for a long moment, then stepped back and turned away.

When the service was over, the members of the funeral party went up to Donna's parents and shook their hands or gave them a hug, and then dispersed. It didn't look like a cozy, supportive group. Most of them seemed to be there out of some sense of duty.

A young Asian woman spoke to Donald Trask. Then she went over to Theresa Durr and spoke to her. Mrs. Durr listened with a look of polite interest on her face, smiled, and gave the young woman a hug. It was the only gesture of real affection I'd seen during the entire service.

After a while, Donald Trask, Jeremiah Strauss, and President Wolf were left on one side of the grave, with Donna's mother and her friends on the other. Trask was looking across the grave at his ex-wife. Theresa Durr seemed to make up her mind about something, walked around the grave, and stuck her hand out to him. He looked at it as if he didn't know what it was, then, greedily, took it in both of his and started to cry. He reached for her, obviously intending to embrace her, but she stepped gracefully back, disengaged her hand, and said something to him with a smile. He stood there, listening to her, his arms still half extended, nodding like a little boy who'd lost something important. Theresa said something to President Wolf and shook his hand, before coming over to Buck and me.

President Wolf followed her with his eyes, shifted them

to Buck, and, finally, to me. He seemed to look at me for a long time; then he left, an important man on his way to yet another task of earth-shaking importance. I wondered if he remembered who I was. We'd met just once, over a year before, when I'd been assigned to keep an eye on the *objets d'art* in the president's mansion during a reception he'd hosted for the regents and some important legislators. His memory for names and faces was considered his most terrifying talent. No one ever got a second chance to make a good first impression on Wolf. I wondered if he was processing the presence of a Homicide cop and a campus cop together at Donna Trask's funeral and, if so, what his computer-like mind would come up with.

After exchanging a few words with Buck, Theresa Durr and I walked back to the parking lot together. As I pulled out of the lot, I slowed to let the young Asian woman I'd seen talking to both of Donna's parents cross the street in front of us. She gave Mrs. Durr a smile and a wave.

"She seemed very sweet," Mrs. Durr said to me. "She asked if there was anything she could do. She said she'd been a friend of Donna's."

"Do you remember her name?" I asked.

"Sumiko, I think. I didn't catch her last name. Funny, I wouldn't have thought Donna would have friends like that. Nice friends," she added dryly. She craned her head, following the black-haired woman with her eyes until we turned a corner. Then she turned back and looked out at the passing scenery. "I guess," she said, after a few moments, "if I'd given it much attention, I wouldn't have thought Donna had any friends at all."

Nine

Theresa Durr didn't need a drink after burying her daughter, so we settled on a coffee shop instead of a bar.

"I go home tomorrow," she said after we'd ordered, "to Santa Fe. I'm staying with people here who used to be friends of mine before I moved away. We don't seem to have a lot to talk about anymore, so I'm in no hurry to get back to them. I'm not exactly sure what campus cops do— try to find stolen bikes? building security?—but somehow I wouldn't imagine you investigate murders. What can I tell you that I didn't tell that Homicide cop you were with at the funeral?"

"Maybe nothing that will help. I don't know. I mostly want to learn something about a young woman who would do what your daughter did: Get up in front of a crowd of very distinguished people and demolish the crowning moment in a man's life."

Theresa Durr looked at me curiously. "Why?"

I concealed the annoyance that question always fills me with. My mother, after a session with one of the various therapists she spent most of her time and money on, came home and announced that, from that day on, she wasn't going to answer any more "why questions." I wished I could use that dodge on Theresa Durr. Instead, I told her, "Because I was there—at the banquet—when she died. And I talked to her a little beforehand, too."

She didn't look as if she thought that was much of an answer. It wasn't. She started to say something to that effect, saw the determined look on my face, and said, "Donna was mad at Strauss, that's all there was to it. She didn't get what she wanted from him, something she felt he'd promised her and she was entitled to. She felt betrayed, and she decided to get revenge." Theresa laughed, and her gray eyes, which hadn't had much expression up until then, sparkled. "What a revenge! Too bad the banquet had to end then. I wonder how Jerry would've handled it, if it hadn't! What kind of a speech could he have made, after what Donna did to him?"

Theresa Durr wasn't your average mother.

"I think I see why Donna was angry at Dean Strauss," I said. "But maybe I'm missing something. What made her expect him to use his influence to override the wishes of a department?"

"Donna's known Jerry Strauss since she was a child," she replied. "Don did some legal work for the University fifteen years ago, in connection with acquiring land the University needed for the New Campus. Jerry was head of the committee that oversaw the expansion. He wasn't such an arrogant man then, or perhaps he concealed his arrogance better than he cared to later. This was shortly before he became Dean of the Graduate School, around the time he inherited all that money from his father. He was at our house a lot in those days, closeted with Don in his study. But he always seemed to have time for Donna. He would even get down on the floor and play jacks with her. She was six or seven years old."

There was a melancholy smile on Theresa's face as she continued. "Oddly enough, Jerry was quite good at jacks. It was fascinating, watching him pluck up the correct number of them with his thick fingers before that little colored ball came down again. And he'd make her laugh sometimes, by dancing for her. He was remarkably light on his feet. It was both comic and, well, bizarre, I guess.

He was like a dancing bear. He and his wife couldn't have children."

She came back to the present. "Don didn't like it at all. He didn't like sharing Donna with anyone. But there wasn't anything he could do about it, just make impatient noises as if he wanted to get down to business. In any case, Donna probably thought she could get Strauss to do whatever she wanted. When it didn't work out, it would have been because he 'tricked' her. That was her favorite line—'You tricked me!' It was remarkably effective, too, because it laid a guilt trip on the person she said it to— usually me, until I left."

"I doubt, somehow, that Jeremiah Strauss is susceptible to being guilt-tripped. Are you?"

"Now? No. Then? Yes."

"Was her father?"

"No, never! But she never accused Don of tricking her, either—at least, not as long as I stayed around—even though he played the biggest trick on her of all: making her think he loved her. All he loved, in fact, was the idea of loving her. Just like at the funeral today. Anyone could see that he was deeply in love with the idea of mourning the loss of his beloved daughter. Donna never had the courage to admit to herself that she'd been wrong about him. She didn't dare examine the nature of her father's love for her, much less hers for him. Everybody else in the world, sooner or later, would trick her, but never Don. Is this interesting to you?" she asked me abruptly. "Is this the sort of thing you want to know?"

"Yes."

"Then I'd better start from the beginning, hadn't I?" she said. She beckoned the waitress for more coffee. The heavy silver bracelet on her arm looked gorgeous against her dark, lightly freckled skin.

She'd married Donald Trask when both of them were graduating from college. He applied to law schools all over the country, got accepted at the University's, so they moved here, and she got a job to support them. About the time he started with a local law firm, Donna was born.

"By that time," Mrs. Durr told me, "Don was already cheating on me. But I didn't find out about it until it was too late to try to get an abortion, and I was too scared and confused to leave him. I also hoped Donna would make things better. At first she did. Don was thrilled to have a daughter, especially one who took after him in looks. He wanted to name her after himself, too, and I went along with that. Don's childish in so many ways, and it was hard not to indulge him. Also, I hoped that by giving in to him I'd turn him into a faithful husband and a good father. That's the way I thought, back then." She said this in a matter-of-fact tone, without bitterness or amazement.

"By letting Donna be his child—by treating her as a form of coinage to buy back Don's love—I lost her to him. She quickly learned to play him off against me. What intelligent child wouldn't? And I doubt he stayed faithful to me for three months after she was born. I saw less and less of him as the years passed, and so did Donna. You'd suppose that would make her turn to me, but it didn't. Starting at a very young age—four, five—she blamed *me* for his neglect. I don't know why. Maybe Don told her lies about me. Whenever Don did have time for her, of course, he lavished affection and toys on her, making the times when he was around seem like Christmas for her, and his absences hell."

"You said he was doing some work for the University when Donna was a child. Do you mean he wasn't at the U then?"

"No, of course not. When it was acquiring land for the expansion to the other side of the river the University hired Don's law firm to provide the necessary legal advice. His firm assigned Don to it. The University made him their chief attorney shortly after I left him, probably on the basis of his friendship with Jerry Strauss."

I suddenly heard myself ask: "What were you doing all the time your husband was playing games with you and your daughter? Just hanging around with a vacuum cleaner in one hand, a feather duster in the other, expecting some kind of deliverance, because you didn't have the guts to walk away from all the perks you got as the wife of a lawyer?"

Her head rocked back slightly, as if I'd landed a blow, but she knew how to absorb it. "No," she said, her calm voice unchanged. "I tried everything I could think of to make things better, for all of us. I even took Donna to a psychologist, but that backfired on me, too. After the second session, she refused to go back, and told her dad that all the therapist wanted to talk about was what a bad father he was. Don, of course, had been opposed to therapy from the start. When he heard that, he refused to let Donna see the psychologist anymore. He just took Donna's word for what went on. I told him I'd get a divorce and ask for custody, but he laughed and threatened me with the best divorce lawyers in town—chums of his, of course. I was scared of him, scared of his power. I felt that he might win her or at least get joint custody."

"Why didn't he want a divorce?"

"Why should he? I was a more than adequate wife for him, in all the areas in which he needed a wife. I kept house, I accompanied him places where he needed to be seen—and I made excellent canapés, an important talent for the wife of a man on the way up!" She laughed bitterly. "I think he thought I'd become reconciled to his cheating and neglect, the way so many of his colleagues' wives were. Besides, he knew the kinds of divorce settlements wives were getting, if they could prove they'd worked to put their husbands through school. He might not have lost Donna, but he would have lost something equally precious: money, a lot of money. So for a while, I stayed, thinking that I could perhaps still be of help to Donna. And I was, sometimes."

"How?"

"Donna would fly into rages that were terrifying, even to her. Then she'd come to me. And when she'd get so depressed that she felt like killing herself, she'd come to me, too, in her confusion and fear. You see—Peggy? Is it Peggy?"

"Yes."

"You see, Peggy," she went on, fiercely, "she knew what was wrong, and yet she wouldn't admit she'd made a mistake about her father. I don't know why, but she wouldn't—couldn't—admit she'd made a mistake. She was determined to have him, to win him over, no matter what it took. She endured almost anything from him.

"Not long before I left, I discovered that he was sharing the details of his affairs with her, flaunting his women in front of her, making her feel that she was his 'partner' in all aspects of his life, including his love life, and I was just an old stick-in-the-mud." Lines that hadn't been there before appeared around Theresa Durr's mouth.

"Then I met a man," she went on, "Mike Durr, a lawyer in Don's firm. There were always a lot of parties, so I got to meet the new people, the ones the firm was grooming for partners. We hit it off well from the first time we met, even though Mike was five years younger than I. We sat alone in a corner of the living room and talked and talked. That was an unwise thing for Mike to do. It was unwise for him to show that much interest in me in front of Don and his friends, of course, but it was just as unwise for Mike to be sitting in a corner talking to a woman, rather than sucking up to the partners. Mike didn't have the personality for a law firm like Don's, thank God for that!" She smiled.

"Mike left the firm, I divorced Don, and Mike and I moved to New Mexico. I gave Donna the choice of coming with us if she wanted to. She stayed with her dad. That was seven years ago. She was fourteen then. I never saw her again until a few weeks before she died. End of story."

"You saw her just before she died?" I asked. "In March?"

"Yes. She came to Santa Fe on spring break, the second week of March. She flew out with her dad, who was going to attend some sort of legal convention in Albuquerque. Donna rented a car and drove to Santa Fe, dropped in on me in my shop completely unannounced, and spent the day with me. It was quite a surprise."

"Why do you think she came? To try to make up with you?"

"That's what I thought at first," Theresa said. "She seemed subdued, almost respectful. She was interested in what I was doing and how I lived. She even wanted to meet my husband. But then she changed, suddenly reverted to the old Donna, the one I'd known when she was a child—Donald's daughter. No matter what I did— showed her my jewelry and how I make it, showed her around my home—a superior little smile played over her mouth, as if all that I'd built for myself was trivial, nothing. By the time she left, I was exhausted."

"Why do you think her mood changed?"

Theresa shrugged. "I think she saw how much I've got now, how happy I am. I think she expected to find a huge hole in my life, the place left by the daughter I'd abandoned."

We sat in silence a while, playing with our coffee cups and spoons. I asked her if she had any regrets.

"No, none!" she replied, her gray eyes wide. "Not even for the wasted years, not even for the mistakes I made. I did the best I could with what I had. What more can anybody do? I lost a lot, of course, but I gained a lot, too. After Donna started school, I had time on my hands, too much time. I started making jewelry. Now I have my little shop in Santa Fe, and I make a pretty good living at it. I don't know how else I could have discovered my talent, if it hadn't been for the years I lived with Don. All the jewelry I'm wearing," she added, "I made." She twisted her wedding ring back and forth on her finger, smiling down at her hand. "I think I must be the luckiest creature on the face of the earth."

Her husband had a law practice in Santa Fe, very low-key. It gave him plenty of time to spend with his wife.

"We're thriving like weeds," she said and laughed. "Life's so hard to figure, isn't it? It's impossible to explain how anything happens. It's stupid to try, don't you think?"

I started to say no, but she interrupted me. "Perhaps you're too young to understand that yet. But you look like you've learned a few things in your life, too. You're not married, are you? Are you living with somebody?"

No to both questions.

As if not hearing me, she went on, talking fast: "I watched Don at the funeral, and saw how he almost fell into Donna's grave. I thought to myself that, if I hadn't had the guts to cut my losses and get out of that marriage, I'd have been standing next to him, and we'd have fallen in together, fallen into Donna's grave together." She laughed, something in the range of small bells. She looked at her watch.

"Strauss would have saved you from it," I said, "the way he saved your ex-husband."

"That was touching, wasn't it," she replied, "the way Jerry practically carried the bereaved father to his daughter's grave and then had to prevent him from falling in! They were like two old vaudevillians, weren't they? And then there was that juggler. That made it almost perfect. I was surprised to see them together, Jerry and Don. I'd heard that their friendship has cooled a lot recently."

I said I'd noticed that there'd been a couple of moments at the grave when Strauss looked as though he wished Trask were underground, too.

"And vice versa," she said. "I guess I should go now," she added. "I hope you haven't been bored."

"I admire you a lot," I blurted out. I'd grown up in a home a lot like the Trask's, except that my mother hadn't run from it. If she had, and if she'd given me the chance to run with her, I'd have jumped at it and never looked back. But she had different strategies for dealing with a husband like Donald Trask, chief among them obliterating her own personality.

"You do?" Theresa Durr said. "A lot of people think

I'm a cold, heartless bitch. And maybe, somewhere deep down, I think I am, too. I think I came to Donna's funeral to try to show those people—and myself, too, I guess—that I do feel deeply about Donna's death. I thought I'd be able to shed tears over my daughter."

She began to laugh again, and then she sat back down in the booth and started to cry. "She was my child, my daughter," she said, when she'd gotten her voice back. "She started out curious and hopeful, the way we all do. But fourteen years later, when I told her I was leaving her and her father, moving to Santa Fe with another man, she stood there and leered at me, as if to say, 'See, I knew you were going to trick me, you, too!' "

"I saw something like that on her face, too," I told her. "It was the last expression on her face before the poison took over."

Theresa Durr stood there and thought about that, looking at me. "Which poison?" She walked away without waiting for an answer. I followed, dropping a couple of dollars on the table.

We drove to her friends' home in silence.

Ten

When I entered the squad room a few minutes before roll call that night, Lawrence and Paula were sitting at a table, playing one of their word games. They were working the dog watch, too, not because they like it, as I do, but because it was their turn. Or rather, it was Paula's turn. Lawrence volunteered, much to Paula's disgust, but from what I'd noticed lately, her disgust was only apparent. He seemed to be growing on her.

Lawrence abandoned the game as soon as he saw me.

"Who was that woman you were with Wednesday afternoon when Paula and I saw you outside Frye Hall?" he asked me.

"Sounds like the start of a very old joke," I said. Even as I said it, I knew what was coming, and my heart sank. When Lawrence had leaned out of the squad car, Edith suddenly remembered a book she had to get from the bookstore across the street and hurried away. Lawrence had been staring out the squad car window while Paula and I were talking. At the time, I'd thought he was stunned by love, but that hadn't been it. He'd been staring after Edith, and Edith didn't want him to get a close look at her.

"You know who I mean?" he asked me.

"Yes," I said. "I know who you mean."

"Well, what's her name?"

"Edith Silberman," I told him, "Professor Edith Silberman."

He nodded, watching me with his large, guileless eyes. "She was one of the people who came into Adamson Hall through the tunnel. At the banquet. Lt. Hansen, your Homicide friend, said he'd appreciate it if I'd tell him if I ever saw any of them."

"Have you talked to him?"

"No. I just thought of it today," he said, "and I wanted to get her name from you. You want to tell Hansen, or you want me to? He'll probably want to talk to her, because she might be able to recall some of the others who came in that way at the same time she did, if anybody else did."

Buck would certainly want to talk to Edith. According to Ginny, she had a motive for wanting Strauss dead, and she'd threatened him, too, and it wasn't just any sort of threat, it was a threat to poison him. And now Lawrence could testify that she had the opportunity to exchange Strauss's apple for one full of poison in the dining room at Adamson. When Buck found out about that, Edith would be brought in and asked some hard questions.

Lawrence was still watching me. I debated whether or not to ask him to give me a couple of days but decided that would be asking him to participate in suppressing evidence, which could get him fired.

I told him I'd call Buck with the information. I didn't say when.

As soon as I could, I went to a pay phone, called Edith to tell her what I'd just learned.

"I recognized him right away," she said sadly. "The boy in the powder-blue suit, in love with the gorgeous black cop who was driving the car. That's why I suddenly decided I had to pick up a book I'd ordered. The ruse didn't work, apparently. The lad has an eagle eye, although a somewhat delayed recollection."

"Do you want to talk to me about it?" I asked her.

There was a long silence, as she thought it over.

"Okay," she said briskly. "It'll give me a chance to rehearse my story in front of an audience, before telling it to the police."

We agreed to meet for breakfast the next morning at a little coffee shop near campus.

The morning and I were both cold and tired. I would have preferred to go home and go to bed, but after returning to headquarters and checking out, I pedaled over to the coffee shop. Edith was already there, in a booth in back that nobody else wanted because the seats were broken. Even though it was a Saturday, the place was crowded and noisy, heavy with the smells of half a century of coffee, a million cigarettes, burnt pancakes and bacon and eggs.

"Watch your food," Edith whispered to me, after the waitress had taken our orders. "I may slip poison into it."

It was a poor excuse for a joke, and Edith wasn't looking all that great either. "That would be like bringing coals to Newcastle here," I replied, playing along.

I waited until the waitress had dropped a battered thermos of coffee on the table. "On Wednesday when we talked, you didn't tell me anything about your run-ins with Dean Strauss over the years. And you didn't tell me you'd threatened his life. A campus cop told me that."

She tried to keep it light. "Well, Peggy, I thought you were interested in Donna Trask. I didn't think my various clashes with Jerry Strauss would interest you."

"Why did you threaten him?" I asked.

"Well, damn it," she replied, her eyes skittering over my face and then down to her cup, "I wouldn't have threatened him if I was planning to murder him, would I? But since I wasn't planning anything of the sort, it seemed a reasonable, even healthy, thing to do. I wouldn't have done it, though, if I'd remembered that Strauss's toady, Bates, is always there, lurking and listening. Without Bates, it would just be Jerry's word against mine—I mean, if it ever went to court. But I was so angry that I hardly heard what I was saying. I just said it, and slammed out of there."

"What did Strauss do to make you so mad?"

Our food arrived. My pancakes were black on the outside, raw on the inside. Edith rearranged her waffle and eggs, as if they were on the table for therapeutic play purposes.

"As I told you on Friday," she said. "Donna Trask tried to get into the Humanities graduate program over the department's objection."

"Over your objection."

"All right, yes, it finally came down to me." She didn't look at all sorry. "In January, after processing the first batch of graduate applications, we rejected Donna. I thought that was the end of it. But a few weeks later I got a polite note from Jerry—Strauss—inviting me to come and see him. I went. He was exceedingly polite, more polite than he'd been to me in years, even a bit nervous. He asked me whether or not we could reconsider Donna's application. I said no. Quite frankly, I didn't understand his humble attitude. I didn't know that he was an old family friend of the Trasks, but I was enjoying the power I suddenly had over him. Then he suggested that maybe I wasn't capable of judging her fairly."

Edith turned pale at the memory. She leaned across her plate and pointed a fork at me. "He's got an uncanny way of finding your weak spots, Peggy. He was playing on my own doubts about my objectivity toward Donna. But then I remembered all she'd done in my class, how she'd treated me in my office, and those two papers she'd written—one for herself and one for that boyfriend of hers, Coombs—and I recovered my balance. I told him Donna Trask wouldn't be admitted to the Humanities graduate program, and that I had the votes in the department to make that stick. So, you know what he did?"

"Threatened to turn you down for a fellowship or something," I guessed.

She laughed bitterly. "You've been hearing things about him. No, Peggy, worse than that, much worse. I have two really bright students who had applied for scholarships from the Graduate School. Jerry mentioned them to me, casually, as if in passing. He was telling me, indirectly, that whether or not they won those scholarships would depend on whether or not Donna Trask got into our graduate program. I myself wouldn't waste any time applying for money from the Graduate School, not as long as he's the dean, but when he went after my students, I blew up. It was the last straw." She lowered her fork and, her hand trembling a little, jabbed out the eyes of her congealing eggs.

"You call him 'Jerry' sometimes," I said. "What's that about? Was he once in love with you, and you threw him over?"

"Good Lord, no!" she said and laughed. "There was never anything like that between us. It's just that, once, we were on a first-name basis, and it's hard to break the habit, even this long afterward."

"But what happened? What's he after you for?"

"I know too much about him," she said, her dark eyes burning into mine, "I'm the only person left in the department who *really* knows how little he deserves the honor of being a University Scholar. He doesn't like having to see me at departmental meetings, bumping into me in the halls every single day, while knowing I'm laughing at him. He'd like me to resign from the University. It's as simple as that," she finished.

"It doesn't sound simple to me," I said. "Why would you be laughing at him?"

"Because twenty-five years ago, when Jerry Strauss and I were both assistant professors, he published a long article in one of the major publications in our field." She pushed herself away from the table, back into the broken plastic of the booth. "Most of the ideas in his article were mine," she said.

She noted the look of shock on my face with grim pleasure. "Even back then," she went on, "it must have been a question of what he had less of, integrity or shame. You see, I thought we were friends. We used to have lunch together, Jerry, several of the other younger faculty members, and I, and we'd discuss what we were working on. He was a little older than the rest of us, and he'd already published a couple of articles. We looked up to him. Well, I'd come up with what I thought was a wonderful idea, a new interpretation of a play by one of Shakespeare's contemporaries, and I spent an entire lunch babbling on about it. Everybody, including Jerry, thought it was wonderful, and asked me lots of questions. Several months later, he published his article."

"But couldn't you have charged him with plagiarism?"

"No. First, the other two professors wouldn't have supported me. They were sweating tenure and promotion themselves, and seemed to have an instinct for when to stick their heads in the sand. Second, they claimed, privately, that they 'honestly' couldn't be sure that Strauss and I hadn't discussed my ideas back and forth, and that he hadn't contributed ideas of his own that modified mine in 'significant ways.' " Edith was speaking in a high, affected voice common to inflated, young academics.

"I was barely able to keep from spitting in their faces," she continued in her normal voice. "But in those days, women didn't do things like that. We were just glad to have been 'brought on board.' And third, in his article, Strauss generously acknowledged that some of his ideas had come out of 'brainstorming sessions' with me and several of the other faculty, and he thanked each one of us for our contributions, 'without which my article would have been much the poorer.' "

I dumped my now cold coffee in my water glass and refilled my cup from the thermos. "I've always known that the University is a place ripe for murder, Edith," I said, "but not quite this ripe. You had a great motive for murdering Strauss. Why didn't you?"

"No guts. Believe me, Peggy, I wanted to. In those days, of course, young and insecure, I could never be sure I'd ever get another really good idea. And he'd stolen the best I'd had up to that time. It was a devastating blow. If I'd had the courage, Strauss would be twenty years in his grave and I'd be about ready for parole from some woman's prison."

"Maybe it's a good thing it's not easy to get hold of cyanide," I said.

Her eyes jumped quickly up to mine, then back down to her coffee cup. "Maybe," she replied. "But now, all that seems like a very small reason to kill somebody. I've had lots of ideas since then, lots of articles and two books . . ."

"But what?" I said.

"But it was such a dirty, evil thing for him to do," she finished, softly. She was deep into her memories. Then she shrugged herself out of them. "I've published more than he has, in fact, our new 'University Scholar.' A year after stealing my ideas, he wrote the book that made him a star in our field. But you know, Peggy, I think there's a kind of nemesis at work in the world. There has to be."

"Why?"

"Because he started to go downhill after that. His work began to repeat itself, he began to publish less and less, and finally he dried up and went into administration. Don't you think there's a kind of divine retribution in that?"

I didn't know whether or not to laugh, because I didn't know how serious she was. Instead, I said: "He later tried to prevent you from being promoted to full professor, and a decade after that, threatened to hurt two of your students if you didn't let Donna Trask into your graduate program."

"Yes." The bitterness flooded back into her voice and she made no effort to hide it. She saw me staring at her, and said, with a nervous laugh, "Yes, I guess I could kill the son of a bitch, after all, now that I think about it. But if I did," she added, her voice rising, "I wouldn't miss and destroy some disturbed kid. If I did try to kill him, you'd never be able to prove it. Besides, I don't need to kill him now. He's retiring as dean, which means I'll be able to get my students their fellowships after all."

"Do you have any idea why Strauss is quitting as dean?"

"He's not doing it voluntarily," she replied. "I can tell

you that much. Most people, once they've got a taste for
the power and money in administration, dread the thought
of having to return to teaching—and Strauss dreads it
more than most, I imagine."

"Then why's he doing it?"

"I think Wolf decided he had to go," she said. "After
fifteen years, Jerry's getting careless in his abuse of power.
I'm not the only person who thinks Wolf made him a University Scholar just to get him out of office without embarrassing him. Jerry probably knows too much dirt about
what goes on in the administration to be dismissed without
getting a big, public reward for it. Jerry would insist on
going out in style."

"The Scholarship carries a fairly large annual stipend,
doesn't it?" I asked.

"Sure, but that's not the important thing to Jerry. He's
got some kind of inheritance that supplements his salary.
The important thing to him is the prestige. He's enormously vain."

She pushed her plate of food away, untouched except
for the damage to the eggs. I'd managed to eat all of mine.
I picked up the check as we got up to go.

"I can't keep Lawrence's information from the Homicide people much longer, Edith," I told her. "I should have
called Lt. Hansen last night."

"What do you think they'll do, when you tell them?"

"It's certainly not enough to get you charged since, according to Lawrence, at least a dozen people came to the
banquet through the tunnel. You've got motive and
opportunity—but there're other suspects with both of
those. The city cops have a stack of abusive and threatening letters from people Strauss has hurt over the years, so
you aren't alone in having threatened him either. Unless
Hansen can come up with something else that puts you at
the head of the pack, I can't imagine that you're in for
more than an unpleasant grilling."

She looked away from me, as she'd done throughout
our conversation. "My son's an attorney," she said. "I'll

ask him to recommend a good criminal lawyer I can talk to. How much time will you give me?"

"I guess it can slip my mind until Monday," I said uneasily.

"Thanks, Peggy." She gave me a tired smile. "That'll have to do, won't it?" We got to the cashier. "I'll buy breakfast," she said, trying to take the check out of my hand.

"We'll go dutch this time," I told her.

"Why?" she asked, trying to smile. "Afraid it would be construed as a bribe for withholding evidence from the police?"

I am the police, I thought, but didn't say it. "Isn't there something else you want to tell me, Edith?" I asked her instead.

"No," she said, not looking up from her purse.

We paid, walked out into the chilly morning. I felt her eyes on my head as I bent to unlock my bike. When I straightened up, I asked her if she could think of anybody who'd want Strauss dead.

"I can think of somebody I'd *like* to see as a suspect."

"Who?"

"Hudson Bates. His office is located exactly between the receptionist's and Strauss's, and he can hear everyting that goes on in that place."

Buck had told me that Bates had stepped on the poisoned apple at the banquet, in the confusion after Donna's collapse. He didn't look capable of murder to me, but then, who does, except in movies? "Why would he want to do in Strauss?"

"Well, I'd like to think that somewhere, deep down in his body—which, I understand, he's going to leave to a health club when he dies—Bates resents all the dirty errands he's run for Jerry, and murdering Jerry would be a kind of warped act of integrity worming its way to the surface."

"Not good enough, Edith," I said.

"No, I guess not."

I walked my bike down onto the street, and she followed me to the curb. I looked back at her.

"I wonder if you'd feel better," I said, "if you told me what's bothering you."

She knew what I meant. She straightened up to her full height, which still put her at eye level with me.

"There's nothing," she said, and she walked away.

Eleven

Edith was hiding something. So was I, from my friend Buck. But I didn't believe Edith had tried to poison Strauss. I knew her too well, or thought I did: She was a passionate woman, not a coldly calculating one. If she'd had the strength, she might have kicked the man to death in a moment of passion, but no, she didn't need violence. She had language, irony, a sense of humor.

I wanted to continue with what Ginny had called my "psychological autopsy." I hadn't gone many waking hours since Donna's death without seeing her on that podium in the final moments of her life. I wanted to know what would drive a person to that place, that time, and to that bizarre death.

She'd had an Asian friend, Sumiko, but Theresa Durr couldn't recall her last name. I didn't know anybody to ask except Bert Coombs. According to the student directory, he lived in the warren of streets beyond the New Campus.

Until recently, the area had been a sprawling clutter of old houses, most of which had been turned into rooms for students and transients, a marginal cafe or two, beer joints, pawn shops, and used clothing stores. Now most of it was being razed, in part to make room for the new conference center that was going to replace Adamson Hall. Rumor had it that the rest of the area would become an apartment and retail complex that would drive the present inhabitants away in search of cheap housing elsewhere.

I biked over, hoping that Coombs's building was still standing and that he was still there. It was possible that he was in jail for desecrating a necropolis at Donna's funeral.

The streets became progressively worse the farther into the neighborhood I rode, for the city had made no effort to repair the potholes left by the winter. It was a cloudy, windy day, with a little blue sky showing in the southwest, and it had rained that night, which made navigating on a bike even more of a challenge.

The address I wanted was on Fairview Street, a misnomer if ever there was one. But a hundred years ago it must have been beautiful, for the river was close by. The building Bert lived in was at the end of the street, looking out onto a field littered with earth-moving equipment like a museum of prehistoric monsters.

I went up the cracked cement steps, pushed open the front door, and entered the chilly darkness. The doors of several rooms on the first floor were open. I glanced into the nearest. It was empty, the occupants having already moved out, either in anticipation of the building's demolition or to seek quieter lodgings. Bert's apartment was number four, upstairs at the front of the building. Loud rock music was playing, so I pounded on the door.

There was a sudden scuttle of activity inside, but the rock music continued. I pounded again. A voice hollered out, "Just a minute, damn it!" It took about that long, and then the door flew open. It was Bert's roommate and fellow juggler, Omaha, looking more disheveled than the last time I'd seen him. He was cinching his belt.

"What d'you want?" he asked me, annoyed.

"I'm looking for Bert," I said.

"He's still at the hospital, I guess. Why?" His eyes narrowed. "Oh, yeah," he said, recognizing me. "You were with him last week, weren't you? On the Mall, or something, when we were juggling." He grinned his slow, not very bright grin. "You wanna come in?"

"Omaha!" It was a woman's voice, angry.

"Sure," I said.

It was a large room, with peeling wallpaper and wires hanging from the middle of the ceiling where a light fixture had once been. The floor was warped hardwood that hadn't been sanded or stained in years. An old sofa bed was open and a woman was sitting on it, holding a sheet up to her chin. The sheet was no advertisement for whatever it had last been washed in, but then, neither the woman nor Omaha were either.

"She wants to know where Bert is," Omaha said to her.

"He told you," the woman said to me. She must have been in her late twenties going on fifty. To Omaha she said, "Your fly's open."

Omaha zipped up without embarrassment.

"What's wrong with Bert?" I asked Omaha.

"You mean, up here?" He tapped his forehead, grinned again.

"No, I mean, why's he in the hospital?"

"He's not in the hospital, he's at the hospital. His little brother's in the hospital. Andy."

The woman flopped down on the sofa bed, still holding the sheet.

"Is that Bert's part of the apartment?" I asked him, nodding at a crude partition of several old blankets strung on a rope across the other side of the room.

"Yeah. You interested in seeing how Bert lives? You never been here before?"

"No," I said, "I've never been here before."

I crossed the room, going around a battered dining room table cluttered with plastic bottles, some of which were cut into pieces, rolls of colored tape, and things I recognized as juggling equipment. I ducked my head around the blankets and looked into Bert's area. Someone had written on a wall, in large, colorful letters, "Beware of low-flying kangaroos." The space contained a thin mattress on the floor with an Army blanket, a desk lamp on a wooden fruit crate, a clutter of books and papers, and a black plastic ashtray, the kind nobody ever buys because they're too easy to steal from bars. It was empty, probably because the police busted Bert for dope last week. A door in the back wall apparently led to a small kitchen. A couple of pairs of old jeans hung over the partition dividing the room.

"Hey, what the fuck's going on in here?" It was Bert's voice. I turned and stepped back out of his space. He came toward me, his pale arms poking out of his torn T-shirt and his bony ankles visible under the too-short pants. "You got a search warrant, or what?"

"I wasn't here to search your place," I said.

"What're you here for, then?" he asked, standing a little too close. I didn't want to step back, since my back was already against one of the blankets hanging there. He was half a head taller than I, which made him about six feet.

"Donna had a friend," I said. "She was at the funeral, an Asian woman. I'd like to talk to her."

Bert blinked. "I wasn't at the funeral long enough to see who-all was there. And what were you doing at her funeral anyway? You didn't know her! What're you so interested in Donna for? What's she done to you? What's your business here? You know, the cops—the real cops, not you dopey campus clowns—were here, too, thanks to you. They took my place apart, and Omaha's, too. And I've been down to police headquarters, too, and they tried to take me apart. But they didn't get nothin', 'cause there ain't nothin' to get. What d'you think you're going to get?"

"She came up to Theresa Durr after the funeral," I said, ignoring the tirade.

"Who's Theresa Durr?"

"Donna's mother."

"She was at the funeral? The woman who ditched her own daughter?"

"That's the one. The Asian woman introduced herself as Donna's friend. Said her name was Sumiko."

Bert laughed. "You're going to have problems finding

somebody named Sumiko," he said. "That's about as common a name in Japan as Ann is here."

"How do you know she's Japanese?"

That one only stopped him for a second. " 'Cause I was in the Army for a couple years, Nancy Drew," he blustered, "stationed in Japan. I had a thing going with a girl named Sumiko, and leaving her was the only thing I hated about coming home."

"Well," I said, "this isn't Japan, so it shouldn't be quite as hard to locate a Sumiko, should it, now that I know she's Japanese." I couldn't help rubbing it in. "How about giving me her last name, too?"

"I told you, I don't know any Sumikos around here. And Donna didn't have no friends, except me, sometimes. Don't you ever listen, or what? And you didn't answer my question. Why're you so interested in Donna Trask all of a sudden?"

"I have lots of interests," I told him. "How's your brother?"

"My—? What d'you know about him?"

"Just that Omaha told me you were at the hospital to see your brother."

"So you're just being polite. Right?"

"I guess so," I admitted.

Nothing I said seemed to lessen his desire to throw a punch at me. I'd managed to maneuver my way over to the door. In their part of the room, Omaha and the woman had decided Bert and I were part of the environment. They were under the sheet together. Modesty was in short supply in this place.

"Was Donna Trask here a lot?" I asked innocently.

"No," he said, "we weren't friends like that."

From under the sheet on the bed behind Bert, Omaha's voice said, mimicking a parrot's, "What d'you know? They weren't friends like that! Sqwaak! They weren't friends like what? Sqwaak!"

The woman chuckled, a low, warm sound.

Bert wheeled on them angrily.

I left.

It was almost two when I got back to campus, and the wind had blown the clouds away for now. The Mall was packed with students snatching sun between classes. It had been a long winter, and the summers are uncertain here, so we grab all the sun we can whenever we see it.

Although he hadn't meant to, Bert had narrowed the field for me from "Asian" to "Japanese." I went into the Union and looked up the International Student Center on the building directory. It was on the top floor, at the end of the hall. I took the elevator.

The door was open. A young Indian woman was sitting at a gray metal desk, writing what looked like a letter. She was dressed in a saffron sari and had a reddish dab on her smooth forehead. I asked her how I would go about locating a Japanese foreign student whose only name I knew was Sumiko.

"I think you cannot," she said, giving me a big smile.

"Why not? There can't be that many Sumikos here, can there? Don't you have a list of foreign students by nationality?"

"Yes, we have that," she said happily, "but we do not give out those lists or the names on them. There is too much possibility of harassment. If you wish, I will have her call you. What is her last name?"

"As I said, I don't know her last name."

"That makes it very difficult," she assured me, frowning with delight.

I wondered what her major was, Red Tape? She pulled open a drawer and rummaged through it until she found a thick sheaf of papers held together with paper clips. She thumbed through it, smiled at a discovery that seemed to please her, pulled two pages with names on them out of the sheaf, and ran a long, brightly colored nail down the names, pausing several times.

"We have three—no, I correct myself—four Japanese

women with the first name Sumiko," she said tantalizingly. "If you give me your name and a phone number where you can be reached, I will tell each and every one of them of your interest. Perhaps one or all will call." She smiled a smile containing all the ancient wisdom of the petty bureaucrat.

Regretting that I wasn't in uniform, I pulled my shield out of my blouse pocket and firmly placed it on top of the list I wanted with just the hint of a slap. "This inquiry is official," I said, my voice grating an octave below normal. I let her take the shield to scrutinize it as I took the list. She started to object, but I headed her off. "You have a Xerox machine in here someplace?"

"There is one down the hall," a tall blond male said, emerging from a side door.

"She is the police, Kurt," the Indian woman informed him. "She—"

"Correct, Rani," he said. "And this is an official inquiry." He spoke with a Teutonic accent that became slightly hysterical on the word "official." To me he explained, "I could not help but overhear."

"Thanks," I told him, and plucked my shield from the woman's hand. I marched out of the room and strode purposefully down the hall. In my ideal state, all civil servants will be German, for they see to it that trains run on time without ever asking their destinations.

It cost me fifty cents to make copies of the two pages of Japanese students at the U. When I returned the original, the woman was gone and Kurt was at the desk.

"She is not experienced in Western ways," he said.

"Different strokes for different folks," I replied.

I called all four Sumikos from the pay phone in the Union basement, but none of them answered. I decided I'd try again that night before going on duty, when they might be home studying instead of in class or out gadding about.

I got to work early that night and called from Ginny's office. Ginny was chewing carrot sticks angrily and typing a report on a party that had gotten out of hand the night before at one of the fraternities. The first two Sumikos lived in noisy student housing of some kind. It took a lot of time for whoever answered the phone to find them, and when she did, they'd never heard of Donna Trask. The third Sumiko wasn't home. The fourth answered the phone herself, and when I'd told her who I was and what I wanted, she asked me politely why I wanted it.

I explained that I was helping the police with the investigation into Donna's death. She responded that Donna's death had been an unfortunate accident. I agreed, but added that even accidental homicide victims deserved our attention. She thought for a moment and then said she'd meet with me. She suggested I come over to her apartment the next day after dinner, since she had classes during the day.

"Still at it?" Ginny asked me, making a face at the little plastic bag of food on her desk. Her eyes were looking for meat and finding only raw vegetables.

"Yep," I admitted. "Psychological autopsy." Her term, while apt, rankled a little.

"Does Homicide know you're helping them in an investigation that they aren't, in fact, conducting?"

"Sometimes," I said piously, "the best help is that which is given anonymously."

"Maybe you should reconsider Al's offer to let you help him raise his son," she suggested.

"No, thanks," I said. I didn't find that particularly funny, but I'm willing to make allowances for Ginny's occasional lapses.

"Then why don't you sign up for a cooking class, Peggy? It might be less harmful to your career."

"You've never seen me try to light an oven, have you?"

That night I patrolled the Old Campus, strolling the elm- and oak-shaded paths, entering the old buildings at random and wandering through them looking for anything out of the ordinary: Doors ajar, for example, and people behind them who didn't belong there. I rarely saw anyone after 1:30 in the morning, not even students in the graduate student offices, nodding into their computer monitors from exhaustion. A strange way to live a life, to earn a living, in my opinion.

At about two A.M., I found myself in the tunnel between Adamson Hall and Jefferson, the building that houses some of the Social Sciences. I climbed the stairs to Jefferson, to explore its emptiness. It smelled of chalk and wax, and the floors glittered like old mahogany in the gloom. A light was on in an office about halfway down the hall. As I came abreast of it, the light went out. The door opened and a man emerged. He took a step back when he saw me.

"You scared me," he said, but he sounded more annoyed than scared. He was tall, at least six feet, and pale, with a long head that was completely bald on top, lusterless dark brown hair on the sides, a thin nose, and thin lips that turned down at the corners. He looked like an undertaker, exactly what I expect to facilitate my move from above to underground, one of the minor reasons I want to put that off as long as I can.

"Sorry," I said, and glanced at the nameplate next to his door: Myles Kruger. The name rang a bell, but I couldn't place it.

"You have a purpose for being here?" he asked me.

"Just on patrol," I answered.

"Excellent," he said. "I'll sleep better tonight, knowing my office is safe."

He seemed to forget me before he finished the sentence, as if he couldn't waste his fine mind even on his own sarcasm. He started down the hall, the way I'd come, toward the tunnel.

As I watched his head disappear down the stairs, I remembered where I'd heard his name. Ginny had mentioned it. Myles Kruger was one of her favorite suspects in the attempt on Jeremiah Strauss's life. Apparently Strauss didn't approve of Kruger's morals, and had damaged his career and wrecked his marriage. Kruger had been caught making late-night anonymous phone calls to Strauss.

I wondered if he'd made them from his office. What was he doing there so late tonight?

I looked down the now-empty hall and then back at Kruger's office door. I had keys that would open it, of course.

Reason prevailed. I continued on my patrol.

Twelve

Sumiko Sato lived in an area of old apartment buildings several blocks north of the Old Campus, hidden behind large oaks and maples. I biked over. The street was lined with sports cars of all ages, kinds, and conditions, a sure sign that the area housed mostly students, but students a lot more prosperous than those in Bert Coombs's neighborhood.

Sumiko's apartment building was four-storied, square, and built of brick that age had turned black. It was called "The Seville." The name appeared on the transom above the front door in flaking gold paint. The security door was ajar. A typed yellowing note taped across the directory announced that the buzzers were temporarily out of order. Somebody had scrawled beneath it in fading pencil that they'd been temporarily out of order since World War II. I climbed to the second floor. A vintage lamp hung from the ceiling in the stairwell, providing a bare minimum of light. There were six apartments on the second floor, three on each side of the hallway. Sumiko was standing in her door, waiting for me.

"He called her 'Princess Donna,' " she said after we were seated and she'd made a pot of tea. " 'My lovely princess,' 'princess this and princess that.' And she seemed to bask—that's the word I want, I think—in this, like a cat."

Sumiko spoke excellent English, but would stop every once in a while to question herself, not me, about the correctness of a word.

"I was new to this country then," she went on, "and I did not know if it was customary for fathers to address their daughters that way. Frankly, I hoped not. And I hoped, too, that it was not customary that fathers touched their daughters as much as Mr. Trask touched his."

"Touched how?"

"Mr. Trask touched Donna as if she were some very valuable object he had only recently purchased. He could not keep his hands off of her, and he would also *pluck* at her—I think that is the word, yes—as if removing very slight imperfections. She liked it. What she did not like was that he also did this, in front of her, to the women he was seeing, although with them his touching could be very sexy also."

I asked Sumiko how she and Donna had become friends.

"When I arrived in this country, the International Student Center found an apartment for me in this building, the same building Donna lived in."

"She lived here?" I said, surprised.

"Her apartment is next door. We met one afternoon on the stairs, as we were coming home from school. She 'adopted' me right there—on the spot, I think is the correct expression. At first, it was good for me to have an American friend like that. But soon I saw that she was not really helping me to make my way here; she was trying to keep me to herself instead. She would meet me after my classes were over, and became impatient if I stopped to talk to another student."

Donna thought of her as a kind of reverse twin sister. She was blonde and fair-skinned and a few inches taller than Sumiko—Sumiko was about five-two—and they both wore their hair short and straight. "She called me her shadow," Sumiko said, 'Sumiko Shadow,' instead of 'Sumiko Sato.' "

"How long did your friendship last?" I asked her, picking through a bowl of cookies, looking for something that didn't have seaweed burned onto it.

"Let me think. From almost the beginning of fall semester until about a month before she died. Yes, we stopped being friends just as March began. However, long before that I was putting distance between us, as I found other friends. She did not like that. But not until March did she stop speaking to me."

Sumiko poured tea for both of us, looked up at me, her dark eyes troubled at the memory. "She demanded, in fact, that I move out of the apartment building, or she would make me sorry. And she began pounding on my walls sometimes and playing her stereo so loud that sometimes it was very difficult for me to study. The walls are thin here. I began looking for another place to live, but now that she's dead, I will stay here."

"You could have complained to the manager," I told her.

Sumiko's eyes widened and she gave me a slight smile. "You did not know Donna very well, I think," she said.

"No, but I'm starting to. She scared you."

"Yes. She could not always control her behavior. When things did not go as she wanted them to, she could be quite frightening. Her behavior was sometimes very childish, but she was not a child anymore, you know, and when somebody who is not a child becomes angry like one, it is more scary than when a child does it. It was as though she were drunk. And afterward, too, she seemed to be—"

Sumiko couldn't think of the word. I supplied it.

"Yes," she agreed, "hung over. As if she had a terrible hangover although she had not been drinking. She looked . . . swollen, like someone who has reacted badly to a bee sting."

"You must have seen quite a lot of them together," I said, "Donna and her father."

"Not as often as Donna would have liked. I turned down as many invitations as I accepted, pretending sometimes to be feeling ill, sometimes that I had too much schoolwork to do. But after the last time I was with them, I did not see them together again."

"Why?"

"It was a party, a big party at the condominium of some rich person who owns so much property here, a man named Harold McCord. I see his name in the newspaper often, and he is on television sometimes, too."

Harold McCord was usually listed among the country's top twenty wealthiest men.

"It was a party to celebrate this McCord's birthday," Sumiko went on. "I think Donna invited me because she wanted to impress me by showing me how many important friends her father had."

Trask took Donna and Sumiko to McCord's party in his car, a large, heavy automobile that looked like a boat that had gone keel up, Sumiko said with a smile—a Cadillac Seville, she learned later, which was funny, since that was also the name of her apartment building. Trask also had his girlfriend with him, a woman he called Kim, about Donna's age. Kim cuddled with him in the front seat, while Donna and Sumiko rode in back. They drove to McCord's newest hotel, on the other side of the river near the New Campus. McCord's condo was the hotel's top floor.

"It was all done in white," Sumiko said, her brown eyes growing wide at the memory, "like a museum. There were paintings on every wall and sculptures scattered around the room, helter-skelter, yes!—helter-skelter. I could see no pattern to it, only that it was very conventional Western art and must have cost this McCord a great deal of money. Mr. McCord himself was dressed all in white, too, like a rock star from the '60s, so that when he stood against a wall, all you could see of him was his jewelry and his dark glasses nesting in his hair like baby blackbirds. It was very vulgar, very grotesque."

Sumiko knew none of the guests except Donna and her father, who didn't seem to be enjoying himself. She felt out of place, and wished she'd been able to find an excuse not to come.

"It was only afternoon, yet everybody was drinking," she went on, "and trying to be very happy. A group of musicians were in a corner of the room, and a few people were dancing in front of them. Donna seemed to—to hover—around her father, as if she were afraid he would disappear if she did not watch him. He drank a lot, but so did she. She sat on a white couch next to him, her father's arm around her, and Kim sat at his feet, between his legs. At one point, I remember, Mr. Trask's glass was empty. So he held it down, pretending to be casual about it, next to Kim's head, but she did not see it. Then Donna reached down and pushed it with her fingers, several times, so that it knocked against Kim's cheek. That got her attention. She got up quickly and refilled Mr. Trask's glass. Several times, Mr. McCord came over and toasted with Mr. Trask. Trask would not look at McCord or return his smiles. It was all very unpleasant. However, it could have been much worse, for at one point Donna almost lost control of her temper and threw a tantrum, and that would have been very ugly, believe me."

I believed her.

"I was standing at the big picture window, looking out," Sumiko continued. "This Mr. McCord has a beautiful view from there. You can see the river, and the New Campus, right below the hotel, and a little bit of the Old Campus, too, across the river. Then Mr. McCord came up and stood next to me, and he stared out, too. He seemed deep in thought. After a while he asked me how I liked it in America—as if he had prepared it especially for me and would be disappointed if I did not like it. I said I liked it very much, of course, but could think of nothing more to say.

"Then Mr. Trask came up and stood next to Mr. McCord and looked out the window. He said to me that Mr. McCord owned everything I could see out that window. He was making a kind of joke, I thought, although I could not be sure for he didn't sound as if he thought it were funny. I pretended to be ignorant, and I said—just because I thought Mr. McCord was so tasteless, you know?—'He owns the University, too?' Mr. Trask turned to Mr. McCord then and laughed harshly and said, 'How would you answer that, Hal?' Mr. McCord laughed, too, and told me that no, he didn't own the University. 'Yet,' Mr. Trask said. I did not understand what was going on between them.

"I was going to leave when Mr. Trask asked Mr. McCord when the groundbreaking ceremony was going to be. Mr. McCord said it was going to be the second week of May, but first they had to finish clearing away what was there from before. Mr. McCord told me that he was going to build the new conference center for the University and that it was going to be where all the old buildings were that were being torn down. He pointed the area out from his window."

I knew where it was, too. I'd been there the day before, when I'd gone looking for Bert Coombs. "What's this got to do with Donna almost throwing a tantrum?" I asked Sumiko.

She held up a small hand to tell me to be patient. She sipped tea for a moment, then went on.

"Mr. McCord said to Mr. Trask that he hoped Mr. Trask would come to the groundbreaking ceremony. He said that President Wolf had agreed to be the main speaker. And that's when the strange thing happened. Mr. Trask said that he assumed that 'Jerry' would be there, too, and Mr. McCord said, 'Why not? It's just too bad we can't name the center after him: the Jeremiah Strauss Conference Center. It's got a nice ring to it, doesn't it, Don?' I could see that he knew Mr. Trask wouldn't like to hear that. He was enjoying some kind of joke at Mr. Trask's expense. Taunting him a little bit, I think.

"Mr. Trask laughed, a very harsh laugh, and said he guessed McCord would name it after himself instead, the way he did all his hotels. They both laughed at that. Mr.

McCord said 'Touché, Donald!' and they touched glasses. I think they were both very drunk.

"But then, unexpectedly, Donna pushed her way between me and Mr. McCord. She must have been standing behind us all the time, listening. She looked from one to the other and said to her father softly, in a cold voice, 'What does he mean, they might name the center after Strauss? What does he mean?'

"Her father was surprised to see her. He said, 'Nothing, princess, it was just a joke.' She said no, it wasn't just a joke. She raised her voice, as if Mr. McCord wasn't there, demanding again what Mr. McCord had meant. It was very uncomfortable. Of course, I had seen Donna that way before, but always when she was mad at me or somebody else, never at her father. So I backed away from them quietly, and went to another part of the room. All her father said was, 'I'll tell you about it later, princess.' "

I asked, "When McCord said it was too bad they couldn't name the conference center after Strauss, do you think he was serious or kidding—just making a joke at Strauss's expense?"

"Why would he want to do that?"

"I'm not sure," I said.

I thought I'd read, probably in the student newspaper, that Strauss had been opposed to the University's putting the conference center on the New Campus side of the river. He'd wanted it built on the Old Campus, where Adamson Hall is now.

"Mr. McCord was drunk," Sumiko said. "How can you tell if people who are drunk are kidding or not?"

I asked her if she'd known Bert Coombs, Donna's boyfriend.

"Yes, except that I don't think 'boyfriend' is really the best word for it. Bert was in love with Donna, but perhaps what he really loved about her was who her father was. But she would not take very much money from her father, so it didn't matter who he was, as far as how she lived went.

"That's why she lived here," Sumiko added with a faint smile, "in this place, this . . . dump, I think is the word. Her father would have put her up in a much pleasanter place, but she would not hear of it. I don't think Donna was fond of Bert. She pretended to be fond of him some-times, when her father could see it. She flaunted Bert—yes, flaunted him—in front of Mr. Trask, exactly as he flaunted his women in front of her. Bert is a juggler and an acrobat, and he goes off to work in carnivals in the summers. He is a kind of a 'dump,' too," she said, looking pleased with her choice of word, "like this building. He was at Donna's funeral with his juggling balls, but then the police came and took him away. They were not a happy couple, Donna and Bert."

"But they never broke up?"

"No. Well, maybe a few weeks before she died, I don't know." She thought about something for a moment, shook her head. "But they'd had such angry quarrels before."

"What do you mean?"

"They had a fight in her apartment. I could hear them. Donna said loudly: 'I don't want money, I don't need money!' She said that she'd told him before that 'This is not about money!' Those were her exact words: 'This is not about money!' He said to her, just as loudly, that she didn't want money because she didn't need it—meaning that he did—and he called her a 'spoiled little bitch.' After a while, her door opened and I heard him shout at her from the hall, in a high, false voice: 'You *tricked* me! You *tricked* me.' He was mocking her when he said that, of course, for those were her own words when she did not get something she thought she deserved—from him, from me, from all the world.'"

"She said them to you, too?"

Sumiko smiled ruefully. "She said them to me, when our friendship ended. She'd come over to my apartment to ask me to go to a movie with her, and I had a friend with me. Donna was surprised, but then tried to pretend she didn't see him, just insisted that I come with her to the movies. I told her I couldn't, that I was entertaining a visitor. She looked at my friend for the first time, and said, 'Entertaining. Is that what you call it?' and she laughed at us, even though we were not doing anything wrong. Then she looked at me and said: 'You've tricked me. I don't like being tricked.' It was scary, so I had to laugh to myself when I heard Bert yell 'You tricked me!' at her. He was giving her a dose of her own poison—is that the word I want?" she concluded with a sweet smile.

I didn't leave the apartment building the way I'd come in. I went out the back way instead, just so I could glance at Donna Trask's apartment door as I walked by. I wondered if the apartment had been cleared out yet. Donna had been dead just over a week. I thought of what Sumiko had heard behind that door, a few weeks before Donna's death, about a month ago: "This is not about money," she'd shouted at Bert. What wasn't?

The back stairs were dark. The back door, which opened onto an alley, clicked shut behind me. Out of curiosity, I tried the door. It was locked, and the lock looked new. The building's owners apparently thought burglars enter buildings only through alleys, since they hadn't done anything about the security door in front. A street lamp at the end of the alley cast a thin yellow glow on its rain-slicked brick surface. It was raining and the temperature had fallen, too. I ran down the alley to the street and my bike.

I live four miles from the University, and bike whenever the weather permits, which is often, even in winter. I don't like biking in rain, though, and I hadn't come prepared for it tonight. "You tricked me," I said to the sky, as the rain ran down my face and neck and into my shirt.

In the distance, between me and downtown, I could see Harold McCord's hotel, in which Sumiko Sato had witnessed the scene between Donna and her father and McCord. You wouldn't be able to see much from the picture windows tonight.

What was Donald Trask doing at McCord's birthday

bash, especially in such an ugly mood? Wasn't it a conflict of interest, to both represent the University and be friends with McCord, who, I supposed, had done a lot of business with the University over the years and—as he'd told Sumiko—won the contract for the University's new convention center?

But maybe it wasn't so surprising. Theresa Durr had told me that Trask had been a real estate lawyer before becoming the University's chief attorney. He'd worked with Strauss, she'd said, fifteen years ago, on something to do with the development of the New Campus. I supposed that a real estate lawyer could have been a friend of Harold McCord's back then.

But it sounded as if McCord knew Jeremiah Strauss, too. They seemed like unlikely friends, if that's what it was—a once and future Humanities professor and a businessman who only knew profits and losses.

I didn't envy Buck his job, if the trail of whoever had tried to murder Strauss led out into the world of Harold McCord and high finance.

Thirteen

I usually enjoy going to work, but not that night. It was Tuesday, and I still hadn't called Buck about Edith, and I wasn't looking forward to seeing Lawrence. I wished that Paula hadn't been assigned the dog watch, or that Lawrence wasn't so smitten with her that he'd signed up for it, too.

They were at their usual table, playing Boggle. The sand was running out in the hour glass and Paula's list was longer than Lawrence's, although not as much longer as usual. Either she was playing with half a mind, or Lawrence was improving. They both glanced up at me as I came into the room, then finished their game.

"I saw Lt. Hansen this afternoon," Lawrence said. His face was pinker than usual. Since mine was turning paler than usual, we managed to keep the same level of rose in the room.

"Oh," I said.

"I asked him what he'd done with the information you gave him about Professor Silberman."

"Turns out you didn't give him the information," Paula said, giving me a chilly look.

I started to say something but couldn't find any words. "How'd you happen to come across Hansen?" I finally managed to get out, stalling.

"He was on campus," Lawrence said, "he'd been—"

"That's not important." Paula cut him off, her voice flat with anger. "What you did wasn't nice, Peggy—except for your friend Professor Silberman."

"Paula . . ." Lawrence said.

"It's okay, Lawrence," I told him. "She's right."

"If she's a murderer," Paula went on, "you've given her time to cover her tracks and time to go after Dean Strauss again, at Lawrence's expense. Did you tell her about Lawrence, too?"

"She's not a murderer," I said, not answering the question.

As far as Paula was concerned, I'd answered the question. She gave me a contemptuous stare. "Cops don't make judgments like that. You're in the wrong business, Peggy."

I don't cry much, and I don't feel comfortable around people who do. I started to cry and simultaneously fight the rage I always feel when I'm ashamed of myself. I liked these two people a lot, and I didn't want them mad at me. I knew I'd behaved irresponsibly. Worst of all, I'd been caught at it.

I wiped away tears with the back of my hand. "I guess I am in the wrong business," I said. "I don't suppose I'll be in it much longer." I was thinking that Buck wouldn't let this pass unpunished. He was in the right business.

Lawrence looked miserable. He said, "I told Hansen I'd only just seen Professor Silberman yesterday afternoon, coming across campus, around the same time and place I saw her with you last week. I didn't tell him you were with her, Peggy. I told him I'd seen you later that night, here, and told you about it, and that there'd probably been a misunderstanding about which of us would call him."

"And Hansen gave Lawrence a look that suggested he was a chump—either for thinking he'd believe such a dumb story so poorly told, or for not passing on the news to Homicide directly," Paula said, showing me no mercy.

I was feeling lower and lower. Lawrence had stuck his

neck out for me and he could easily get it chopped off along with mine, if Buck got the real story out of Edith.

Mercifully, it was time for roll call. We went out on patrol separately—Paula, Lawrence, and I—into the rain.

I'd told Edith at breakfast on Saturday that the fact that she'd been one of the people who'd gone into Adamson Hall through the kitchen and dining room probably wouldn't get her more than a hard grilling from Buck. I was wrong. She was arrested and taken to jail, almost as soon as Buck had finished talking to Lawrence.

As I'd suspected, Edith had held out on me. She'd held out something big: Her late husband, Paul, had been a chemistry professor at a small local college until his death.

It took up most of the six o'clock news the next night. Unaccountably, the reporter gave the story from Edith's front lawn, a breeze mussing his hair, making him look as if he were bringing us this report under difficult, possibly hazardous, conditions.

Paul Silberman, the reporter told us, had kept a laboratory in his home. It might well have contained cyanide, he added, for the benefit of the slower among us. One of the late professor's colleagues had informed the police that when he visited Edith less than two months ago, the lab was still in the house and, as far as he could tell, just as Silberman had left it.

"Damn," I whispered.

The lab was gone now, the newshawk droned, arching a meaningful eyebrow. Edith Silberman had shown it to the police herself. Police technicians had gone over the room, to see what they could learn, but they'd offered nothing more than a significant "no comment" to the media representatives.

The television cameras switched back to the anchorwoman, who filled in the background. Edith was brought before a magistrate that morning and released on her own recognizance that afternoon. We were treated to the sight of newspaper and television reporters following her out of the courthouse and waiting for her in ambush when she arrived home. Children and adults, leaning against cars and milling around, waved at the television cameras and looked at each other with self-conscious grins. They were probably doing that now, as they sat and watched themselves and Edith.

Although she was small, Edith had never looked short to me. She was compact, like a bundle of contained energy. Now, as the reporters blocked her way into her home, she looked even more compact, like some kind of black hole that has so much energy that it endangers everything around it. She stared into the cameras and stated that, on the advice of her attorney, she would say nothing at this time. She said this in a steady voice, her dark eyes hard and unblinking, and it seemed to me that the television cameras switched away from her in relief. The patch of white hair at her temple was like a burst of flak.

The anchorwoman was speaking again. Edith Silberman had reportedly held a grudge against Strauss for years. According to one of her younger colleagues, she'd said in an agitated manner that she deserved a University Scholarship more than Strauss. And, in front of witnesses, she'd once threatened to poison Strauss, too.

A studio portrait of Donna Trask appeared on the television screen. It was a recent photograph, but Donna looked no more than sixteen, sweet and ethereal. I recalled Sumiko Sato's description of her when she didn't get her own way—bloated, as if hung over, her eyes hidden behind black lenses—and how I'd last seen her, ready to explode a bomb in a banquet hall of distinguished people, a leer of triumph on her face.

Finally the anchorwoman introduced us to a tame and telegenic University psychologist, who came on to explain the psychological reasons for why homicidal women throughout history have favored poison.

"Until the advent of the so-called 'women's movement,'" he said, as if speaking through a mouthful of overripe persimmon, "knives and guns might have been considered 'unladylike,' if you will. One must normally stand to use them effectively and assume an aggressive pose—".

I assumed an aggressive pose and zapped, if you will, the TV with my remote.

So, I thought bitterly, as I forked down an icy lunch that I hadn't left in the microwave oven long enough, Edith had tricked me again. Then I heard myself and said aloud, "Oops!"

But she had tricked me. She'd asked me to give her a couple of days before going to Buck with what Lawrence had told me, and then she'd rushed home and cleaned out her husband's chemistry lab.

The phone rang.

"I'm sorry, Peggy. I should have told you about Paul."

"Paul who?" I said. I was being childish again. Or still.

"My husband," Edith said, pretending not to hear the chill in my voice. "I'm not sorry I didn't tell you," she went on, "I'm just sorry it might hurt you."

"What's the difference?" I demanded, fighting not to shout at her. "What kind of meaningless distinction are you striving to make here?"

"I don't like the criminal justice system," she answered. She sounded exhausted. "It scarcely works in the case of the guilty. For the innocent, it's a nightmare. You're supposed to be innocent until proven guilty. That sounds nice, doesn't it, but if it's true, why do they take you away from your home in handcuffs, book you, haul you before a judge, and expose you to the media's prurient curiosity? And now I'm going to have to pay an enormous sum of money I don't have to a lawyer who's going to defend me in an arena where victory goes to the biggest ham, the one who can perform best in front of a bunch of people who know all about guilt and innocence from watching soaps, game shows, and sitcoms."

She stopped to catch her breath, went on: "I was willing to do anything to try to avoid having 'my day in court,' Peggy. I was even willing to lie to you. And I'm not sorry—I'd do it again. I'm just sorry I didn't do a better job of it, and I'm sorry if you get hurt."

I didn't say anything for a while, because I agreed with her about the legal system. I just don't know an alternative to it. Maybe Paula was right, I thought, maybe I'm in the wrong job.

I said, trying to sustain my anger, "I guess you've been busy since I last saw you, spring cleaning."

"Yes, I have," she said. "I've already admitted that to the police, since they were going to find out anyway. Unfortunately, I went about 'spring cleaning' in a rather crude way, and some of my neighbors seem to have told the police that they noticed me hauling boxes and sacks out to my car over the past several days. I was surprised by how much Paul had in there."

"It must have been painful," I said, "to have to get rid of all your husband's stuff in a rush like that."

"Not really," she replied. "I didn't leave the lab intact for sentimental reasons. When Paul first built it, I hated having it there, because you could smell it everywhere in the house. But then I got used to the smell and forgot about it. Since his death, I've just been too busy to get rid of it. But after you told me what your campus cop friend remembered about me, I went home and cleaned house. Foolish, to say the least, especially since I didn't do a very good job of it."

"Was there cyanide in there, Edith?"

"You think I'd tell you if there had been?" She tried to make a joke out of it. "No," she went on, "there wasn't, at least not under that name, and I don't know any other name for it. There were some bottles with poison warnings on them, but I don't know what they were or what they were for. I poured all the chemicals down the toilet, washed the bottles, put them in paper bags, and took the bags to one of those dumpster things behind a gas station."

"You admitted all that to the police?"

"Why not?" She laughed shortly. "My lawyer looked like he was about to cry when I did, but so what? He'll cry his eyes out in a courtroom, if he thinks that'll get me off. He'd do that even if he thought I'd poisoned an entire child-care center. So it was good practice for him."

"Did they find the stuff you put in the dumpster?"

"I haven't heard. If not, they've probably got people out at the landfill looking for it, even as we speak. But I don't see that it matters, one way or the other. I'm not about to recant my testimony that there was a lab in the house full of chemicals at the time somebody tried to slip Jerry Strauss a poisoned apple."

She'd disposed of the evidence as soon as she could after I'd warned her. The way she put it, it made me sound like an accomplice. I *was* an accomplice!

Maybe Edith could read minds over phones. She said, "This cop, Hansen? He asked me why I'd suddenly cleaned out Paul's lab on Saturday—as if he suspected I'd been warned, or something, although he didn't come right out and say so. I pretended to misunderstand the question. I told him I wasn't religious, that it didn't bother me to work on the Sabbath."

"Oh, by the way," she added, the casualness in her voice sounding forced, "I'm on leave from the University, with pay, until this business is settled. Jerry Strauss's little toady, Hudson Bates, called me with the news this afternoon. It's running mean little errands like that that empowers Hudson. And my guess is that Strauss listened in on the call, just for kicks."

I told her I was sorry. She lied and said she wasn't, that she could use a little time off. It wasn't a convincing effort.

"Did you really tell somebody in your department that you deserved to be a University Scholar more than Strauss?"

"In an 'agitated manner?' I can think of several of my younger colleagues who would have happily told the newshounds that one. Yes, I did say it, but I was joking. But only *half*-joking. I'm afraid I don't quite deserve the honor, at least not as the Scholarship was originally defined. I'm not a great scholar and teacher, just an honorable toiler in the fields. But Jerry isn't even that. You don't sound mad at me anymore. Peggy," she added.

"No, I'm not mad at you anymore, Edith," I said. "I'm sure I would have done the same thing you did."

I couldn't bring myself to confess to her that I had done the same thing to Lawrence.

"Do you have any idea how Jeremiah Strauss got to be a University Scholar in the first place?" I asked her.

"I don't know, to tell you the truth," she replied, sounding relieved to change the subject. "All I can think of is Wolf must have been under tremendous pressure to make him one. After all, the prestige of the University depends, to some extent, on the quality of our University Scholars. Wolf had to feel that diluting the Scholars' ranks with a man like Jerry Strauss was necessary."

"So it was Wolf's doing?"

"Well," Edith answered, "the regents had to approve it, of course."

"What are *their* qualifications for making those kinds of judgments?"

"They have none," she said flatly. "The board of regents is composed of prominent members of the community, and they're supposed to oversee the workings of the University, but they have no special qualifications for the task. Over the years, there have been a lot of rich businessmen among them, sports boosters—is there anything lower than a sports booster, I wonder?—a handful of failed politicians with important contacts, a token sprinkling of women and minorities, and even some ex-jocks who once played for our team. A skillful university president can play the regents like a not very complex musical instrument—a sweet potato, for example. When it comes to selecting University Scholars, I'm sure they vote for whomever Wolf tells them to vote for."

"Some of the regents are wealthy businessmen, you said?"

"A couple. Why, Peggy? What's buzzing around in your head?"

"Nothing. Harold McCord's never been a regent, has he?"

"No, and he never will be. He's done too much business with the University for that to happen. The University may be the most corrupt and cynical institution in the state, but at least it tries to be circumspect about it."

"I just learned that McCord recently told Donald Trask that it was too bad they couldn't name the new conference center after Strauss."

"What? That must have been a joke at Strauss's expense."

"Yeah, maybe. My informant thought it was at Donald Trask's expense, too. Either way, I don't get it."

"Jerry Strauss chaired the committee that recommended that the conference center be put on the New Campus," Edith said. "He was on record as being strongly against it—he wanted it on the Old Campus, for some reason. But he got voted down by his own committee. As you might imagine, that hasn't happened too often in Jerry's career! I don't know what role Trask might have played in all of that, other than as the U's legal beagle." She yawned noisily. "I'm tired now, Peggy, and I don't see how any of this is going to help me."

"Maybe it won't," I told her. "But Strauss was involved in more than just trying to mess up your life. You're not the only one who wanted him dead."

"I didn't want him dead, damn it!" she protested, suddenly angry.

"I'm sorry."

"You're probably right," she said, her voice resigned. "I probably did—do—want him dead."

We were silent for a few moments. "It's none of your business, Peggy, what happens to me," she said finally. "But if you did want to help me, you could try to find out who besides me had access to cyanide. Maybe one of your Homicide cop friends knows—Hansen? That's one of the tacks my lawyer's going to take. But there's no reason for you to get involved."

"Does your lawyer know that Hudson Bates stepped on the apple that killed Donna Trask?" Buck had told me that. He didn't say it was confidential, although the media hadn't mentioned it.

She laughed. "How disgusting! And his wife wasn't even there to scrape it off his Oxfords! You think he did it deliberately, to destroy evidence?"

I said I didn't know, I was just passing on what I'd heard.

We exchanged a few hollow, encouraging words, and hung up.

Fourteen

No, Edith's problem wasn't any of my business, I thought as I walked my beat that night. And it wasn't my business, either, to pick Buck Hansen's brains and pass on the harvest to Edith or her lawyer.

Since watching Donna Trask die, I'd gone to her funeral, and interviewed her mother, her boyfriend, and her friend Sumiko. None of that had been my business either.

Her ex-boyfriend, I corrected myself. And her ex-friend. And, in a sense, her ex-mother, too. Donna had put an X through a lot in her life.

Why had I gotten involved? One reason was a large empty space in my life since Al and I had split up. It needed filling, and learning to cook, as Ginny had suggested, wasn't likely to do the trick. Al had been fun and comfortable to be with. And predictable and sometimes boring, too. We'd never lived together. He'd made marriage-type noises occasionally, but I'd managed to put him off without causing irreparable damage.

Everything was fine until Al's son came to live with him. Then he no longer wanted me coming and going at his place, and of course he could no longer stay at my place either. I wasn't interested in marriage or in moving in with Al—I'd tried that once, with somebody else, with awful results—and I wasn't ready to be a mom to a boy with facial hair starting to sprout up around his acne either. Which left me feeling lonelier than I'd felt in a long time.

But the loss of Al didn't explain why I'd become obsessed with Donna Trask. I'd talked to her briefly, and a while later I'd watched her die a horrible death, her face suffused with a mean, exulting rage. I'd wanted to know the source of that rage, and now I thought I did. It wasn't really Jeremiah Strauss she was mad at. She was mad at the father who'd never been there for her except in all the wrong ways, and mad at her mother who'd gotten away. And she was mad at herself, too.

I knew a little about those things, but I'd been lucky. My anger hadn't consumed me the way it had Donna. I'd managed to grow up—in some important ways, at least.

Donna had destroyed a triumphant moment in a man's life, and in the process she'd been destroyed herself. Now her rage was going to destroy Edith Silberman, a friend of mine and the best teacher I'd ever had. I was going to do what I could to prevent that from happening.

The Campanile bells struck the half hour—2:30—as I went down into the tunnel system. The morning wasn't unusually cold and I didn't really think about what I was doing down there. Sometimes it's best to surprise yourself a little.

I passed the entrance to Adamson Hall and continued on until I came to the stair leading up to Jefferson Hall, where Ginny Raines's favorite suspect, Myles Kruger, had his office. No light showed under his door, but I knocked anyway and waited a moment, before using my passkey. The room smelled of stale tobacco, like a dirty ashtray. Opposite where I was standing, behind Kruger's desk, a window faced a courtyard and the dark windows of the Language Arts Building on the other side of it. I crossed the room and twitched the venetian blinds shut, then used my flashlight to look around. I didn't know what I was looking for, just something that would throw suspicion on somebody besides Edith, and Kruger was the only viable suspect I knew of.

I ran my flashlight over the walls covered with bookshelves. From the titles, it was obvious that Kruger's speciality was early American history.

I tried his desk drawers, but they were locked. He'd have to be stupid to hide cyanide in his office, but then, he'd had to be a little dim, or a little nuts, to make more than one anonymous phone call to Strauss. He should have assumed that after the first one, there'd be a tap on Strauss's phone. Maybe he'd been just as stupid about the poison. If he'd tried to poison Strauss once, he might be planning to try again. If so, where would he keep his poison hidden, if not at home or in his office?

I went over to the old oak file drawers next to the window. They weren't locked. As I started to pull the top one open, a key turned in the door behind me.

There wasn't any place to hide. There wasn't any point in trying to hide. The door opened and the silhouette of a tall man filled the doorway.

He saw me against the window, and stopped in the act of turning on the overhead light. "Who are you? What are you doing in my office?"

"I'm a cop," I told him. "I heard a noise in here. I came in to investigate."

"The hell you did! And what'd you find? A bat?" He let the door shut behind him, switched on the light.

"Funny," he said, "until recently, I'd never talked to a cop, campus or otherwise, in all the ten years I've been here. And now all of a sudden they're everywhere I turn. And I've seen you before too. You were lurking outside my office at this same time on Monday. Didn't you find what you were looking for then?"

"I didn't come in," I said, "I was just patrolling the building. But tonight I heard something. It must have been your radiator. I'll be leaving now."

"You'll leave when I say you will." His voice was loud in the room and there was a glitter in his dark eyes that I didn't like. He looked even more like an undertaker than he had the first time I'd seen him.

He left me with three choices: Try to push him out of the way, use my walkie-talkie to call for help, or stay there until he let me go. The first option might get me hurt, the second trouble. Only the third option might get me something useful.

"This has to do with those phone calls I made to Strauss, of course," he went on, when I didn't say anything. "But I thought you just nailed somebody for trying to kill him. Edith what's-her-name, Silberman."

I hate it when people don't believe me, especially when I'm lying. "I told you—" I began.

"No," he said, as if I hadn't spoken, "that doesn't make sense. Not even the cops are stupid enough to send somebody in without a search warrant. You don't have a search warrant, by some chance, do you, and it just slipped your mind to show me?" He cocked his pale undertaker's head and twisted his thin lips into a mocking smile.

"I came in here on my own," I told him. "Edith Silberman's a friend of mine."

He ran his long fingers through what was left of his lusterless hair and shook his head in bewilderment. "She's a friend of yours! And in order to try to get her off, you're hoping to serve me up to justice instead." He seemed to think that was the most outrageous thing he'd ever heard. "She must be one hell of a friend!"

"I guess she is. Anyway, why not you?" I asked. "You had a motive. This building's connected by the tunnel to Adamson Hall, so you had the opportunity. And making threatening phone calls to Strauss doesn't rank very high on the rational scale, does it?"

"You know all about me, don't you?" He reached into his jacket pocket, pulled out a package of cigarettes. "Do you also know that Jeremiah Strauss destroyed my marriage? I suppose that ranks high on your rational scale, doesn't it?" He poked a cigarette between his sour lips and lit it, blew out a stream of smoke, and then walked through it into the middle of the room. Resting his knuckles on his desk, he leaned across it at me. "Do you know the story," he asked me, "or do they omit details, wind you up, point you to a suspect's office, and order you to go in late at night and search it?"

"I don't know why you were mad at Strauss," I said.

"Really?" he replied, not caring if I did or not. "Then you don't know that I once had a good marriage, do you?"

I nodded.

"Kate's a marvelous woman, a wonderful wife. She worked to help me through graduate school. She even agreed to postpone her career—she's got a degree in child development—until the kids started school."

He paused, looked at me, sucked smoke. "Get to the point, I hear you say," he said. "Why? Does the smoke bother you? Maybe I'd be able to quit, if you'd all just leave me alone. Well, after I got tenure and we had a house and two children, and everything was going exactly as planned, I decided, for some inexplicable reason, I wanted to know how it feels to live for a while, just visit, you know, the sewer. And I found just the woman to show me around." He laughed, a mirthless, nutty laugh. "Sewer guides are everywhere," he assured me, lowering his voice to a confidential whisper. "Divorced women of a certain age, most of them . . ."

The Campanile bells struck three. Kruger cocked his head, as if to hear better. Then he nodded, said, "Perfect! It's always three o'clock in the morning, isn't it, in the dark night of the soul? Who said that, I wonder?"

"Huckleberry Finn," I told him, just to see if he could hear any voice but his own. He couldn't. He was no longer suffering for what he'd done. He was suffering in his struggle to put a little style into it and doing a piss-poor job of it, in my opinion.

"And you liked it in the sewer," I said impatiently, "and you might have stayed there a long time, except that your wife found out about it, and then the jig was up. You had to choose—your sewer guide or that wonderful woman, your marvelous wife. Or was it a wonderful wife, marvelous woman? I can't remember."

He straightened up, as if I'd landed an uppercut. Good. What I really wanted to do was throw up on his shoes.

He came around his desk. I moved, too, keeping it between us. He pulled out his chair and slumped down into it. "Right," he said, deflated, "my wife found out. You really know how to cut through the bull, don't you?" Kruger poked out his cigarette, only half-smoked, the expression on his face saying that it had disappointed him. "It was Strauss who told her. An anonymous phone call."

"How do you know it was Strauss?"

"Oh, it wasn't Strauss himself," he replied. "My wife knows his voice. Besides, Strauss wouldn't do his own dirty work. It was Hudson Bates, his gofer."

I asked him how he knew that.

"I didn't, until the Graduate School turned me down for a research and travel grant. It didn't make any sense, since my proposal was a good one. So I went to Strauss to find out why. He didn't even get up when I walked into his office. He sat there, looming over his huge desk, and watched me approach with complete indifference. I started to tell him why I was there. He didn't even wait for me to finish. 'You're an adulterer,' he said. 'I don't like adulterers on the faculty—it gives the University a bad name.' "

Myles Kruger barked something in the way of a laugh, but his long face didn't lose its mournful expression. "That was the last thing I expected to hear. I just stood there, staring at him. He didn't say anything else. Finally I crawled out of there. Later, it occurred to me that it might have been Strauss who tipped off my wife, using Bates. So I called Bates at his home and, without saying anything, I handed the phone to my wife when he came on the line. She talked to him, pretending to be a telephone solicitor. She said he was the anonymous caller."

"And then you started making anonymous phone calls to Strauss," I said.

"That was later, after my wife decided to go ahead with the divorce anyway. She just quit counselling and hired a lawyer," he added, still incredulous.

Are there any love stories left with happy endings? I asked Kruger where he was on the day of the banquet.

"The cops have already asked me that," he replied, fishing out a new cigarette. "I was right here, in my office. And I was right here that night, too, while all the dignitaries were—supping, I believe the word is—and the young woman died. I wasn't invited, alas. The cops know all that, too."

"Did you know Strauss would be using an apple for a prop at the banquet?"

"No, I guess I was one of the few people on campus who didn't." He lit his cigarette while he waited for me to ask him something else. When I couldn't think of anything, he said, "I don't think I've ever met Edith Silberman. She's in the Humanities Department, isn't she? Strauss's department. How does a campus cop like you happen to know her?"

I told him I got my B.A. here and that Edith had been my adviser for my senior thesis.

He nodded, not really listening. "You want to hear another funny story about what goes on in the Graduate School?"

"Sure."

"A couple of months ago, Strauss let a secretary who worked in his office go. Kevin Ames. He didn't give a reason, but Ames thinks it's because Strauss doesn't think men should perform work like that. Adding insult to injury, he gave Ames a negative evaluation, which meant he'd never get another job on campus. Well, Ames knew about Strauss and me—the secretaries in the Ad Building know everything that goes on in that place. A month or so ago, Ames and I bumped into each other in a restaurant downtown, and he told me his story—sympathizing with me, you know?"

The cigarette smoke was getting to me, making my eyes smart and my nose run. "Yes, I know," I said, to urge him along.

"He told me something else that ought to make a proper little moralist like you gag. You want to hear it?"

Nobody'd ever called me a proper little moralist before. I almost liked the sound of it. "Sure," I said.

"Shortly before he was let go, Ames stumbled onto two people kissing in an elevator. Passionately. You want to guess who the man was?"

"Not Strauss," I said, quite firmly. Maybe if, someday, they wrap up an expensive call girl operation in this town, they might find Strauss's name on the list of johns, but he'd never be caught making out in an elevator.

"No, not Strauss." Kruger laughed at the thought of that, choked on smoke. "It was that little prick, Bates! Making out like a beaver in the elevator with a secretary or a student."

This didn't sound like Bates, from what I'd seen of him and heard from Edith.

"Strauss must not have found out about it," I said, "since Bates is still the assistant dean." I knew enough about assistant deans to know they only serve at the pleasure of their masters.

"He found out about it," Kruger said grimly. "I told him, in one of my late-night phone calls to the son of a bitch."

"Then he must not have believed you," I said. "Why should he?"

"With Strauss, it doesn't take fire, it just takes smoke. It's more likely that Bates is too useful to Strauss for Strauss to let moral considerations get in the way. Faculty members like me are a dime a dozen, whereas a faithful administrative toady is a prized possession. It's always possible, of course," he added, "that Strauss found some other way to punish Bates—which would give Bates a motive for murder, too, wouldn't it?"

"If the story's true," I said, "and if Strauss did punish him."

"Yeah." The expression on Kruger's face said he wanted the story to be true.

I asked Kruger why he was in his office so late.

"I live alone now, and I can't sleep. So I came in to do some work. Now that Strauss has resigned as dean, I'll apply for another grant. Maybe I'll get it. You really expected to find something incriminating in here?"

"Desperate times require desperate measures," I said.

"I suppose you could get into trouble for this." His deep-set, mournful eyes lit up a little at the thought.

I said that I could.

"From what I read in the newspaper, there's been bad blood between your friend Silberman and Strauss for a long time. So I guess she can't be all bad. I hope you're right that she's not guilty, but I don't want to go back to being a suspect." He waved his cigarette around the room, filling the air with poisonous little whorls. "You're free to look around some more, if you want to. I won't tell. But you won't find anything." He switched on the goose-necked lamp on his desk and opened a book.

"Thanks," I said, and left.

Fifteen

I rode to campus the next day after lunch and locked my bike to a lamppost in front of the Administration building. It's six stories tall, with the offices of the president, Vice President Hightower, and their staff occupying the entire top floor. The public elevator doesn't go that far up. The fifth floor belongs to Donald Trask, the University's chief attorney, and his staff of lawyers, along with the many lesser vice presidents, assistant vice presidents, and assistants to the vice presidents that clutter up the place. The fourth, third, and second floors house the various deans, associate deans, and assistant deans of the colleges that make up the University. The Ad Building's a fortress, its inhabitants united in their desire to never go back to the classroom and face students again.

The Graduate School offices were on the fourth floor, and that's where I was heading. I wanted some information quickly and hoped I could get it from Strauss's secretary without Strauss finding out about it. Even if he did, I had a story ready.

Jesse Porter was sitting at a card table set up in the hall outside Strauss's office. He looked surprised to see me. Jesse's got brown hair, eyes to match, and a head that's almost perfectly round. For a while we called him Jesse James because he shot himself in the leg while practicing quick draws in a campus building late one night in his rookie year. The teasing stopped when, unarmed, he took on two muggers with knives a few months later.

"I didn't think bats came out during the day," he said.

"Ha-ha. How come you're still here?"

"This'll probably be my last day. Dean Strauss thinks the danger's past, now that they've arrested somebody."

I looked at the clipboard on the card table. A sheet of paper on it registered times in and times out for everybody who'd been in Strauss's office. I wondered how that knowledge would keep anybody alive.

"What are you up to?" he asked me.

"Unofficial business," I said, "on behalf of a friend. Stay alert, because they arrested the wrong person." As I went past him through the door, he dutifully wrote down my name and the time.

There were three desks scattered around the large outer office, but only one of them was occupied, by a woman who was staring down at a sheet of paper on her desk as if it might contain a revised answer to the riddle of the Sphinx. Her eyes were following the finger of the man behind her, who was leaning over her shoulder and talking as he pointed things out to her in a low, creamy voice. She didn't look as if she enjoyed his closeness any more than I would have, but she kept her face carefully blank, a *sine qua* for the compleat secretary.

They both looked up as I came in, the man with a mildly pained expression on his face, as if I'd broken his concentration and, with it, shattered an unusually fine idea beyond repair. It was Hudson Bates, the associate dean. He had a pleasant face, blow-dried hair of no particular color, and he was wearing a dark, three-piece suit, beautifully tailored. He looked like a clothing store dummy, before they started personalizing them.

The secretary asked if she could help me. I said I wasn't in any hurry, and I could wait.

"That wasn't what she asked you, was it?" Bates said, as if he really hoped that, with a little gentle prompting, I'd be able to answer the question. His voice was rich and pleasant, like suntan lotion, and seemed designed to project to an audience larger than just the three of us.

I felt my face start to grow hot. A few years ago, a question like that would have reduced me to babbling, but I no longer allow people to do that to me without at least trying to make them pay a price. I said, "I hate it when somebody returns politeness with rudeness. It's so easy to do, so why bother?"

He started to say something, then realized he could only bluster something incoherent. His eyes turned down to the back of the secretary's head. "We can finish going over this later, Janine," and he walked through a door just beyond the secretary's desk, without looking at me again.

Victories are measured by the size of your opponents, which made this victory very small, but I savored it anyway, even as I noticed that Bates didn't close his door after him. In the window in his office I could see his reflection as he sat down at his desk and bent over some papers.

I recalled the story Myles Kruger had told me the night before, about a secretary surprising Bates kissing a young woman in an elevator. No, I thought, Bates wouldn't put himself into a position like that.

"Yes?" the secretary said, interrupting my reverie. There was a nice smile on her face.

"I wonder if you could help me," I said. "I'd like some information." I wasn't happy having Bates within listening distance, but it would be worse if I whispered. "I'd like to know who was on a committee Dean Strauss chaired last year, the conference center committee."

"I don't see why not," she said. "That's not confidential information."

In the window in Bates's office, I saw his ghost pick up a phone and punch some buttons. He only punched four, which bothered me. I listened hard, but couldn't hear a phone ringing behind Strauss's door, down the long hall behind the secretary's desk.

Meanwhile, she went to a file cabinet and picked

through it until she found what she was looking for. I asked her if I could copy down the names on the list, but she offered to make a Xerox copy for me. Saying she'd only be a minute, she left the room. I sat down at the chair by her desk and waited.

Dean Strauss's door opened. He filled the doorway, then lumbered down the hall toward me like a bear coming out of hibernation early. From my seated position, he was even bigger than I'd thought, and I got up instinctively, prepared to run. I remembered, irrelevantly, what Theresa Durr had said, about how quick he was with his hands, and how light he was on his feet. His mane of reddish-gray hair seemed to blow about the sides of his head as if he were running.

"Where's Janine?" he asked. He looked around the room, as if she played funny little games with him sometimes, and was perhaps hiding behind one of the empty desks.

"She went to make a copy of something for me," I said. "She'll be right back." My voice was flimsy, like onionskin.

He grumbled something, turned back toward his office, then paused. "You work here?" He seemed to be asking the wall. I'd heard that one of the most disconcerting things about Strauss was that he never loked directly at anybody he was talking to. His eyes moved around the room as he talked or listened, never resting anywhere for long.

I said no.

"I've seen you before. Where?"

"I was at the banquet in your honor in Adamson," I told him. "I'm a campus policewoman, but I wasn't in uniform then."

"What's your name?" he asked, speaking to a painting on a wall and then to the telephone on Janine's desk.

"Peggy O'Neill."

"What's Janine doing for you?"

"She's getting me a list of the members of the confer-

ence center committee you chaired last year," I said. I
went on without waiting to be asked: "I have a friend
who's writing her senior thesis on 'Decision Making at the
University.' Her chief example's going to be the way the
University decided to place the conference center over on
the New Campus instead of here. It was a pretty contro-
versial decision at the time, she tells me, and there was a
lot written about it. I don't know anything about it, myself," I added, "since I don't read the *Daily* much." I threw
him that, as if tossing a baby to the wolves, since I knew
he hated the *Daily*. Once I get warmed up, I give good lie.

"What's she going to do," Strauss demanded, "interview
everybody who was on the committee?" His eyes had suddenly fastened on me.

"I don't know," I said. "I guess so." I could feel the
sweat starting to trickle down my sides from my armpits.
This was the hardest person I'd ever lied to. I promised
myself that, if I made it through this time, I'd never ever
lie again. "She did tell me she planned to try to get an appointment to talk to you," I added, fighting to keep my
voice steady and relaxed.

Strauss continued to stare at me. Then his head turned
slowly, this way and that, his eyes again moving around
the room. It was as if he smelled the blood of an English-
man, but couldn't figure out where it was coming from.
"What's her name?" he asked me, abruptly.

Won't he ever quit, I wondered, but I answered without
hesitation, struggling to keep desperation out of my voice.
"Anita Torres." I do have a friend with that name, a junior.
She's the sort of student who might start her senior thesis
in her junior year. She's ambitious, and in a hurry. If I
could get out of Jeremiah Strauss's clutches alive, she
would be getting a call from me.

Janine returned with the copy of the list of committee
members. Strauss interrupted her before she could tell him
what I wanted.

"I know all about it," he said, and explained it to her
with a meat-handed attempt at humor. He had small, even

teeth, which he showed in something that might have been a smile. Then he turned and lumbered back the way he'd come, having forgotten that he'd come out initially on the pretext of looking for Janine.

Janine walked me to the door, followed me into the hall. "He really put me through the third degree!" I said. "You'd think I'd asked for the plans for the atomic bomb, or something. Is he always like that?"

"Always," she said quietly, moving down the hall, away from where Jesse Porter could hear us. "How else could he have survived all these years as dean? We don't even gossip about him in the women's lounge," she added, even more softly. "We think he's got it bugged."

"He said he'd seen me before. How could he, when he never seems to look at you directly?"

"Don't let yourself be fooled by that," she said, more softly yet. "He doesn't miss a thing."

As I took the stairs down to the first floor, I considered what to do next. I intended to interview at least some of the people who'd served on the conference center committee with Strauss, to try to get some idea of what kind of problems there might have been. There must have been problems, if Strauss had been on record as wanting to put the center on the Old Campus, and the committee, apparently against expectations, had voted to recommend putting it on the New Campus. I hoped I'd be able to stir up something that would help Edith Silberman.

On an impulse, I checked the Ad Building's directory and located the University's publicity office. It was in the basement. I walked down, found the office I wanted, and went in. A man came over to the counter. I explained that I was a reporter for a consortium of neighborhood newspapers, working on an article on "Movers and Shakers at the U," and I wanted photographs of a cross-section of University administrators. He said he'd be happy to give me the pictures and asked who I was interested in.

I wanted to show Lawrence Fitzpatrick pictures of Hud-

son Bates and Donald Trask, to see if he might remember
if either of them had come to the banquet through the
kitchen. The thought that Donald Trask might have poisoned his own daughter, meaning to kill Strauss, was horrible but not impossible. And the more people I could find
with possible grudges against Strauss who'd come through
the kitchen, the better for Edith. I didn't know what
Trask's problem was with Strauss, but it was obvious their
friendship was creaky, to say the least.

Just to muddle things up a bit, I gave the man at the
counter the names of several regents, the dean of the Medical School, President Wolf, and Strauss, in addition to
Bates and Trask. He went to a file and brought me glossy
publicity photographs of each of them, spreading them out
on the counter between us as if they were cards in a magic
trick. He shuffled them around, until he had Bates and
Trask side by side. "They'll be out of office by fall," he
said. "At least this one'll be, for sure," he added, dropping
a finger on Bates's bland face. "Dean Strauss," and he
moved his finger to Strauss's photograph, "is going back
to teaching. I'm sure you know who he is. Somebody tried
to knock him off a couple weeks ago and got a student instead. The new dean will want his own assistant, so Bates
will have to go back to teaching, too. I hear he's not
thrilled by the prospect," he added, lowering his voice,
"but don't quote me." He glanced over his shoulder. Nobody else in the office was paying us any attention.

"What about Donald Trask?" I asked him. "He's on the
way out, too?"

"That's what I've heard." He leaned across the counter.
"Off the record, right?"

"Right."

He wrapped a thumb and index finger around an imag-
inary shot glass, knocked it back, said, "He drinks, and
Wolf doesn't like that." He glanced down at Trask's picture. "He looks kind of like a drinker, too, doesn't he?"

I looked at Trask's portrait. It had been retouched, eras-
ing not the years, but the dissipation. He looked a lot like

Donna in the picture they'd shown of her on television, and as she'd looked the night of the banquet.

I gathered up all the photographs and thanked the man for his help.

It was almost two o'clock. I called Edith. I asked her how things were going and, to my surprise, she laughed.

"I find myself living in a vacuum all of a sudden," she said, "and facing the prospect of having to do so for the rest of my life. So I've put myself on a reading schedule. I'm planning to read all the books I've wanted to read or reread for years, but have been too busy writing and teaching about literature to do it. It was either that or kill myself," she said, still sounding cheerful, "and it's already paid off immensely. The very first book I started with gave me a line that's going to allow me to survive, no matter what."

"I'd like to hear it," I said.

"It's from Flaubert's *Sentimental Education*. 'He found that the happiness merited by the goodness of his soul was slow in coming.' " She barely made it through the quote before she started laughing.

I laughed, too. "So much for wallowing in self-pity," I said. I wondered what Donna Trask would have made of a line like that. Can you really feel you've been tricked by everyone—by life itself—if you have a sense of irony? I can't imagine a life without a sense of irony. It would be like being color-blind.

"What d'you want, Peggy?" Edith asked me. "Have you found anyone else who deals in cyanide? If not, I'd like to get back to my book."

I told her I wanted to talk to somebody who'd been on the conference center committee with Jeremiah Strauss.

"Why?"

"I want to find other people besides you who might have wanted Strauss dead. The more the merrier."

She didn't bother to deny she'd wanted him dead this time. I read her the names on the list I'd got from

Strauss's secretary. She'd been around the University a long time, and I assumed she knew at least one of them.

"Curtiss Naylor," she said finally, when I'd read through all the names. "He retired last June. I'm sure he'd be glad to talk to you."

"What's he like?" I asked.

"He lives alone, always has. An art historian. You'll like him. He's an oddball."

Sixteen

Curtiss Naylor lived in a neighborhood of tidy little homes. Those around his were all done in dull colors that had mostly faded into some virtually identical beige with the years. Naylor's house seemed to have been newly redone, the stucco a lively pink and the trim a green that was almost glossy. I liked it, but I wondered if his neighbors did.

A man was in the yard, his unruly white hair glittering in the afternoon sun. He was on his knees, which were fitted with colorful plastic knee protectors—one a bright red, the other a bright blue—and digging in the soil with a trowel. At first, I thought he must be resodding his lawn, but as I came closer, I realized that it wasn't a lawn, it was a rock garden.

"Professor Naylor?"

He looked up. "Not with the city, are you?" he asked me.

"No, I—"

"Because I haven't planted prairie grass yet this year. Until I do, and until it gets higher than eight inches, you can't cart me off to jail. You'll just have to wait."

I told him who I was and that I was trying to gather information that would help Edith Silberman's defense. She'd suggested I talk to him. I was interested in what he could tell me about the conference center committee he'd served on with Jeremiah Strauss.

He rubbed his high forehead, leaving a slash of mud just above his tie-dyed sweatband. His grin was wide and full of teeth that were friendly and clearly his own. "What put you on our trail, mountie?" he asked, trying for gruffness that wasn't in him. His eyes were a remarkably clear blue.

"I'm just playing long shots," I told him.

He thought about that for a moment, then scrambled to his feet. He was lean, and a good six inches taller than me. "I'll do anything I can to help Edith," he said.

I asked him what he'd meant about the cops and prairie grass. He explained that, the previous year, his neighbors had called the police on him because he'd included prairie grass in his rock garden.

"They hate my guts," he told me, "because I don't have a lawn. But there's no law says you have to have one, so they couldn't get me—until I stuck some prairie grass in among my wildflowers. There's a law against letting your grass grow higher than eight inches." He looked up and down his street, at all the little lawns that were just beginning to turn green. "You come over on Saturday sometime," he said, "when they're all out working on 'em with their gasoline-powered this and their gasoline-powered that. They look like the dead, cursed to mow their own graves."

He led the way into his house, poured two cups of tea from a thermos. "How's Edith holding up?" he asked when we were seated in his living room.

I told him I'd talked to her an hour or so ago, and she'd sounded fine.

"She'll survive this, too," he said, nodding. "She's no killer. It wouldn't surprise me," he added, "to discover that Jerry Strauss was behind it, somehow. Bad blood there, always was, between Jerry and Edith. He's about ready to retire, I hear. After almost getting himself murdered, I should think he would!"

I didn't quite see how Strauss could be blamed for

Edith's being arrested for attempting to kill him, but I didn't say anything. "He's retiring as dean," I told him, "but not because somebody tried to kill him. He's returning to the Humanities department to finish out his career, teaching and writing."

"Jerry, teaching and writing?" Naylor snorted. "Not voluntarily, he's not. The man always loathed teaching, and he's probably forgotten how to write anything more profound than a memo. When I read in the paper that they'd made him a University Scholar, I thought, 'For what?' For sitting in that big, luxurious office of his in the Ad Building and throwing his enormous weight around for fifteen years? Is that what it takes to be a University Scholar in this day and age?" Curtiss Naylor was still wearing his knee protectors, except now they were down around his ankles.

Before he could catch his breath to continue, I asked him how Strauss had been appointed chairman of the conference center committee.

"Wolf appointed him," he replied. "I suppose he thought Jerry'd be the natural choice. After all, he chaired the committee that recommended the University expand across the river in the first place—create the New Campus—back in the mid-'70s. A stupid decision, in my opinion, since it split the University in half and turned it into a schizophrenic monster, the humanities on one side, the sciences on the other. Reduced the possibility of a dialogue between them—not that that's been possible since the sciences stopped speaking in the vernacular about a hundred years ago. They figured it'd be more profitable to speak in gibberish. And they were right, which is why the humanities are starting to follow suit."

I didn't say so to Naylor, but I've always been grateful that the University chose to expand across the river, rather than try to put up new buildings among the old ones on the Old Campus or, worse, tear down the old ones to make room for the new. I love the old buildings, the way I love the night. So I had something to be grateful to Jeremiah

Strauss for if, as Naylor said, he'd used his influence to spare the Old Campus fifteen years ago.

"It wasn't a popular decision, you know," Naylor went on. "There was plenty of land available around the Old Campus, and a few of the older buildings there that are so expensive to maintain could have been razed, too, and we could have had the expansion we have now, but without crossing the river."

"But Strauss's view prevailed," I said.

"Strauss's views have usually prevailed through the years, haven't they? His argument was that expansion could be unlimited across the river. The area was run-down—old houses falling apart, firetraps, most of them, and marginal businesses—whereas on the Old Campus the U is surrounded by a well-established middle-class community that it would be costly for the U to invade."

"That sounds plausible to me," I said.

"It was plausible. That's why Strauss managed to win, although it was a near thing. The counter-argument was that the University didn't need unlimited expansion. A university can only grow so much, after all, and the so-called 'baby boom' had to come to a screeching halt someday, which it did. We didn't need all that space on the other side of the river, especially when it would cost us our cohesiveness."

"Okay," I said. "Because Strauss chaired the New Campus committee fifteen years ago, Wolf made him chair of the conference center committee last year. Wasn't that almost guaranteeing that it would end up on the New Campus?"

"You'd think so, wouldn't you?" Naylor replied. "And that's the odd thing! Strauss made it clear he was no longer convinced it had been a wise move to expand to the New Campus. He even went on record as being committed to putting the new conference center on the Old Campus, if at all possible. He led me to believe that, in his heart of hearts, he'd seen the light, realized the error of having split the University. He led me to believe that he thought that putting the new center on the Old Campus might do something to restore unity to the University."

" 'He led you to believe,' " I said.

"What?"

"You used that phrase twice in two sentences," I pointed out to him.

"I did?" Naylor frowned, thinking about it. "Yes, I suppose I did." He cocked his head, as if trying to see himself from the side. "Why?"

I couldn't tell him, so I decided to let him figure it out for himself.

"When it came to the vote," I said, "the committee voted the other way, against Strauss. How do you think that happened?"

"Well, stranger things have happened, I suppose. You see, the committee members fell into three factions right from the start: those who favored moving to the New Campus, those favoring building the conference center on the Old Campus, where Adamson Hall stands now, and a couple of undecideds. Frankly, I must confess that those who favored the first option did their homework much better than we did ours. We relied too heavily on Jerry to carry the burden—after all, he'd done it so well in the past."

Naylor's high, muddy brow furrowed. "But the experts he brought in," he went on, "to give us estimated costs, environmental impact statements, et cetera, were simply not as convincing as the experts brought in by the other side. Even so, I was quite surprised at the final vote: Five in favor of the New Campus, only three votes in support of the Old Campus."

"A defeat for Strauss."

"Yes, indeed. And the student newspaper made hay out of it, too. They've been after Strauss's scalp for a long time—no love lost there, on either side. The city newspaper raised questions about the choice as well, but President Wolf supported the committee's vote, the regents supported Wolf, and the legislature went along with the regents."

"My impression is that Strauss doesn't handle defeat gracefully," I said.

"That's an understatement! Jerry was in an ugly mood for a long time afterward, unapproachable, unless you wanted your head bitten off."

"Strauss himself chose the committee members?" I asked.

"Well, Jerry proposed names, but they had to be accepted by Wolf, naturally. Jerry chose me because we'd worked together before, on the New Campus committee fifteen years ago."

I showed him the list of committee members I'd got from Janine, Strauss's secretary. "Who else was on your side?"

He fished in his shirt pocket, brought out a pair of half-glasses people use for reading, and hung them on his nose.

"Will Sheridan, here, was on the New Campus committee, too," he said, pointing to a name with a mud-caked finger. "Back then he was an avid supporter of expanding across the river, and wouldn't listen to any arguments against it. Len Bartlett was on the New Campus committee, too. He hated the very thought of starting up a campus on the other side of the river, and he and Sheridan scarcely spoke to one another. It was quite funny to watch the courtly way they attempted to knife each other in the back. I assume Len agreed to serve this time because Strauss convinced him he favored building the center on the Old Campus. He didn't attend committee meetings very often, however, and napped through the ones he did attend. Like me, he retired last June."

Naylor ducked into the list again, pointed to a couple of names. "Carol Madson and Margaret Penny could've gone either way. They kept their minds open, but I thought that Penny, at least, would vote for the Old Campus, when it came to the vote. They were both bright young things. Carol's in Psychology, Margaret's in Anthropology—or was, I should say; she's left the University. She was a fighter, Margaret, and I liked her."

He looked down at the list again. "These other two fellows, Meyers and Webb, supported building the Center on the New Campus from day one. Couldn't be budged. Meyers is a surgeon—believes only in cut, cut, cut! Webb's an economist, a cold fish with a sausage moustache that barely hides a tiny, sucking mouth."

I ignored the editorial comments, counted the names, said, "So you think that, when it came to the vote, there were three sure votes in favor of building the center on the Old Campus—Strauss, you, and Bartlett—and three sure votes in favor of the New Campus—Sheridan, Meyers, and Webb—and two undecideds, the two women?"

"That's right."

"The New Campus side must have won over both women."

"The vote was anonymous, of course, so there's no way to know."

We sat there a while, drinking tea, each of us preoccupied with our own thoughts.

"Nobody on the committee bore Jerry enough of a grudge to want to kill him," Naylor said, sadly. "The issue just wasn't that important."

He pulled himself up out of his chair and adjusted his colorful knee protectors. He wanted to get back to his garden. I headed for the door. "You were around the University a long time," I said when we were back outside in the spring sunshine. "And you know Strauss pretty well, too. Can you think of *anybody* who might want to kill him?"

He looked over his rock garden from the front stoop, still mostly rocks and twigs green with new buds, and mud. He turned his attention to the question reluctantly.

"Badly enough to actually do it? Some of my neighbors wish I were dead, and they'd probably kill me, too, if all they had to do was press a button and nobody'd know who'd done it. Love of lawn is an all-consuming passion around here. You could be dying of a wasting illness, and none of the neighbors would notice, but let a dandelion pop up in your lawn, and they're all over you with advice about which poison works best."

He looked at me. "Where was I? Ah, yes. Oh, I suppose even I've sometimes wanted Jerry dead. He's an arrogant and uncaring man who's ridden roughshod over anybody who gets in his way for fifteen years. I'm a gardener, though, and if I used poison, it'd be arsenic, wouldn't it? I guess there're still quite a few bug killers containing arsenic around. But cyanide!" He shuddered. "Now where do you get that, d'you suppose?"

"Okay," I said, "so you didn't do it—not your *modus operandi*. Who might have?"

He gave me a conspiratorial look and, in a whisper, barked: "Wolf!" as if a wolf were lurking behind one of the trees next to his house.

I played along. "Wolf!" I echoed. I was glad we didn't have an audience. God knows what it would have thought. I wondered if some of Naylor's neighbors were watching us from behind drapes, and could read lips.

"Why not?" Naylor asked. "Jerry Strauss has been in administration a long time. He knows a lot of dirt about a lot of people. He doesn't like sex between consenting adults, if they're not blessed by a clergyman first—that's a well-established fact. As far as anybody knows—and I believe it's true—Jerry's been faithful to the memory of his wife ever since she died. And he expects that kind of behavior of others, too. Now Wolf, on the other hand, has been divorced a while, you know, and no one believes he rattles around in that mansion of his alone—not all the time, not even often."

"You're suggesting that Strauss may use some knowledge he has of Wolf to blackmail him."

"That's not the right name for it, Peggy. That's much too crude. You blackmail people for money. Jerry Strauss would never do that. For one thing, he doesn't need it."

"But for something like a University Scholarship?"

"Yes," he said, grinning, "something like that. And it

wouldn't be any kind of direct threat, either. He'd just mention to Wolf—very offhand, you know—that he'd like to be appointed to the vacancy left by Emily Cauldwell. I knew her, by the way," Naylor added. "She was a delightful woman, and I'm sure she's spinning in her grave at the thought that Strauss now occupies her place among the Scholars. I seriously question whether she would have died, had she known."

I reminded Naylor that, at least according to rumor, Strauss wasn't resigning as dean voluntarily. Wolf had pressured him to quit. "Surely," I said, "if Strauss had any hold over Wolf, he wouldn't be resigning."

"Jerry must realize that his time is up. Otherwise, he wouldn't go. He's been dean of the Graduate School longer than anybody else ever has. He's beginning to slip, there's more muttering now than ever before. Maybe Wolf would bow to threats from Jerry to keep him on, but I suspect that Jerry's decided it'll be more comfortable to return to the Humanities department for the few years he has left, loaded down with honors."

"The only problem I have with your scenario," I said with a laugh, "is that I can't see President Wolf succumbing to that kind of pressure—not unless Strauss had color photographs of Wolf cavorting naked around the president's mansion with chorus girls."

"The sex example," Naylor said, somewhat huffily, "was just that. But what about this? Take something that, to you or me, is just a rumor, just something a secretary in the Ad Building thought she'd heard a vice president tell his wife on the phone—but maybe not, maybe she heard it wrong. But she tells one of her less fortunate sisters the story as she thinks she heard it—in all confidence, of course!—and that secretary tells her boss, the chairman of—just suppose, now—*my* department! Eventually, *I* hear the story, too. It's only a garbled rumor to me. I just shake my head, willing to believe anything of a base nature about what goes on among the high mucketymuck."

"The what?"

"Mucketymuck. Look it up."

"I wouldn't even know where to start."

"With an m." He leaned into me, spoke into my face, "As I was saying, it's just a garbled rumor to me. But Jerry Strauss *knows,* you see. It's not just a vague rumor that comes to him, all out of shape and missing the best parts. He's got names, dates, places, *prices*—that sort of thing." Curtiss Naylor sagged down into his dirt and picked up his trowel.

"Hey," I said, "come *on!* Out with it. Fill in the blanks!"

"It was hypothetical," he said, not looking up.

"My ass!"

"Well! If you're going to get vulgar about it, I'll have to ask you to leave."

"I won't leave without saying a lot worse things than that, if you don't tell me the whole story."

He got up again, his knees creaking, glared down at me, arms akimbo. "A nice old man," he said, "thirty-some-odd years ago, died in his sleep—without issue, as the lawyers say. He left the University an island in the middle of a lake up north. Quite a beautiful island, I understand, on quite a lovely lake. He didn't want it developed because it had been in his family for several generations. It held fond memories for him from when he was a kid.

"So, as stated, he left it to the University—for research purposes, ecological studies, things like that. He thought that would preserve it, that it would be safe in the University's hands, forever and ever. And he died in that belief." Naylor almost crooned those last words.

"The island was sold five years ago," he went on. "You want to guess who bought it?"

"Wolf."

"Wolf, yes. And Donald Trask. They went in on it together. Trask arranged it, of course, as a former real estate lawyer and the U's chief attorney. But here's the really good part. The two of 'em turned around and sold it to a land developer, who parceled it up into small lots just large enough for people to put up little cabins and boat houses and docks. Now the lake's abuzz with every kind of gasoline-powered vehicle imaginable, and the only things living on or near the island are the people in their A-frame cabins with their powerboats and boom boxes."

"How'd it happen?" I asked, aghast.

"Easy," he said, his deep blue eyes flashing angrily. "It's the Devil's marketplace, the University. You can get anything you want there, if you know the right people and are willing to pay the price."

"Could you be a little more specific?"

He calmed down, looked a little shamefaced. "Oh, if you insist! The University decided to sell the island. None of the science departments were interested in using it for research. The U has plenty of that kind of land for research and besides, it's short of funds. When the University decides to sell something off, it's required to advertise prominently and accept anonymous bids. Somehow, Wolf's and Trask's bid won."

"Strauss could use knowledge like that," I said, "if he had the proof."

"And Wolf wouldn't like being the victim of that kind of genteel blackmail," Curtiss Naylor said.

"A man of integrity wouldn't give in to it," I said.

Naylor smiled as he sank back into his soil on his colorful knees.

Seventeen

I called Anita Torres as soon as I got home, told her I'd taken her name in vain with Dean Strauss. She said, "Decision Making at the University" sounded like a fine topic for a senior thesis except that, since she was a Chemistry major, it might be difficult to sell her adviser on it. I asked her to just sell it to anybody who asked about it, and she promised she'd try. We agreed to a racquetball match on Monday at noon, one of our several-times-a-month meetings in which we take turns beating each other up. Anita's a converted tennis player, which makes playing racquetball with her an adventure.

I thought about calling Buck, to sound him out about how much damage I'd done to our relationship and what it would take to repair it, but I didn't feel up to it. I might slip up and confess that Lawrence had lied to him—shame has that effect on me—and I didn't want to risk getting Lawrence in trouble. I took a nap instead and didn't wake up until it was almost time to go to work. Sleep is sometimes the wisest course of action, especially if you can't think of anything else to do.

Before roll call that night, I showed Lawrence the pictures of Donald Trask and Hudson Bates. He shook his head, said he didn't think Trask had come through the tunnel and kitchen. He wasn't sure about Bates; there wasn't that much to remember about his face. So much for that.

I was assigned the New Campus. It's not my favorite assignment. The buildings are less than fifteen years old, but they look as if they were put up yesterday, and they'll never look any older. Nothing grows on them except graffiti, and very little grows around them either.

I tried to imagine what the University would have been if the New Campus had never been built. Maybe some effort would have been made to design new buildings on the Old Campus that respected the old architecture. In which case, it was too bad somebody hadn't fed Jeremiah Strauss a poisoned apple fifteen years ago.

It was a cold night, with a fat third-quarter moon hanging over downtown, and I hadn't seen anybody out and about since about 1:30. Using my walkie-talkie, I checked in regularly with the dispatcher, telling her which buildings I was entering and leaving. At about three A.M., I went to the faculty lounge of the Physics Building and bought a cup of coffee from a machine. I sat down at a table in the corner and nursed the coffee for a while, warming up for the remainder of my watch.

The river winds through the University here. Out of one window, to my right, I could see the roofs of buildings on the Old Campus and the Campanile that rises out of the trees above everything else, while on this side of the river, to my left, lay the land being cleared for the new conference center. I'd known a woman who taught piano in a house in that area. I wondered if the house was still there, and where she was now.

Bert Coombs lived there, too, on the edge of the demolition site. Once the center was built, the land around it would be worth too much to leave as cheap student housing, so Bert and his roommate Omaha would soon be looking for a new place to live, if they weren't already.

Rising up behind the cleared land was Harold McCord's hotel, most of its windows dark. The windows in the top floor, though—McCord's condo—were lit. Maybe he worked all night, or maybe he was afraid of the dark. The brightest star in the night sky out there read "McCord." He'd named the hotel after himself.

Harold McCord was going to build the new convention center for the University. I thought of what Sumiko had told me about McCord's birthday party a few months ago. Donald Trask and his daughter had been there. An odd friendship, if that's what it was. But maybe not. Trask had been a real estate lawyer before the University made him its chief attorney, and McCord had made his fortune in real estate.

Donald Trask. According to Curtiss Naylor, he was a man who had facilitated questionable, if not down-right illegal, dealings for President Wolf, and for himself, too. Trask did seem to get around. Fifteen years ago, according to Theresa Durr, he and Strauss had spent a lot of time closeted in Trask's study, just when the University was considering building the New Campus. She hadn't said anything about seeing the other members of the New Campus committee there, just Strauss and Trask.

I thought of asking Naylor if the committee sometimes met at Trask's home, but I remembered that Trask wasn't working for the University then, he was working for a private law firm. Why would the committee meet at his house?

What did McCord mean, I wondered, when he told Trask that it was too bad they couldn't name the new conference center after Strauss? Was it just some kind of joke at Strauss's expense? Or at Trask's? It was too bad Sumiko's English hadn't been quite good enough to tell whether he'd meant it seriously or not.

I felt the hair rise on my neck and arms, as I realized that Donna Trask, before me, must have wondered the same thing. She threatened to cause a scene at McCord's party, until her father promised to tell her later. I wondered what his explanation had been.

Why had Strauss pushed to expand to the New Campus fifteen years ago, but this time opposed building the conference center there?

He led me to believe ... Those were Naylor's words, twice. Strauss had led him to believe that he was in favor of putting the center on the Old Campus, where Adamson Hall was, to restore some of the unity that had been lost fifteen years earlier, he'd said. And yet the people who wanted the center on the New Campus had won.

What if Strauss had packed the conference center committee, so that most of the effective members were on the side of handing the center over to Harold McCord? Both people who'd started out openly in favor of building on the Old Campus had been about to retire. According to Naylor, Strauss had selected them for the committee because they'd served with him in the past. Somehow, I didn't think sentimentality was one of Strauss's motivating influences. Two other committee members—both women—were newcomers to the University, and might have supported putting the center on the Old Campus, if Strauss had come up with strong enough arguments. But he'd failed to do that.

Of course, there didn't have to be anything sinister about it. After all, Strauss was fifteen years older now, so maybe he'd just been tired, too, like Naylor and Leonard Bartlett.

Or maybe it wasn't Strauss who'd picked the committee. Maybe it was President Wolf, working with his chief attorney Trask, who'd appointed Strauss to head the committee in the first place.

How much was it worth to McCord, I wondered, to build the conference center on the New Campus side of the river?

A cloud sailed in front of the moon, then moved away again, indifferent to human concerns, since it was just going to evaporate soon anyway. A barge, as silent and indifferent as the cloud, glided down the river in front of me. I was reluctant to go back out into the cold.

It was close to four o'clock, which meant the New Campus had gone unguarded for nearly an hour as I sat and brooded. I got up, crumpled my Styrofoam cup into a

ball, and put it in the contribution box for a landfill somewhere, turned to go.

" 'If her eyes are blue as skies, That's Peggy O'Neil, If
she's smiling all the while, That's Peggy O'Neil.' "

The song was coming from the darkness outside, in the
hall. It was Bert Coombs's voice, an eerie parody of an
Irish tenor's. He stepped into the room, juggling knives.

"How'd you get in here?" I asked, trying to keep my
voice steady.

"Came through the door, same as you." His eyes flickered back and forth between me and the knives, moonlight
glittering on the blades.

"You're lying," I told him. "The door locked behind
me."

"The song lies," he said. "I don't. You don't smile
much, Peggy O'Neill."

"I don't have blue eyes either, Bert," I told him, "and
I've got two l's in my name. The other Peggy's got only
one. What do you want?"

"You're sayin' you're not kin. That kind of figures." In
his high, thin tenor voice, he sang another snatch of the
song my father, in a moment of drunken inspiration,
named me after: " 'If she walks like a sly little rogue, if
she talks with a cute little brogue, sweet personality, full of
rascality, that's Peggy O'Neil.' No, you're right," he went
on, "no similarities anywhere, except maybe you're full of
rascality. Are you?"

"I asked you what you wanted, Bert."

"Hey, nothing! Honest. I was just passin' by outside,
and saw you in here, all alone."

That was a lie, too. He couldn't have seen me from outside the window; it was too dark in here. My skin crawled
at the realization that he must have been following me as
I made my rounds, and perhaps watching me from the
door for at least some of the time I was sitting there drinking coffee, busy with my own thoughts.

"I like walkin' around nights," he went on. He'd made
two of his knives disappear into his pants, and he was flip-

ping the third up in the air, idly catching it with one hand. "Hey, I just thought of something! Maybe I should be a campus cop like you! You spend your nights just strollin' around campus all by your lonesome, don't you? And you get paid for it! I'd like that kind of job, since it's what I do anyway. The juggling cop! But don't you get scared sometimes—a woman out at night, all alone? Oh, I forgot, you've got a gun, don't you?" His humorless grin flashed in the moonlight, as if he were daring me to reach for it.

I did have a pistol, and it was in the forefront of my mind, but I'd never get it out and pointed at him before he'd put a knife into me, and we both knew that.

"Back up," I said, and started for him. He'd had plenty of opportunity to kill me before now, but he hadn't, so maybe he was just playing some kind of game, maybe he enjoyed scaring people, women. Or maybe he liked the idea of killing me in this empty building after playing with me a little first. I took another step toward him.

"Sure," he said easily, and backed up, out into the hall, his eyes jumping back and forth between me and the knife. He was grinning, showing his long, irregular teeth and the muscles in his gaunt and pale face.

"Put the knife away, too," I said.

The third knife followed the others into his clothing. I debated whether or not to beat him up and decided against it since the skin on my knuckles tears easily. Besides, he was probably a lot stronger than he looked.

"How'd you get the door open?" I asked him. "You got lock-picking equipment?"

"I don't need stuff like that to get into a place like this," he said scornfully, slipping into his shoes, which he'd left just inside the door. "You can search me if you want, but it'd be a waste of your precious time."

I believed him. "You've tried to scare me, Bert," I said. I was backing him out the door and onto the steps, moving slowly. "And you've succeeded. But you could have done worse than that. You're just reminding me how vulnerable I am, walking around alone at night. Why?"

"Man, I'm not trying to scare you! I like you too much for that, Peggy O'Neill. I like you a lot, I really do."

"Where'd you find the lyrics to the song?" I asked him. "They aren't easy to get hold of these days."

"I know lots of weird and wonderful things," he replied. "For instance, I know that everybody's happy now, right? Except Professor Silberman, of course, the poisoner." His face knotted into an ugly grin, probably beyond his control. "I like that. I can sleep better nights, knowin' she's off the streets. After all, I was a student of hers, too—and a friend of Donna's."

"But she's not behind bars, Bert, she's out on bail."

"Hey, I didn't know that! Ol' Strauss better watch out then, right? She missed him the first try, maybe she'll try again. They better not call off his guards, huh?" He winked, his face a veritable museum of twitches. "What're you goin' to do to keep busy, now that the police have got ol' Silberman?"

"I'll think of something," I told him. "I'm still kind of interested in Donna Trask—and you," I added.

"Me?" He tried to look shocked. "What for?"

"I'm thinking about the first time I met you," I told him, "in the tunnel outside Adamson Hall. You were begging her not to go in—to come away with you instead."

"Hey, I wasn't begging. I just wanted her to come with me—to a movie or a bar or something."

I shook my head. "No," I said.

"All right!" He was twisting and turning inside, trying to find the right formula. "I was begging her, a little. I knew what she was gonna do, right? I thought it was stupid. I didn't want her to do it, to make a fool of herself in front of all those people."

I was quiet for a moment. He watched me anxiously, his entire face wrinkled with concern. "That was really nice of you," I said, "to be so worried about her reputation. My mother was like that, too, always worried about what other people would think. Funny, you don't look anything like my mother."

His eyes ran all over my face, trying to figure out if I was kidding. "It's true," he said finally.

"I found the Sumiko I was looking for, by the way," I told him. "She told me she overheard you and Donna quarreling in Donna's apartment last month. Donna said something like 'I don't want money, or need it,' and you said that you did. Care to tell me what you were talking about?"

"Sumiko's got a problem with English," Bert said, his voice tight. "You have to take something like that with a grain of salt."

"I thought her English was excellent," I said. "Want money for what, Bert?"

"Look, what's this all about?" He was suddenly outraged, his voice rising, loud in the emptiness of the night. "What's your big interest in Donna? It's all over. We can just go about our business now, right? Silberman tried to kill the guy, Strauss, he'd been bugging her for a long time. She got Donna instead. *C'est la vie!*"

"I'm going to learn the entire story," I assured him, pretending to ignore his outburst. "I'm going to find out why you begged her not to go into Adamson Hall that night, and what it was you wanted money for."

"Why?"

I shrugged, gave him a pleasant smile. "I guess it's just because I'm dying to know," I told him. We were at the bottom of the steps outside the Physics Building. He suddenly advanced on me. His face glowed in the moonlight like a dead man's. I reached for my pistol, backpedaling, wondering if he were high on something. His right hand moved quickly and something came toward my face in a blur. We were too close, and I couldn't duck in time. It hit me on my left cheek, not particularly hard, but enough to disorient me anyway.

A bright light splashed in my eyes.

"What's going on up there?" It was Paula's voice. Shielding my eyes, I could see her getting out of a squad car, her hand on her pistol. Lawrence was climbing out of the other side.

Bert started running in the direction of the river, his green pants flapping around his bowlegs.

Paula pulled up beside me, breathing hard. She looked a question at me.

"We'll let him go," I said, taking her arm. "He's that juggler we saw outside Adamson. He was just trying to scare me."

"Why?"

"I think so he can stop being scared himself."

"What's it about?" Paula demanded.

I told her I'd let her know when I found out.

She wasn't satisfied with that, but I didn't see any point in telling her any more. I also couldn't see any reason to go after Bert. For what?

After Paula and Lawrence had driven off, I looked around to find whatever it was he'd tossed at me. I found it in an empty cement planter next to the steps. It was a ball, about the size of a tennis ball, but rubber and solid. I'd seen balls like that before: red, green, and yellow. Bert Coombs had lost the yellow one at Donna Trask's funeral. Unless he'd replenished his supply, he only had the red one left to play with now.

Eighteen

My phone rang, shattering a vivid dream I'd never remember anyway. Still mostly asleep, I groped for the phone, picked it up.

It was the dispatcher, Ron. "That you, Peggy? Lt. Bixler wants to see you in his office at eleven." There was a kind of muted panic in his voice, and he cracked no jokes, which meant Bixler was standing next to him, making sure he got it right.

"Wants to give me a raise, I'll bet," I said, "wants to apologize for all the—" I knew that wasn't it. Condemned prisoners probably talk to their lawyers like this, passing the time until the reprieve or the prison chaplain arrives.

"Get the lead out, O'Neill!" That was Bixler's voice, coming from somewhere close to Ron.

"Okay," I said, and hung up. I looked at my clock radio. It said 10:22. I'd had less than three hours sleep.

Bixler wasn't alone. Hudson Bates was with him, the assistant dean. He was lounging in a chair, his feet sprawled out in front of him. He made it look like a position he practiced a lot in front of a mirror.

Bixler wasn't looking well. He was looking like the contestant standing next to the host of a program called "Guess My Disease."

"You know who this is," he began, giving Bates a respectful nod.

"We've met," Bates said pleasantly.

I nodded. Payback time.

"Dean Bates is assistant dean of the Graduate School," Bixler said, an edge to his voice. "He—"

"Why don't you let me handle this, Sergeant?" Bates asked, giving Bixler an easy smile. It was the weirdest thing. Everything he said sounded as if he'd memorized a script beforehand. What did that make Bixler and me?

"Lieutenant," I said, feeling a little hysterical, wanting to personalize the scene as much as possible.

"I'm sorry?" Bates said, rearranging muscles in his face slightly to make the smile express mild puzzlement.

"He's a lieutenant," I said, gesturing awkwardly at Bixler, "not a sergeant."

"Excuse me, Lieutenant," Bates said, without missing a beat, "I stand corrected—again," he added, to remind me that he hadn't forgotten yesterday. "What do you do in your free time, Officer O'Neill? May I ask?"

I pursed my lips, frowned, and pretended to think for a moment. "I play a little racquetball, ski a little in the winter, sail in the summer, lunch with friends. Let's see, what else—"

"That's not what he meant," Bixler stuck in. "Answer Dean Bates's question. Don't be cute."

I wondered why I couldn't be cute, if Bates could. "What did you mean, then?" I asked Bates.

"I said I'd handle it, Lieutenant Bixler," Bates said, his voice shifting from mellow in the key of phony to steely in the same key. He smiled encouragement at me. "You do a little detection, too, I imagine?"

"Detection?"

"You lied to Dean Strauss yesterday," he said, finally coming out with it.

"Lied? How?" Christ, I thought, they hadn't wasted any time checking my story!

"Stop playing games with the dean, O'Neill," Bixler

couldn't help interrupting. "You're in big enough trouble as it is."

What he meant was that Jeremiah Strauss was mad at one campus cop—me—and, in his rage, might use his influence to do something to hurt the entire police force, such as get our budget cut. Bixler was going to do whatever he could to prevent that. I was sure he hoped that stomping me was what it would entail.

"Yesterday," Bates continued, as if Bixler hadn't spoken, "you came to Dean Strauss's office. You asked for some information under a false pretense. You told Dean Strauss that you were there to help a student gather material for her senior thesis." He paused, waited for my response.

I've been caught telling lies more than once in my life. When I was a kid, and one of the nuns eager to warp me into what passed in her mind for the straight and narrow caught me, I turned to thin Jell-O and puddled on the floor around her sturdy Red Cross shoes. But I don't do that anymore. With practice, you get better at facing the consequences of getting caught telling the lies you think are necessary, and you try not to tell the other kind.

"How do you know?" I asked Bates, because I was curious.

"That's none of your business, O'Neill," Bixler blustered. "Answer the question!"

"We know because I made a point of looking up your friend's academic record," Bates replied calmly. "Anita Maria Torres, I believe it is. A chemistry major. I called her adviser and asked if a thesis on "Decision Making at the University" would be an appropriate senior thesis in the Chemistry department. He said no, Miss O'Neill. If you'd like, we could call Ms. Torres right now and break this news to her. It would be a shame, if she's already begun work—"

"Please," I said, flinching at the sarcasm. "I confess. I did it. But I was only interested in helping the city cops try to find out who wanted to murder Dean Strauss."

"Ah," Bates said. "In other words, doing a little detecting. It took us a while to get that out of you, Officer O'Neill, didn't it?"

"I did it on my own time," I said.

"No," he corrected me, quite earnestly. "You did it on *our* time—my time, the dean's time, and the dean's secretary's time."

He paused, waiting to hear what I had to say to that.

"I'm sorry," I said. Being contrite might get this over with faster. "I was only trying to help."

"How were you going to do that?" Bates wondered aloud. "You aren't satisfied that the *real* police have arrested the right person?"

"No. Edith Silberman didn't do it."

"You have reasons for thinking that?"

Through the phoniness, it sounded to me as if Bates were really interested in my answer.

"You don't?" I asked. "After all, she's been an excellent teacher here for twenty-five years! Are you so easily satisfied that she's a cold-blooded killer?"

I'd gotten him again. He turned pink around the edges. "That's neither here nor there. Scholars don't let sentiment get in the way of facts, Peggy."

Peggy! I felt my fingernails digging into my palms.

He went on. "I'm asking you if you have any evidence, any substantive proof, that Professor Silberman is not the guilty party, other than that you think she's an excellent teacher, of course." From the way he said it, it was obvious that excellent teachers were a drug on the market in Hudson Bates's world.

"Not yet. But, after all," I added, "it's in Dean Strauss's best interest to get the guilty party, isn't it? Otherwise, his life's still in danger."

He ignored that. "So you decided to begin by talking to members of the conference center committee that Dean Strauss chaired. And to whom did you talk on the committee?"

"I only got around to one person," I said, "a retired professor named Curtiss Naylor."

There was a faint look of disappointment on Bates's face, and I realized that he, or Strauss, had already called the members of the committee, and Bates had been hoping to catch me in a lie.

"Nobody else?" he persisted, but the fire had gone out of him. He already knew the answer.

"Nobody else."

"What other 'leads' are you pursuing?"

I fought back a smile. In spite of his feigned indifference, he *was* interested in finding out what I was doing. I thought of asking him if he'd managed to get the cyanide off his dress shoes.

"I'm not pursuing any other leads. Actually," I went on, earnestly, "I lost interest after talking to Curtiss Naylor. That was a dead end. It all seems so hopeless. I guess I just don't have what it takes to be a detective. The patience and determination . . ." I let it trail off with a shrug of resignation.

'You just wanted to help, you said," Bates went on. "But in doing so, you lied to Dean Strauss. Why didn't you simply come out and explain to him what you wanted the list for?"

"I was afraid he'd tell me no," I said, "order me to leave it alone."

"Why would he do that?"

I didn't say it was because I thought Strauss was probably thrilled that Edith Silberman had been charged with the attempt on his life and wouldn't like anybody trying to get her off the hook. I said, "Nobody likes amateurs sticking their noses in. I figured he'd just laugh at me." I thought of turning in the toes of my shoes, to look gawky and helpless.

Bates emitted a stage laugh. He picked up his thin briefcase, hugged it to his chest, and got up. He turned to Bixler, to see if Bixler were impressed with how he'd reduced me to a soft-spoken little girl—a flute-player, perhaps, they're the nicest. I wished I were wearing a gingham dress, so I could spread my knees as far apart as possible and drop my hands helplessly in my lap. You can only do that in gingham, I think.

"And you hoped that maybe you'd get lucky and find out that the police were wrong, and you'd be a hero," Bates went on, almost chortling. "Maybe even put the University Police Department 'on the map,' as it were." His face turned serious again. "But Dean Strauss doesn't like being lied to, even for what might be considered a good cause. Nobody likes being lied to, do they? Do you?"

I stood up, too. Nobody likes being stared down at either. "No," I replied, and finally did turn my toes in ever so slightly.

"I'll report back to Dean Strauss," he announced. "I'll tell him that you were only trying to help, and you felt the need to lie to do it. I'll do what I can for you," he added.

He'd humiliated me completely, so the look he gave me was one of affection, almost love. He smiled, trying not to show any real interest as he let his eyes move up and down my body, then lifted his right hand away from his briefcase, still clutched to his chest, presumably in case I wanted to shake it, or kiss it. I didn't want to do either, so he flapped his hand back onto the briefcase, nodded to Bixler, turned, and left.

Bixler had expected something much worse than this. He sagged into his chair, which protested loudly. Not according to any script at all, just according to the various low-energy neurons that drive him, he said, "You've gone too far this time, O'Neill, lying to Dean Strauss. I'm going to see about getting you disciplined. Fired, if I can."

"How can you do that?" I asked him. "I did it on my own time, and I didn't try to pass myself off as a cop."

He ignored that. His face was glistening with sweat. "I'll wait to see what the Dean's going to do first," he said. "If he wants your ass, he gets it. On a platter. Now get out of here."

I left, fighting not to let the image of my ass on a platter break me up before I got out of earshot.

Nineteen

The weekend passed, the third since Donna Trask's death, bringing Edith's arraignment two days closer. I was feeling grumpier and grumpier. I thought of trying to talk to other members of the conference center committee, but I was certain that either Strauss or Bates had contacted most of them, and I couldn't count on them not tattling on me.

One thing was sure: Strauss didn't like loose ends. Probably within minutes of my leaving his office on Thursday, he'd had Bates check my story and discovered that I'd lied to him. Then he sent Bates to step on me. Did he really want Edith out of his hair so badly that he'd let her go to jail for the rest of her life, even if she wasn't guilty? Of course, he probably thought she was guilty.

Nobody seemed to want me poking my nose into the attempt on Strauss's life and the death of Donna Trask. Even Bert Coombs had tried to scare me off.

Monday morning was rainy, but by the time Anita and I finished our racquetball match and I showered and changed and was walking back across campus to police headquarters where I'd parked my car, the sky was starting to clear up. I was coming around the side of the Language Arts Building, across the Mall from the Administration Building, when one of the Ad Building's front doors opened and Dean Strauss came out. He was trailed by

150

Hudson Bates, holding his thin, expensive briefcase to his chest.

I stopped to study them, blending in with the students passing around me. They made an interesting contrast. Strauss was wearing a suit that must have been two decades out of style, heavy tweed, the coat flapping open. I recognized Bates only by his beautifully tailored suit and his modish hairdo. The poodle was better trimmed than its master.

They turned down the Mall toward the Union. Strauss seemed preoccupied with whatever serious business he was off to take care of, and Bates looked preoccupied with the back of Strauss's head. Students made way for Strauss, and Bates appeared sucked along in his wake. I wouldn't want Bates behind me, if I were Strauss and I knew there was somebody out there who hated me enough to have tried to kill me.

The thought of their offices being empty interested me: just Janine, alone at her desk. She'd liked me for the way I'd put Bates down last week. Maybe she could give me some idea of what Strauss planned to do with me, if anything. My career as a campus cop would be over for sure, I knew, if Bates or Strauss returned suddenly and found me with Janine. For some reason, that was a risk I was willing to take. Maybe I'd had enough of being a campus cop, but didn't have the guts to quit on my own.

I took the elevator to the fourth floor. The card table where Jesse Porter had been sitting the last time I was up there was gone. Janine was alone in the office.

"Hi," I said, my lips ready with a lie in case I'd misjudged her and she was one of them. "Where are the boys?"

She seemed happy to see me. "Gone for the day. An important meeting. They only attend important meetings, isn't that interesting? What can I do for you this time? More research for your friend?"

"I lied about that," I told her. "I wanted that list for reasons of my own. I assumed you'd know that by now."

I explained the whole business to her, including my belief that Edith Silberman wasn't the poisoner.

"Golly!" she said, shocked. "Lying to Dean Strauss, right to his face! He could snuff you!"

"But he hasn't," I said, "not yet. And he didn't tell you I'd lied, either. Wouldn't you have set up the meeting between Bates and Bixler, my boss?"

"Who else? I didn't, though." She worried a pencil eraser with her teeth. "Maybe it was Bates, running some little errand of his own. He does that sometimes, I think."

That put an entirely new slant on the episode, but one that made no sense at all. "What would be the point?" I asked her.

She shrugged. "Maybe Bates wanted to handle it himself, show Strauss that he could perform brilliantly on his own. Maybe he reported back to Strauss everything that went on between you and him and your boss. But if Bates was trying to earn brownie points," Janine added with a laugh, "it's way too little, way too late."

"Why?" I suddenly remembered the story Myles Kruger had told me about Bates caught kissing a woman in an elevator.

"Strictest confidence, okay?" Janine said, lowering her voice. "Little Hudson Bates is married, you know. One of those 'commuter marriages.' His wife's a professor at some dinkwater college in California and during the academic year they only see each other at Easter and Christmas and sometimes on long weekends, which gets kind of expensive, you know? Well, Bates wanted Strauss to use his influence to get the College of Arts to create a position for her here."

I asked her what made Bates think Strauss could do that.

"Well, because it can be done, you know, and, if he wanted to, Strauss could probably do it." She glanced again over her shoulder at the empty offices of the two men she was gossiping about. "A year or two ago, President Wolf used his influence to get Bennet Hightower's wife a position in the Botany Department," she went on, "because Hightower threatened to go somewhere else if his wife couldn't get a job here. Wolf just leaned a little on the dean of the College of Arts and—poof! Botany's got a position it doesn't need and Hightower's wife's got a job where she can come home nights to her hubby."

"I thought that was illegal," I said. "I thought the affirmative action regulations say you have to conduct a nationwide search before you hire somebody for an academic position."

"You're right, it is illegal, strictly speaking. But who's going to complain? After all, it was a woman who was hired, wasn't it? There'd be a big stink if the position had been filled with a man, of course. The University probably couldn't have gotten away with that. The Botany Department's happy to have the new position, of course, even though they didn't really need it, and they're also happy to have a vice president's wife, because that gives them a little more clout around here than they had before— especially if Hightower should someday become president, which I've heard is possible."

Curtiss Naylor had called it the Devil's marketplace. I'd thought he was exaggerating.

"That makes her just another woman getting something through her husband," I said. "She didn't have to compete with anyone for the position."

"True." Janine glanced over her shoulder again. "Anyway, Hudson Bates thought he could get Strauss to use his influence to do the same thing for his wife. She's got a Ph.D. in folk music, you know."

"But Strauss turned him down."

"Not at first. At first, he gave Bates reason to think he'd do it." Janine grinned at a memory, something secret she wanted to tell. "And then he changed his mind."

She wanted me to ask why. I said, because I'd been waiting for this to come up, "Because Strauss heard a nasty, nasty rumor involving Hudson Bates, a woman, and an elevator."

"You're good," Janine said, slightly crestfallen. "I suppose you already talked to Kevin. He used to sit at that desk over there," she added, nodding at the empty desk in question.

"He's the former clerk-typist who saw Bates making out in the elevator?"

"Don't you know?" The mystery of how I knew the rumor about Bates deepened for her. "Kevin Ames," she said. "That was his desk, over there by the window. But 'making out's' too strong. The way Kevin told it was, the girl waited until the elevator door had opened just enough so she could see Kevin standing there, looking in. Then she reached up quickly and kissed Bates on the cheek—or on the side of the mouth. Like old lovers, Kevin said, not old friends."

"What did Bates do?"

"Bates was so shocked, Kevin said, he couldn't move at first. Then he looked like he wanted to kill her. He stepped out of the elevator, shoved Kevin aside, and stalked down to his office, his face white as death, Kevin said. The girl strolled after him, grinning like a Cheshire cat—Kevin's words again, not mine. When Strauss fired Kevin—he made Bates do it, of course—Kevin told Strauss the whole story."

"And that ended Bates's chance of getting his wife here."

"Right." Janine was looking at me with an expectant smile on her face that I didn't understand. "Well," she said finally, "aren't you going to ask me who the girl was?"

Oh damn, I thought, I'm getting slow!

She saw the look on my face. "Some detective you are," she crowed.

"Donna Trask," I said.

"Right."

"Why was she with Bates?"

"Because when Donna Trask came to Strauss and asked him to get her into the Humanities graduate program, Strauss turned it over to Bates, told him to deal with it, the way he always does. But poor Bates couldn't do a thing. You can't just override a department's wishes in matters like that, you know, especially if the student's grades aren't really good, and Donna's weren't. Strauss knew he couldn't do anything, so he ordered Bates to stall Donna until she cooled off. But she didn't cool off, she just got madder and madder as time passed and she didn't get what she wanted. She was in here a lot, in Bates's office over there, and it was all the poor chump could do to keep her from breaking furniture! She kept demanding to see Strauss, and Bates kept telling her Strauss was busy, or at a meeting or something. It got pretty hairy around here in January. Finally, Strauss called Professor Silberman in. I don't know what happened between them, but that's when Professor Silberman blew up at him and threatened to poison his slop." Janine laughed happily at the memory.

That was when Strauss had threatened to deny fellowships to Edith's graduate students. "And after that Kevin saw Donna planting a kiss on Bates."

"No, it was a couple of days before Strauss called her in and told her she was out of luck, he couldn't do anything for her."

"How'd she take that?"

Janine said, with heavy emphasis, "It was very quiet in Dean Strauss's office. I didn't hear a thing. She was in there about half an hour. And then she marched out without saying a word, her face absolutely expressionless, her nose in the air. It was spooky, considering how angry she sometimes got with Bates. And that's the last I saw of her. I didn't see Dean Strauss the rest of the day, either. For all I knew, he could've been in his office, dead. But I didn't go to see."

I was sitting and facing the two empty offices, Bates's just behind Janine's, Strauss's down the hall behind her, Bates's door ajar, Strauss's closed, probably locked, even though he thought he was safe now.

"If Strauss had taken a bite out of that apple, instead of

Donna Trask," I said, "Donna would be a prime suspect, wouldn't she?"

"That's the first thing I thought of, when I heard what happened at the banquet," Janine agreed. "She'd have been my favorite suspect."

I asked Janine if she'd told this story to Buck Hansen. "Oh, sure," she said. "I told him everything I could think of. But if you're thinking it was Hudson Bates who poisoned that apple, forget it. He doesn't have the guts to try to kill anybody. He could've sent the threatening letters, though. That's his style."

She was probably right about that. According to Myles Kruger, Bates had called his wife anonymously, on Strauss's orders.

"You bought the apple for Strauss that he was going to use at the banquet, didn't you?" I asked her.

Her face darkened. "Yes. But the police don't think it was the same apple that killed Donna Trask, you know. They think somebody—Professor Silberman, probably—sneaked into the banquet hall and replaced my apple with the poisoned one. But the police didn't show me the apple that killed Donna. Bates stepped on it, they said."

"The apple you bought," I said. "You brought it to Strauss in his office the day of the banquet. Where'd he keep it?"

"On his desk, with his speech. By the way, I polished that apple. There wasn't a thing wrong with it. No needle holes, nothing. I told the police that, too."

"You left the office around 4:30?"

"About then, yeah. To catch my bus. Strauss had already gone home by then, to rest up and change for the banquet."

"And Bates? Was he still in his office when you left?"

She laughed. "I see what you're getting at. You think Bates could've poisoned the apple after I'd left for the night, right?"

"I couldn't have put it better myself," I said modestly. She shook her head. "He left just after Strauss did. He had a meeting over on the New Campus. He told me he wouldn't be coming back to the office. He was going directly home from the meeting to get ready for the banquet. Besides, I told you . . ."

"So he knew the apple would be there after you'd left, when the office was empty," I interrupted her.

"Yes, that's right. When you put it like that . . ."

"Was Strauss's office locked?"

"Strauss's office isn't ever locked—wasn't, I mean. It is now, of course. I suppose Bates could have come back here before Strauss did, on his way to the banquet, and replaced my apple with the poisoned one, but how would anybody be able to prove it?"

I thought that Edith Silberman's lawyer wouldn't need to prove it, only need to raise the possibility. The apple had been accessible to a lot of people, so it could already have been poisoned when Strauss came back to get it, and the speech, on his way to the banquet. Edith wasn't the only person with a strong motive for wanting Strauss dead. Hudson Bates was a prime candidate, too. Much better than Edith, in my book. After all, he'd destroyed the murder weapon.

I went home and made the hardest phone call of my life.

Buck was in, but he kept me waiting almost five minutes. I decided to believe it was because he was busy, not vindictive. When he came on the line, his voice was rough with an anger he was trying not to show.

"What is it, Peggy?"

I told him I was sorry, added that everything he'd guessed about my holding back on him about Edith Silberman was probably true.

There was just silence on the line, meant for me to fill by talking or end by hanging up. I could see him at his cluttered desk, the phone crushed—no, don't get melodramatic, stupid, I told myself—held to his ear, his blue eyes surrounded by the laugh wrinkles that were probably making him look reptilian at the moment. I knew he'd never been this angry at me before. A part of me was glad we were speaking on the phone, so I couldn't see his face, but another part of me wished he could see how I looked, so I could use that as a weapon to try to soften him.

The silent treatment wasn't working, so I said, "I'm in the wrong line of work, I know that. But I don't know what else I can do. I knew Edith Silberman wasn't guilty, so I couldn't see any reason to clutter up your investigation with irrelevant information."

"The relevance of the information is my business, not yours," he said. "Professor Silberman used you. If she'd done a better job of cleaning up after her husband, it might have weakened our case considerably. You're a cop, Peggy. I agree with you that you probably shouldn't be."

So I started to cry again, as I did with Paula and Lawrence last week. But I didn't let Buck hear me. He'd have no way of judging the sincerity of my crying, and the only way I could judge its sincerity was if I didn't let him know.

"I know she was using me," I admitted. "I even knew it then, when she was doing it. But doesn't the fact that she waited until the last minute, and then did such a crummy job of cleaning up after herself, prove that she's not guilty? Nobody would keep a goddamned chemistry lab in the house, especially after they'd used it to poison somebody. Do you really think she's guilty, Buck?"

"It's not my job to make decisions like that. The district attorney thinks she's guilty. I work for him, not for myself."

That was the big difference between us, between this man I loved so much, and me. I asked him to excuse me for a moment while I blew my nose. Then I told him of my interview with Myles Kruger and what I'd learned from Janine about Hudson Bates.

He said Homicide knew all that. Both Bates and Kruger had been suspects, but neither had any known connection to cyanide.

"That's the big thing for you, isn't it?" I said bitterly.

"The cyanide. Even though Strauss's behavior drove Kruger to do something as crazy as make threatening phone calls, it still comes down to who had access to cyanide."

"Sure. If Donna Trask had been killed with a Colt .45, anybody in possession of that kind of gun, with motive and opportunity, would become the prime suspect. You see anything wrong with that?"

I told him about being summoned into Lt. Bixler's office and being warned off the case by Bates. "He was there to find out what I was up to and what I'd learned, Buck. And he may have been doing it on his own, behind Strauss's back."

"I'm bogged down in work," Buck said. His voice was no longer angry, just impatient. I'd accomplished something by calling him. "There've been a few murders committed since we arrested Edith Silberman," he went on dryly, "some of which I'm being asked to solve."

I told him I was sorry again, he mumbled something about it being okay, and we hung up.

I called Edith, told her what Janine had told me about Hudson Bates. She listened and was silent for a moment or two. Then she started laughing.

"So it's true, what I told you. All these years little Hudson has run thug's errands for Jerry Strauss, and for what? Nothing. Jerry returns to teaching loaded down with honors, and Hudson returns to teaching with nothing to show for his loyalty but a well-earned reputation as a weasel. What a pity! My lawyer will find that interesting. I don't suppose your hawk-eyed friend Lawrence saw Bates coming to the banquet through the kitchen, did he?"

"I showed him a picture of Bates," I told her. "He didn't recognize him."

"You should've shown him the clothes Hudson was wearing," she said. "Who'd recognize his face? Well, every little bit helps. Thanks, Peggy!"

I also told her what I'd heard about Bates and Donna Trask.

"Interesting, if true," she said, "in a *National Enquirer*-ish sort of way. I don't suppose your informant, this admirable Janine, could find out for you if Bates has a hobby making jewelry?"

I laughed, puzzled. "I don't think Bates wears jewelry. Why, what's the joke?"

"Silversmiths keep cyanide around, my lawyer tells me," Edith replied. "It's very effective in removing tarnish."

People, too, I thought, as we hung up.

Twenty

When I woke up the next morning, it was raining heavily. I made coffee and zapped a sweet roll into hot mush in my microwave, took both into my living room, and sat and stared at a bird hiding from the rain in a bush outside my window. It stared back at me. I tried to put myself in its place, to try to experience the utter differences between us since, for some reason, I wasn't able to do it from my own perspective. Fortunately, the phone rang before I got sucked too far into that. It was Curtiss Naylor.

He said, "That little twit, Hudson Bates, called me the other day, to ask if you'd been in touch. I thought of lying, but it's always dangerous to lie when you don't know why, so I said that yes, we'd talked. He wanted to know what about, and I thought that was a bit officious of him—after all, I *am* retired and no longer need to kowtow to cowpats, as it were—so I asked him what business it was of his. He said that you'd been passing yourself off as something other than what you are, and the dean was naturally curious to find out why. 'In what sense "naturally?"' I asked him, for it has been many years since Jerry Strauss has done anything naturally, and of course Hudson pretended he hadn't heard my question and repeated his. I told him that we'd only discussed some of the later Impressionists, especially the Americans, and hung up on him." Naylor paused for a well-deserved deep breath.

161

"Thanks," I said, feeling better about the day.

"If you want to pick some more of what's left of my brains after a lifetime of teaching and research, why don't you come over? You could wear a false nose and moustache to throw off Strauss's spies, and a kerchief to cover your hair."

Why not? I didn't have anything better to do. "Do you have coffee," I asked him, "or shall I bring a thermos?"

He was standing in his front window, gloomily staring out at his rock garden, which the rain had turned to mud, when I got there. He handed me a cup for my coffee. He had a pot of tea next to his easy chair.

When we were settled, he said, "I gathered that Jeremiah Strauss assigned Bates the task of calling former members of the conference center committee to see if you'd been in contact with them, and to try to find out what you were after. Jerry doesn't usually waste effort—even Hudson's effort—on completely trivial things. So he must not think you're a completely trivial thing."

"Maybe not," I said. "But I'm not even sure Bates was calling you on Strauss's orders. He may have been doing it for some reason of his own." I told Naylor what I'd found out from Janine, about Strauss creating a position for Vice President Hightower's wife, but refusing to create one for Bates's. And I also told him Janine's theory about why he'd refused to help Bates.

Naylor chuckled. "I can just see Hudson sticking a hypodermic full of cyanide into an apple and cackling horribly, like the witch in *Snow White*. Except that Hudson's a lot prettier than the witch. He's even a lot prettier than Snow White." Then he shook his head. "But it won't fly, Peggy. Revenge isn't enough of a motive for a man like Bates. He's capable of murder, of course, and poison's probably the way he'd do it, too—something low-down like that. But he'd only resort to murder if he felt trapped and couldn't think of any other way out. He doesn't have the guts to murder somebody just because he's mad at him for not giving his wife a job. What else have you come up with?"

"Nothing," I said, suddenly angry, "not a damn thing that adds up to anything. I've been wasting my time."

"Don't be so hard on yourself, my dear. Maybe you're asking the wrong questions," he suggested, trying to be helpful. "You always get wrong answers that way. It never fails."

"You know," I told him, "when I started out, I was only interested in Donna Trask. It must've taken a lot of guts, and a lot of anger, for her to do what she did. I wanted to find out more about her. I was curious, too, to see if I could find out what she was planning to say before she died."

"I hadn't heard that she'd planned to say anything more," Naylor said.

"That's because nobody but me thinks she was. I thought I saw her start to pull a piece of paper out of her pocket just before she died."

"Now I wonder what could have been in that speech," Curtiss Naylor said, sinking his long chin into his hand. He seemed to accept my theory without any hesitation, possibly to humor me. He glanced up at me from under bushy eyebrows. "I imagine Donna Trask would pick up a great deal of dirt in high places over the years, as the daughter of the University's chief attorney. And it sounds as if that young lady was quite capable of hacking and slashing both this way and that, without regard for the child in its mother's womb, etc., etc. It would have been quite a speech!" He sat up, poured himself tea. "If you're right," he added, "it sounds like it might have been a lucky thing for a lot of people that she died when she did, Jeremiah Strauss included."

"Yes."

"Under what bush do you intend to look now?"

"I was wondering that myself," I told him, "when you called. I'd like to look into the possibility that Strauss only pretended to favor putting the conference center on the

Old Campus, but that in reality he wanted it on the New Campus. And, if so, why'd he try to hide his interest? Who was he trying to fool?"

"Since you were last here," Naylor said, "I've been wondering the same thing myself. You put me onto that line of thought when you pointed out that I'd said twice that Strauss 'led me to believe' he wanted the center on the Old Campus. He led a lot of people to believe that. Maybe we aren't the first to suspect he was lying."

"You think it's possible he profited from it and cut somebody else out?"

"Somebody on the committee, you mean?" Naylor asked, grinning faintly. "Me, for example? No wonder you brought your own coffee and won't eat my cookies."

"I wasn't thinking of you," I assured him. "Would it have been worth a lot of money to Harold McCord to get the center over on the New Campus?"

"Well, McCord's building it for the University, of course," Naylor replied, "but he could do that no matter where it's located. You'd have to ask somebody else about that."

"When you were serving on the New Campus committee with Strauss fifteen years ago, did the committee ever meet at Donald Trask's home?"

"Now why would we do that? Fifteen years ago, Trask wasn't even connected with the University."

"He was the lawyer the University hired to negotiate the acquisition of the land for the New Campus," I told him.

"Was he, indeed? Who told you that?"

"Donna Trask's mother."

"She was sure?"

"She sounded sure to me. She said Strauss was often at their home during the period when your committee was meeting. I suppose she could have the dates wrong. Maybe Strauss was there after the committee had voted in favor of the New Campus, working out the details with him."

Naylor was silent for a long time. Then he said: "No. That wouldn't have been Strauss's job. Once our committee had done its work, we were finished with it. Strauss, too."

"Then perhaps they became friends at that time," I suggested.

"That could be. Jerry's salary wasn't much back then—he hadn't come into his inheritance yet—but even then he loved to be around power and money. Donald Trask, as a real estate lawyer for a big law firm, was a member of the class to which Strauss aspired."

"And now Strauss has money and belongs to that class, whereas Trask's fortunes seem to be heading downward."

"Bashing the bottle can do that to a person," Naylor said.

We listened to the rain beating on the windows of his living room for a moment, and then suddenly something he'd said struck me, and I laughed.

"What's so funny?"

"You said Strauss came into his inheritance back then, at the time he was working to get the University to expand across the river. Donna Trask's mother told me the same thing."

"So?"

"We have quite a number of coincidences here," I said. "Fifteen years ago, Strauss used his influence to get the University to expand across the river, and fifteen years ago he inherited a lot of money from his father. He spent time, unaccountably, with Donald Trask in that period. Trask became the U's chief attorney shortly after that, and he's also a good enough friend of Harold McCord's to attend his birthday party, although he doesn't seem very happy with McCord. McCord suggests to Trask, jokingly, that it's too bad they can't name the new conference center after Strauss. I thought the joke was on Strauss because he'd been so opposed to putting the center on the New Campus. What if it wasn't a joke at all? What if it really was too bad they couldn't name the center after Strauss, because he'd been instrumental in getting it on the New Campus?"

Curtiss Naylor thought about that for a little while, then,

a glitter in his eyes, said, "I hate being played for a sucker."

"There may be somebody else out there who doesn't like being played for one, either," I told him. "I think maybe I'd like to know more about the history of the New Campus—for instance, who owned it fifteen years ago, before the University acquired it."

"I'll bet you think you know."

"I'd like to know for sure."

"Perhaps I can point you in the right direction," Naylor said. "I play bridge with one of the law librarians. He's been around the University a long time and knows everything about the legal history of the place. As a consequence, there are few people on campus more cynical than Raymond Clough. I'll give him a ring for you."

He found the number he wanted in his address book, dialed and explained why he was calling, and handed the phone to me. Clough agreed to see me as soon as I could get to the law library.

He was in his late fifties or early sixties, and gray from the top of his head down to his socks and loafers.

"You want to know who owned the land that's now the New Campus before the University acquired it?" he repeated my question. "Harold McCord owned it, or most of it."

He looked at me, waited for my reaction. I didn't have any. It didn't come as a surprise.

"Most people today," he went on, "would be surprised to know that. When we think of McCord now, we think of the hotel magnate, the philanthropist, the University benefactor and sports 'booster.' " He smiled as if the words tasted sour. "Above all, perhaps, we think of the man with extensive land holdings in the city, without thinking of what the term 'extensive land holdings' might encompass. But that's today." The tip of Raymond Clough's tongue came out and touched up his lips with some much needed saliva.

"In the '60s and '70s," he went on, "Harold McCord was a slumlord. What's now the New Campus was mostly tenements then. Firetraps, cheap housing for students and the poor. And liquor stores, 3.2 bars, so-called adult bookstores and movie houses. As a matter of fact," Clough added, "McCord was able to buy a lot of that land cheaply because the owners needed the money to defend themselves against charges of illegally producing and selling pornography. McCord closed the pornography businesses down—he didn't want that headache—but he kept the rest."

For ten years, Clough said, McCord ran the buildings into the ground, never doing any but the most necessary repairs, and then only when the housing inspectors or fire marshalls insisted; strangely enough, they didn't come around often. He was lucky that no students died in any of the fires.

"A landlord wouldn't be able to get away with that today, of course," Clough told me, "at least not as easily, but that was before rent withholding became legal. When the University decided to expand over to that side of the river, it had McCord's land condemned. 'Eminent domain,' it's called, the state's right to take what it needs, or thinks it needs."

"But McCord couldn't have made much of a profit off it, could he?" I asked. "When the state condemns land, doesn't it pay the owners only what it's worth? 'Fair market price,' or something like that?"

Clough gave me a look which implied that I was some new species of innocent, just crawling into the ugly light of day. "Why yes, certainly," he agreed, "but what criterion do you use to determine 'fair market price?' If they'd gone according to what McCord paid for the land a few years earlier, or what the buildings were actually worth, he wouldn't have made a large profit. But he was able to show that the land was potentially worth far more than he'd paid for it, and that he had been planning to develop it. Indeed, he was even able to produce, as from a magician's hat, some nice architectural drawings of a development—something he called 'a city within a city'—complete with moderately priced student housing, apartments in a variety of price ranges, office and store space, restaurants—and even a hotel."

"He did build all of that," I said.

"Yes, of course he did. Because, you see, Harold McCord also owned the land adjacent to the land the University took, and when the University moved in, that land increased in value tenfold. And that was where he put up his big development, using the money he got for the land the University took. People a lot more cynical than I am suspect that the plans he showed the state were never meant for the land the University took at all, but for the land just beyond it."

"Gee," I said. "Why aren't I that smart?"

"You may be, Miss O'Neill," Raymond Clough said reassuringly. "However, you may not be as bent."

"Now, in order to build the new conference center, the University is leasing Harold McCord a big chunk of its land. Is that right?"

He nodded.

"Land he sold the University, fifteen years ago."

He nodded again, pleased with the progress I was making.

I had to laugh. "He must have had a good lawyer back then," I said. "You wouldn't happen to know who it was, would you?"

"He had a number of good lawyers, Ms. O'Neill, then as now. However, the lawyer whose name most frequently appears on the documents relating to the transfer of ownership of McCord's land to the state was that of our own honorable chief attorney, Donald Trask."

"Jeremiah Strauss's friend."

"I've heard that rumor, too," Clough said.

"It's not a rumor."

"Nor is it illegal."

"But if Strauss took a big bribe from McCord to persuade the University to expand over onto that side of the river, that must be illegal."

"Must it be?" Clough asked, scratching the side of his nose. "No. In very bad taste, certainly, but not illegal, if Strauss could show that there were persuasive grounds for expanding onto that side of the campus, and that wouldn't be so hard to do. The 'bribe,' as you so slanderously call it, if it exists, would only have been a gift. Harold McCord has given many such gifts in his time."

"All right," I said. "So Strauss wouldn't have gone to jail for it, but he'd have been exposed as a man of no integrity. He'd have been disgraced at the University."

"Yes, indeed he would. And he wouldn't have liked that at all. Like all men without integrity, Jeremiah Strauss is overly sensitive to public opinion. That's why he wanted the University Scholarship so badly, I suspect."

And, I thought, that's why he'd worked so hard to conceal his interest in putting the new conference center on the New Campus. He'd never have been made a University Scholar, if it became known that, fifteen years ago, he'd delivered the University into Harold McCord's hands and, less than six months ago, he'd done it again.

I thanked Clough for his information and got up to go. He waited until my back was turned. Then, in his soft, dry voice, he said, "I heard that Strauss and Trask aren't as tight as they used to be."

"I've heard that, too," I said. "Now that Strauss has got all he possibly can from the University, and Trask's drinking is getting out of hand, there seems to be a falling out between them."

"Do you think that's all there is to it?" he asked me.

"You think there's more?"

"I don't know anything, of course," he said in the same dry voice. "Does anyone, around here? But you might want to ask yourself this: What did Jeremiah Strauss need Donald Trask for this time?"

He waited to hear my answer. I didn't have one. He seemed to like that.

"After all," he went on, "the University already *owned* the land, didn't it—thanks to the efforts of Strauss and Trask fifteen years ago. But this time, all Strauss needed to do—if, indeed, he did it—was to get his committee to recommend that the University, in effect, give some of that land back to McCord, to build and operate the conference center. He didn't need Donald Trask's help for that, did he?"

"Which means," I finished for him, "that Jeremiah Strauss didn't have to cut Donald Trask in on whatever it was McCord paid him this time."

"This is all very irresponsible of us, Ms. O'Neill," Clough said. "Besides, I'm sure that Jeremiah Strauss would have felt a moral obligation to Donald Trask to share with him some of his ill-gotten gains, for the service Trask performed for him fifteen years ago. Don't you think so?"

I laughed at the thought of Strauss feeling a moral obligation to anybody, and Clough managed to work up a smile as faint as bird breath.

Twenty-One

It was time I paid a call on Donald Trask, a condolence call. After all, I'd come to know his daughter nearly as well as I'd know my own sister, if I had one. I waited until after dinner the next night, and then drove up to his home.

Trask lived on a hill. We have a few hills in this town and they're prime real estate, I don't know why: The view from any of them is just of the roofs of houses that aren't on hills.

Trask's house was small, but it looked expensive, with natural cedar siding. A huge bay window jutted out above the steeply terraced yard like a ship's prow, all lit up. A white grand piano filled the bay. Flagstone steps wound up from the street to the front door.

The mailbox was on the street. I peeked inside. Nobody had collected the mail, so I took it with me as I climbed the steps, thumbing idly through it. It wasn't all that different from mine, just more bills. A postcard advertised take-out pizza on one side, a lost child on the other. I wondered if there was a connection.

I was a little out of breath when I got to the top of the steps. Trask certainly never walked up: A driveway circled up to an attached garage on my right. A white Cadillac, Sumiko's upside-down boat, was parked in front of it. It wasn't a new car, and it needed body work. Small patches of rust grew along the sides like lichen, and there was a dent in the front fender next to the headlight.

The woman who answered the door had the generic look of the woman who'd been with Trask at McCord's party, as Sumiko had described her to me. She was barefoot and wearing a man's white dress shirt that reached mid-thigh. She came up to my eyes, which made her about five-five, and her figure was boyish. The woman Sumiko had seen with Trask had been named Kim, but I couldn't count on this being the same one.

I gave her the mail and asked her if Mr. Trask was home. I almost said "your father."

"May I know your business?" she asked me, hugging herself because she wasn't dressed for the cold air I'd let in.

"I knew Donna, his daughter," I said. "I just wanted to pay my respects."

She looked a little confused, as if Donna's death were last season's distraction, and we were into something else now. "Just a moment, please," she said, and closed the door in my face.

It opened a minute later, and she let me in and led me though the living and dining rooms to a large four-season porch.

The porch was glass on three sides. The back windows looked onto a deck that ended at a cut in the side of the hill. A deck light illuminated a rusting portable grill, a table with a glass top, and lounge chairs with muddy cushions. They all looked as if they'd been there since a final barbecue last fall.

Trask was sitting in a black leather recliner that didn't fit the room, his slippered feet up on the matching ottoman. The white shirt he was wearing was open at the throat and hung out of his trousers. A coat and tie were draped over the television set, and his glasses were pushed up into his thick, sandy hair. Close up, I could see that his once strong chin was in the process of becoming a bag, and the blood vessels in his pale face looked like crazing on a Japanese vase. His eyes were small and red-rimmed, as if he'd been crying a lot recently, but they watched me steadily as I approached.

A newspaper was scattered on the floor around him, and he was drinking something dark with ice in it.

"I've seen you somewhere," he greeted me. He took a lot of time looking me up and down.

"I was at Donna's funeral," I told him. "I was also at the banquet when she—died."

He paid no attention to the pause. "The banquet? Why?"

"I came as somebody's guest," I said.

"Whose?" I started to name a professor I knew slightly whom I'd seen there, but he interrupted me with, "Never mind, the professors all look alike. I can't tell one from the other or remember their names. Can you? I suppose you have to, you're a student. Kim!" he hollered and, back to me, "What's your name again?"

"Tammi," I told him, "with an i."

He nodded approvingly. "That's a nice name," he said. "You want coffee or a drink? I think we've got wine, too, Kim, right?"

"Coffee would be nice," I said, and added, the way my mother always did, "if you've got some already made."

"Bring Tammi coffee," Trask said to Kim.

"I'll make some," Kim replied, and disappeared.

He said I couldn't have been a friend of Donna's, I was too old for that, and besides, he knew most of her friends. He watched me as he said that, his eyes unblinking.

I replied that I'd been a teaching assistant in the Humanities department and had talked to her on a number of occasions. I'd been impressed with her work and was shocked at her death, especially since I was there when it happened.

I'd said something he liked hearing. He nodded, and his expression softened. "She was a brilliant student, Tammi," he said. "Right from the start, from grade school. You know what she did once? She couldn't have been more than five. She toddled up to the blackboard during a PTA meeting—all the mothers were there, you know?—and she wrote, 'Donna is the best student in her class.' It caused quite a stir. Everybody laughed and clapped. And she was right. No other kid her age could've done that! She was precocious." It took him two tries to pronounce the word correctly. He knocked down a hefty slug of his drink, no doubt to sharpen his wits, and then let the glass down with a thud on the leather arm of his chair. "I hoped she'd go to law school when she finished her B.A. I was planning to quit this damned university, and we'd go into partnership together."

"She had that kind of a mind," I said, hoping he wouldn't ask me what I meant by that.

"Gone now! My only child, gone," he said, his voice a teary, angry rasp. "Why don't we have the death penalty in this state? Bleeding-heart liberals!" And then he added, "Death's too good for the bitch." He thought about that for a few moments, and then shot me a suddenly bright look. "It's been three weeks since Donna died. What brings you up here to see me now, Terri?"

"Tammi. I guess I didn't want to intrude on your sorrow, but I haven't been able to get her off my mind."

I was going to go on to say that this was a part of the grieving process for me—a line I felt sure would work on him—but fortunately, Kim returned with a cup of coffee. The coffee was instant, with undissolved crystals floating on the surface like little bugs. Kim took a step toward Trask, giving a practiced pantomime of refilling a glass. He shook his head. "No more for me," he said. "Business, remember?" He flicked a look at his watch.

Kim left the room. A few moments later, piano music floated softly out to us from the living room. "Chopsticks," one of my favorites.

"I hope I'm not keeping you from anything," I said.

"I've got a little business coming up later tonight," he said. "We're finalizing the plans for the groundbreaking ceremony for the new conference center. You know about it?"

I said I did, wondering who "we" were.

"It's a week from this Saturday. You coming?"

I said I hadn't been invited.

"I'll see that you get tickets. Two be enough?"

More than enough. "Fine," I said, "thanks."

"Kim!" "Chopsticks" stopped and Kim appeared in the porch door. "Get Tammi's address for me, will you?"

I gave her a fake address and Lt. Bixler's last name and then she returned to the living room and resumed her playing.

"You're in the Humanities department, right?" Trask asked me. "I suppose you know all about how Donna tried to get into the graduate program and got turned down by the woman who killed her, Silberman. I suppose you knew her?"

I said I did. I told him I'd never worked with her because she was too rigid in her views for my critical taste.

I added that it wasn't just Silberman who'd rejected Donna's application, it was a committee. I've found, in my career as a liar, that it often works best to tell the person you're lying to something she or he doesn't want to hear. Nobody believes you'd do that unless you're compulsively committed to telling the truth regardless of the consequences.

"She was chairman of the committee," he said, glaring at me, struggling to bring his recliner into the upright position and setting his empty glass on the floor. "We all know the power the chairman has!"

Probably nobody, I thought, knew more about that than Jeremiah Strauss's friend Donald Trask.

"The way Donna described the situation," he went on, "Silberman wouldn't let her students get away with saying anything she didn't agree with. Donna paid the price for that. She was stubborn and stuck to her guns no matter what."

"I've heard Professor Silberman could be pretty opinionated, all right," I agreed, feeling a little uneasy speaking about Edith as if she were dead. "But you must know more about it than I do, considering that you saw the paper Donna wrote for her and everything."

"I couldn't make heads or tails of what Donna wrote," he replied, waving it away with a hand. "It was all gobbledygook to me. But she said she'd shown it to another Humanities professor, and he'd said it was brilliant. To be honest, I never understood her interest in the humanities. I kept telling her, 'Princess, you don't want to go to grad school in a dead-end field. Forget it. Get your B.A., and I'll help you get into any law school you want.' " He shook his head and reached down for his glass. "I couldn't get her into the grad school here," he said bitterly, "but I could've gotten her into any law school in the country. Kim!"

"Chopsticks" stopped again. Kim came in, took his glass, retreated.

"Where was I?" he asked me. "Oh, yeah, law school." He brooded on that for a while, saying nothing. Then, with sudden, suppressed anger, he exclaimed, "That goddamned Jerry! You know him? Jeremiah Strauss?"

I said I'd seen him at the banquet in his honor.

"In his honor! In his honor! What a joke! I could tell you a few things about Jerry Strauss and honor!" He was silent a moment. Kim returned bearing a fresh drink. He took it from her, trembling slightly. "I tried to tell Donna about that," he said to me, still holding the drink in front of his face, "about honor and Jerry, but she didn't believe me. She believed him instead, believed he'd get her into the Humanities graduate program over the whole fucking department's objection."

He brought his mouth to his glass and tipped a little of the drink into it, swallowed, continued. "I talked to him about it," Trask went on. "I warned him not to play games with my daughter! He assured me he wouldn't. He assured me! The son of a bitch tricked me, too!" he blurted, and then laughed, a hollow, meaningless laugh. "Well," he added, almost to himself, "it wouldn't be the first time for that, either." He shot me a sly look. "But you don't know anything about that, do you?"

"No," I said, feeling suddenly cold. I'd heard a ghost: Donald Trask, like Donna, claiming he'd been tricked.

"No, you wouldn't," he said, sounding disgusted that I hadn't personally experienced Strauss's perfidy. His look changed from sly to hard. "You see," he went on, "I knew Jerry hated Silberman's guts. So I thought that'd be an additional reason for him to override the bitch Silberman and help Donna."

I started to say something about his language, in spite of myself, but he waved his free hand at me to shut me up.

"All right, all right!" he continued, raising his voice to answer the objection he thought I was going to make. "So maybe Donna's grade point average was borderline! So what? Jerry's fixed more than that in his years as dean; he could've fixed that, too, if he'd wanted. But instead, he strung her along. He handed her case over to one of his stooges, instead of dealing with it personally. He got her hopes up, then pulled the rug out from under her." He took another swallow of his drink, leaned in my direction, and, in a loud whisper, said: "And she died in place of him, too. How much longer will his luck last, do you think?"

He was staring at something behind me. My impulse was to turn and look to see what it was, but I knew that all I'd see was a blank wall.

"You're convinced it was Silberman, then?" I asked him. "That she hated him enough to murder him?"

"Aren't you?" The question surprised him.

I shrugged. "Well, I don't know anything, of course," I said, "and probably the police haven't told us everything they've got against Professor Silberman, either. But it doesn't seem like very much," I added, "at least, to someone who knew her, as I did. And I've heard rumors that Strauss has made a lot of enemies more powerful than Professor Silberman."

"For example?" His gaze was trying to focus on me

through his half-closed eyelids, and something was coming through his drunkenness, something not unlike intelligence.

"In his business dealings," I said.

"What business dealings? Are we talking about the same person, Jeremiah Strauss, dean of the Graduate School?"

I plunged ahead, since there'd be nothing to gain by plunging back. "He had a lot to do with the U's move to the New Campus side of the river," I pointed out, "and with the decision to put the new conference center over there, too."

"And?"

"He could have profited from those things," I said.

He stared at me, his fingers digging into the leather of his chair, turning his knuckles white. Something seemed to be telling him he had to try to sober up now, quickly, like a scuba diver who's just realized he's out of oxygen and the surface is way, way up there.

"How would that have led somebody to want to murder him?"

I shrugged.

"A moment ago," he said, squinting up at me, "you mentioned that you'd known Silberman well." He began struggling out of his chair. "That was a slip, wasn't it? You didn't mean to say that, did you? When you first came in here, you said you didn't know her very well at all. Who are you? What do you really want?"

He was out of his chair now. He took a step toward me, stopped, waited for me to answer. I didn't recall saying I'd known Edith well, but I didn't see any point in arguing about it.

"I told you," I began.

"You're no friend of Donna's!" he interrupted me. "I said, what do you want here?"

"I don't know about that," I replied, trying to ignore the threat in his voice, "but there's another thing I want to ask you about before I leave. At the banquet, I got the impression Donna intended to say more than she did, before she died. I thought she was going to give a speech, and was reaching into her pocket to bring one out, or notes for one. I wonder if you found anything like that in her clothing."

"You're wrong, there wasn't anything like that." Then, in spite of himself, he asked, "What kind of a speech? She'd already given a speech, a great one-line speech about Eve and the apple. What more could she do to wreck the banquet for poor Jerry? Why would she want to say anything else?"

"I'm just guessing," I said, not quite accurately. "Maybe she planned to go on to spill dirt she'd collected on some of the people at the University."

"Dirt," Trask repeated, as if that were a word he didn't know. "I don't get it. What kind of dirt had Donna 'collected?' "

"I have no idea," I assured him, again whittling a little off the truth. "But I figure that—being your daughter, and all—she might have heard quite a lot over the years. Heard it from you, I mean," I added, to be sure he knew exactly what I meant.

For a moment, Trask didn't move or say anything. "Chopsticks" reverberated through the house.

"What could she have heard?" He didn't like that question, for some reason. He started over. "You don't know what you're talking about, do you? You're here to try to help that woman who killed my daughter, Silberman, aren't you? Donna didn't know anything! How could she? She wouldn't do anything like that to her father even if she did!" That came out in a rush, too fast to stop. It even startled him, leaving him with his mouth hanging open.

"They're here!" Kim was standing in the dining room doorway. She almost sang the words, looked as though she was going to enjoy the impression they'd make on Trask.

"What?" He looked over at her, a different kind of panic growing in his eyes.

"Harold McCord and President Wolf," she told him. "They're coming up the steps right now."

Twenty-Two

For a crazy moment, I considered dashing out onto the deck, jumping over the side, and sliding down the hill to my car. I doubted, however, that would do me any good. Wolf would probably see me, and even if he didn't, the chances of his recognizing me from Trask's description were good. He knew who I was, and he'd seen me at Donna Trask's funeral with Buck and Theresa Durr.

"Pick up in here," Trask said to Kim. He was stuffing his shirt into his trousers. "I'll let them in." He followed me through the dining and living rooms, running his fingers through his hair, trying to stand up straight. The fear and anger I'd aroused in him were forgotten. He had other, more pressing, concerns. As he opened the front door, I took a deep breath and stepped outside into the yellow glare of the porch light.

Wolf was almost at the top of the steps, moving quickly as always. Harold McCord, easy to recognize from his frequent appearances in the media, was ten or twelve steps behind. Wolf was a trim, athletic man of medium height, about fifty-five, and showing almost no effects of the long, steep climb. McCord, on the other hand, younger than Wolf by a few years, resembled somebody who wasn't going to survive the Bataan death march, although his body managed to imply that he worked out at an expensive club several times a week.

180

They both looked up as I came down the steps toward them. My sudden appearance must have startled Wolf, but he didn't show it. He just paused and flashed me his signature smile, a cocaine smuggler's smile that had disarmed countless people whom he'd later left for dead.

"Officer O'Neill," he said.

"Yes. I'm just leaving." I gave McCord a smile and he smiled back, the meaningless kind that wonders where we've met. I'd never been that close to a multi-millionaire before.

At the bottom of the steps, I turned and looked back up. The three men were together on the porch. Trask was staring down at me and his mouth was moving. Wolf's head was cocked and he seemed to be listening to Trask intently. McCord was peering over his shoulder to get a look at the subject under discussion, who got into her muddy, beat-up Rabbit and drove off, wondering what the harvest was going to be this time. Somehow, I didn't think it would be tickets to the groundbreaking ceremony for the new conference center.

Before roll call that night, Paula was showing off a new silver bracelet, letting it slide up and down her arm. It wasn't hard to guess where it had come from: Lawrence was looking like he'd just purchased the Koh-i-noor diamond and then casually tossed it to her. A superior smile was playing around his mouth. It was a nice bracelet on an even nicer arm, but I thought Paula was overdoing the expression of pleasure. She saw me looking at her, read my mind, and gave me a wink. She hadn't forgiven me entirely for Edith Silberman, but at least our friendship was on the mend.

As I walked my beat, I thought about my talk that evening with Donald Trask. He was clearly on the way down—mentally, financially, probably physically as well. Everything about his house—Kim included—pointed in that direction.

It had upset him when he'd discovered that I wasn't

who I pretended to be. And it had angered him to discover that I didn't think Edith Silberman was guilty of trying to kill Strauss. But it had done more than make him mad, it had frightened him when I mentioned the possibility that Strauss's involvement with the New Campus could have been the reason somebody tried to kill him. Why? He obviously hated Strauss. Was it just because he thought Strauss had "tricked" his daughter? Maybe Raymond Clough was right. Maybe Strauss had profited from the decision to put the conference center on the New Campus and hadn't shared whatever McCord had given him in the way of a bribe with Trask.

When I'd suggested to him that Donna was going to give a speech that would expose some of the shady things she'd learned about the University, which she'd learned from him, he'd blurted out, *She wouldn't do that to her father.* He was wrong about that, I thought. Curtiss Naylor said that Donna sounded like the sort of person who wouldn't spare the child in its mother's womb. From everything I knew about Donna and her relationship with her parents, she had no reason to spare her father, if she decided to spill everything she knew.

The squad car pulled up alongside me around 1 A.M. Lawrence rolled down his window and asked me if I wanted to let the Old Campus take its chances for a half hour or so while I warmed up with a cup of coffee. I got in, and we drove off to a White Castle that was close to campus and open all night. I was aware that I was a distant second choice of coffee-break partner for Lawrence, but I didn't mind.

As we sipped our coffee, the poor moonstruck guy asked me what I thought of Paula's bracelet. I said I thought it was lovely.

"It's got both our names on it," he said, "and the date."

I hadn't noticed, I told him, and he said that was because those extra touches were on the underside, next to her skin. Do all men in love talk like this, I wondered. Do women?

I sipped my coffee and thought of the bracelet, the way it had slid up and down Paula's arm in the squad room before she'd put on her uniform jacket. It reminded me of something else I'd seen recently. Then I remembered: Theresa Durr, Donna Trask's mother, had been wearing silver bracelets on her suntanned arms at her daughter's funeral.

The realization struck with a force that almost took my breath away.

"Where're you going?" Lawrence asked me.

I went to the pay phone in the corner, yanked open the door, and stepped inside. My fingers fumbled trying to press coins into the slot, and I had to get down on my hands and knees to look for a dime I'd dropped.

"What's wrong, Peggy?" Buck asked, when I managed to get him on the line. He was at home. He'd been asleep, naturally.

"Jewelry makers use cyanide," I said, trying to speak very slowly.

"I know that."

"Donna Trask's mother is a jewelry maker. Did you know that? And did you know that Donna visited her mother in Santa Fe a few weeks before she died, and spent time with her, both in her home and in her studio?" I took a deep breath. "I just thought I'd share this with you before I share it with Edith Silberman's lawyer," I added sarcastically. I couldn't help it. Buck hates the word "share," as in "communicate," as much as I do.

I thought he must have left the phone, the silence dragged out so long, but he was just letting some of the ramifications develop in his head. Finally, he said, "Thanks."

"You're welcome," I replied. I felt better, now that I'd gotten it out, as if I might have died before telling him, and nobody would ever know. "Do you have any objections to my telling Edith about this?" I thought I'd try to rebuild my shaky reputation for responsible behavior and willingness to cooperate.

"I'd rather you waited until we talked to Mrs. Durr. Can I call you tomorrow, I mean, later today?"

"Sure," I said, happy to do him this small favor.

I didn't hear from Buck that day. The day after, though, Friday, he phoned to invite me over for dinner.

I knew things were okay between us when I saw he'd cooked spaghetti, something he knew I liked. Buck doesn't hold grudges as long as I do, and I don't hold them very long.

After we'd eaten, and were once again sitting on the couch and looking out his big picture window, I asked, "What's going to happen now?"

Buck poured coffee. "Edith Silberman's lawyer has asked the D.A. to postpone her arraignment," he replied. "I'm sure he will. I should have asked Theresa Durr more questions, the way you did. You may have noticed that I gave you full credit to the media."

I tried not to look smug. I'd tried not to sound smug for the reporter who'd called to interview me, too. I'd bored his ear off with the kind of clichés athletes layer on their adoring public: I'd gotten lucky, I'd just happened to be in the right place at the right time. The article, understandably, couldn't pinpoint exactly what that place was.

Edith had been unavailable for comment. I could have told the reporter that she was staying with a sister, to avoid the hostility radiated by some of her neighbors.

After I'd called him, Buck flew a man to Theresa Durr's home in Santa Fe. She'd checked her jewelry-making supplies and told him she believed a two-ounce bottle of cyanide was missing. She'd bought it, she said, along with other chemicals, from a local supplier, not long before Donna had come to visit her in March. She was able to find a receipt to prove it. Yes, Donna had seen her mother's supply closet and had had access to the closet while Theresa Durr was out running an errand. Theresa had told

Donna about the cyanide back when Donna was a child, when she'd tried to interest Donna in what she was doing then.

"What else?" I asked Buck.

He shrugged. "Mrs. Durr believes Donna could have committed suicide. She thinks that killing herself in front of a large crowd of University dignitaries might be just the sort of thing she would do."

"You mean," I asked incredulously, "she thinks Donna flew out to Santa Fe simply to steal cyanide from her? Intending to use it later to kill herself?"

"Mrs. Durr thinks she went out there in the hope that they could make up, but something kept her from going through with it, perhaps seeing how happy her mother is now. She thinks Donna took the cyanide on an impulse— because it was there, because it was her mother's, because it was dangerous."

"What's her father's theory? He saw a lot more of her than her mother did."

"He doesn't seem very happy with the idea of suicide, naturally, but he admits it's possible. He told us his daughter had started seeing a therapist a couple of months before she died."

"What for?"

"He said he didn't know. She wouldn't talk to him about it."

He wouldn't have heard her if she had, I thought. "And what about you? What do you think?"

He didn't answer for a few moments, then shrugged. "It's a bizarre way to commit suicide," he said. "Cyanide's not all that easy to get hold of, you know, unless you know where to look for it. I find it hard to believe that Donna's stealing cyanide from her mother and her subsequent death by cyanide were just an odd coincidence. I don't like coincidences, Peggy."

"I don't either," I said. "But how does suicide explain the fact that the apple sat in front of Jeremiah Strauss all through dinner? It's an odd place to put an edible suicide weapon, isn't it—in front of somebody who just might take it into his head to eat it? What if Strauss hadn't liked Chicken Kiev any more than I do and decided to eat the apple instead?"

"But he wouldn't have done that. He needed the apple for the speech he was so proud of, remember? Where would he have found another one on such short notice?"

"Still," I said, "she was taking a risk, if all she wanted to do was kill herself."

"The theory is that she may initially have intended to kill Strauss in revenge for his not helping her get into the Humanities graduate program. But at the last moment she changed her mind, and decided to kill herself instead." Buck's voice was expressionless.

"Do you believe that?" I asked him.

Instead of answering, he asked me if I thought it was possible.

My father blew his brains out outside my bedroom door when I was a kid, so I know a little about suicide as a form of communication. Buck knows that.

"Sure," I said, "it's possible. Suicides are hopelessly confused people, most of them. I've come to know Donna Trask pretty well in the last three weeks. I'm sure she was capable of such a confused and creatively sterile act. There's just one thing about it that bothers me."

"What's that?"

"Her death came as a surprise to her. And I've told you before, Buck, I think she was planning to give a speech."

"Did it ever occur to you that you're wrong, that you only imagined the speech?"

"Briefly," I replied, "but I was watching her pretty closely, remember? I don't imagine things like that."

"That would make it murder again," he said, "with Edith Silberman our number one suspect. Because, as far as we know, Silberman was the only person, other than Donna Trask, who had access to cyanide. And where *is* the cyanide Donna stole from her mother, if she didn't use it herself?"

"I've had two interesting encounters with Bert Coombs," I told him, not answering the question—at least, not directly. "Most recently at about 3 A.M. last Thursday. He was juggling knives and was quite upset with me for not being content with Edith's arrest. I think he was trying to scare me into minding my own business."

"Why?" Buck asked.

"I don't know. His role, if any, is hard to figure. He tried to talk Donna out of going to the banquet. If he'd succeeded, Strauss would have died, and she'd still be alive. Does that mean he knew the apple was poisoned, knew Donna was either going to use it to commit suicide or to murder Strauss?"

"Probably not," Buck said. "He just didn't want her getting into trouble by wrecking the banquet for Strauss. But I'll have him brought in, and have his apartment searched again."

"He's been brought in twice," I reminded him. "He's probably getting to like it. I doubt you'd get anything out of him, unless you've got some new interrogation methods you haven't told me about."

"They aren't exactly new."

"They wouldn't work on Bert anyway. He's tougher than he looks."

"You're right. He earned a dishonorable discharge from the Army for doing drugs—using and dealing. He served a little time, too. He learned to juggle in a military jail."

"Donna had an interesting lover, didn't she?" I said.

"He's trying to turn over a new leaf," Buck said, his voice flat. "But it's just so hard, 'cause we won't let him forget his past. We're always hassling him. Poor guy! But he does seem to have a genuine tragedy in his life. His kid brother's dying."

I recalled Omaha telling me something about Bert's visiting his brother in the hospital, and Bert had flared at me when I'd asked him about him. "What of?"

"Liver cancer. Incurable. Coombs doesn't want to believe it. He thinks his brother just isn't getting proper treatment because he can't pay for it. Coombs has been thrown out of the hospital twice for making a fuss, threatening the personnel."

I told Buck what Sumiko had told me about the fight she'd overheard between Bert and Donna a few weeks before the banquet. "His brother might be the reason he wanted money."

"That doesn't explain how he thought he was going to get it," Buck said.

We sat in silence for a while, looking out at the night. The name "McCord" was burned into the sky north of us, and it occurred to me that perhaps Harold McCord was staring out his picture window across at us. More likely, he'd be looking down at the land he owned sprawled out before him, gloating over it and his own cleverness.

"What are you going to do now?" I asked Buck.

"Until I'm told to lay off," he answered. "I'm still treating it as homicide and attempted homicide. What about you? Now that it looks as though your friend Edith Silberman is off the hook, I suppose you'll have to find something else to do in your free time."

"She's not off the hook," I said. "I'm like you, Buck. I'm still treating it as murder."

I got up, went over to his big picture window, looked out at the night, the river, the lights of the University. I thought back over the time I'd spent with Donna Trask and the people who'd known her, one way or another, and the people I'd come into contact with because of her. "If the suicide theory holds up," I said, "that would mean there never was an attempt on Strauss's life, doesn't it?"

"It could end like that," Buck said.

"No," I told him, "it can't end like that."

Twenty-Three

Edith called the next day, Saturday, to thank me for getting her off the hook. She'd stayed at her sister's a few extra days to avoid being harassed again by the representatives-of-the-people's-right-to-know-thrilling-things-that-aren't-any-of-their-business. She explained that she'd been able to stand without flinching in the glare of publicity when practically everybody assumed she was guilty, but she didn't think she could do it again, now that everybody assumed she was innocent.

I told her I wasn't sure she was off the hook. "What if they find the cyanide she stole from her mother?"

"They haven't found it yet," she said. "There are only so many places she could have hidden it, and apparently it wasn't in her apartment. Don't try to scare me, Peggy. And don't be such a pessimist. Donna Trask committed suicide. When you think about it, it makes perfect sense."

It did, except for one thing. I said, "I still think she was going to give a speech before she died. Maybe it was going to be some sort of swan song, a 'suicide speech,' but, if so, she wouldn't have killed herself before delivering it, would she? And they haven't found a suicide note, either. Everything *I* know about her suggests that, at the very least, she would've left a note blaming everybody—you, Strauss, her mother, her father—for what she was doing.

189

The Donna Trasks of this world do not go quietly into that good night."

"Gentle," Edith said.

"What?"

" 'Do not go gentle into that good night,' " she recited. " 'Old age should burn and rave at close of day. Rage, rage against the dying of the light.' Dylan Thomas. He went young and plastered, of course."

"Donna would have gone burning and raving," I said, "if she'd known she was going. I think she planned to burn and rave, but died before she could."

"You don't know that for sure. According to the newspaper, both of her parents said she had problems with depression."

"Did she look depressed to you at the banquet, just before she died?"

"It's none of your business, Peggy," she flared. "You're not a psychiatrist. You aren't a Homicide cop, either. You could get hurt."

"Why do you say that? Because you agree with me that there's a killer loose, don't you, Edith? You knew Donna Trask. You know she didn't kill herself."

"I don't care, one way or the other! It's not my killer who's on the loose. Let Jerry Strauss wonder and worry about the suicide theory. Forget it, Peggy, it's not your problem."

"You told me, not so long ago, that you believe texts can be interpreted, Edith, and that we have a moral obligation to try to interpret them. Isn't that what we have here, a kind of text? Don't you think it can be figured out?"

"I meant fiction," she said, impatient with me. "This is real life. That's why we read fiction, because it gives us something real life doesn't: a sense of an ending, a sense that everything that happens has a purpose we can figure out."

"I look for those things in life, too, Edith," I said.

Long pause. Finally, quietly, "Okay, Peggy. Good luck."

* * *

When I got home from work Tuesday morning, there was a message on my answering machine from Buck, asking me to call him.

"Jeremiah Strauss got another death threat," he announced.

"What?"

"You heard me. But take it easy, it might not mean anything. It might just be the work of a crank. So could the first ones, of course."

"When did he get it?"

"It came yesterday, Monday morning. It's creepy, short, and to the point. 'You're going to be very sorry you tricked me, Jerry. I'll see you at the groundbreaking.' It's signed, 'Donna.' "

I could feel the hair rise on the nape of my neck, but not because I believed the note had come from beyond the grave.

"When she was a child, she called Strauss 'Jerry,' " Buck said.

I told him that "you tricked me" was also one of Donna's favorite expressions. "She apparently defined everything bad that happened to her in terms of people tricking her," I said. "And her father does that too—he used the same word about Strauss to me last week."

"Do you think Donald Trask sent this note?"

"Why not? He had plenty of reason for hating Strauss. What if he'd sent the first threatening notes, too, and they inspired someone to try to kill Strauss—but got Donna instead? Trask would be living with that knowledge right now. It might explain his red-rimmed eyes."

Even worse, what if Donald Trask had poisoned the apple meant for Strauss and killed his daughter?

I told Buck what I was thinking. He listened, then said that maybe he'd pay a call on Trask. "If you're right, Peggy, maybe all it will take is a little nudging, for him to break down and confess." I was surprised how quickly Buck was picking up on my suggestions now, after I'd been in his doghouse for so long.

"Do you think the same letter writer wrote the first notes?" I asked him.

"It's virtual certainty," Buck said. "This one was typed on one of the University's rental typewriters, in the basement of the library, just like the first one. We never made that public knowledge. We wanted to try to identify and weed out the copycats."

"It's not clear that it's a death threat," I said. "The first ones were quite explicit on that score."

"It's explicit enough for me, Peggy."

"How's Strauss taking it?"

Buck laughed angrily. "He thinks it's the work of a crackpot. If it had been up to him, the police wouldn't even know about it. His secretary opened it and read it before he could get his hands on it. He was at a meeting, so she called me before he got a chance to see it. When we talked to Strauss, he was annoyed his secretary hadn't consulted him first."

Poor Janine.

"Is he going to the groundbreaking?"

"Couldn't keep him away."

I told Buck what, with the help of Curtiss Naylor and Raymond Clough, I'd learned about how Strauss must have gotten the conference center into Harold McCord's hands without seeming to, at least publicly.

"He'll be kind of an invisible guest of honor this time, too, won't he?" Buck said. "They can all sit around and smirk and wink together. Kind of a nice parallel to the last time, in Adamson Hall."

"How so?"

"Well, the last time he was guest of honor without deserving it. This time, he deserves to be guest of honor, but he won't be—except to a select few of his cronies. The irony ought to appeal to him."

"I suppose he'll be surrounded by security people."

"Oh, he'll have plenty of protection," Buck assured me, "but that's not my job. It only becomes my job if the protection fails. Besides, I'm taking a week off starting Friday. I'm flying to Boston to visit my parents.

"I'm not leaving till Saturday, though," he added. "I'm going to spend Friday sailing. How about coming along? The weather's supposed to be good. I'll try to get you back in time for the party at President Wolf's mansion that night."

I love sailing. I've been saving to buy a small catamaran since early last winter. "Sounds great. What party?"

"Wolf's hosting a warm-up party for the groundbreaking ceremony—to celebrate the fact that the center's going to be named after him. Gee, I thought you'd have been invited."

"You mean, Wolf's resigned as president?" You couldn't get a building named after you if you were still active on campus.

"Don't you read the newspaper, Peggy? It's on the front page of this morning's paper. He announced it last night. He's accepting a position at a 'think tank' somewhere in California."

"I don't take the paper anymore," I told him. "Donald Trask offered me tickets to the groundbreaking on Saturday, but he didn't say anything about the party the night before. Somehow, I doubt I'll be attending either." I told him about my visit to Donald Trask's home.

"Christ, Peggy! You know you're probably finished as a campus cop, right? What're you going to do? Apply to us for a job?"

Even though it wasn't particularly funny, I had to laugh at the panic in his voice as he hit *us*. Then I sobered up. "No, that would just be out of the frying pan and into the fire for me, wouldn't it? Except that I'd lose you as a friend for sure. I don't know what I'll do if I get canned. I'll wait and see if it happens first."

"Well, you may not be going to the groundbreaking, but you might be going to Wolf's party whether you want to or not—assuming you're still a campus cop on Friday."

"Why?"

"To keep Strauss alive, of course," he said, and hung up.

Damn. I'd been assigned to that once already. The results hadn't been good.

Twenty-Four

After roll call that night, I walked with Paula to our assigned beats. We were both on the Old Campus. My discovery about the cyanide, triggered by the silver bracelet Lawrence had given her, had completed the process of restoring our friendship, even though she couldn't see how that had any connection with my suppression of evidence. She made sure I knew her feelings on that subject and then things returned to normal between us. I doubted, however, that she'd ever trust me again to pass on information in an investigation.

I asked her how things were going and felt her shrug in the darkness. "Pretty good, I guess. I took Lawrence home with me last week."

"To meet your folks? This is moving pretty fast, isn't it? It's only been a month since he noticed you seemed to be sexed differently from him."

"Not to meet my folks," she insisted. "But they were there, of course. And it's not moving too fast." Another pause. I thought the subject was closed. "He's fun, though," she went on, "in a kind of clutzy, low-key way, and sweet. I think he was curious about what my folks are like. He came as something of a surprise to them."

"So I would imagine," I said.

"That somebody that good-looking could be so nice. So genuine," she added, as if I hadn't spoken.

"I've always been surprised by that, too," I said, recovering quickly.

"Mamma's concerned that he might not be smart enough for me, though."

"Smart enough for you for what?"

"She's concerned about the family gene pool. Mamma's a member of Mensa—you know what that is?"

"It's that organization of people drawn together by their high IQs, isn't it?" I shuddered at the thought. Sooner a bowling league.

"Yeah. Mamma wants me to join. Apparently my high school counselor told her my IQ, and it's high enough. Don't you think that's a violation of privacy?"

"Probably not. You were a minor at the time."

We got to where we were going to have to split up, Paula going in the direction of Frye Hall and the buildings around that part of campus, while I headed over toward the river. We talked for a few more minutes, standing there in the cold spring air, the moon a wedge of tangerine in the clear night sky.

"So your mom's afraid Lawrence wouldn't be capable of doing his part, DNA-wise," I said. "In the event."

"Right. I pointed out that Daddy can't get into Mensa, either, but she replied that we can't go on marrying beneath ourselves intellectually forever without paying a price. So I asked her if she was sorry she'd married Daddy. She didn't answer, just fluffed off." She changed the subject abruptly. "Is it still all over between you and Al?" Paula likes everything nice and clear, a consequence, perhaps, of her high IQ.

"Yep."

"You finding something to do with your time, now that the Trask business is all cleared up?"

"Nope."

I spent the first hours of my watch uneventfully, walking the empty paths between buildings, using my passkey to wander through dimly lit and deserted buildings, occasionally encountering students—the men often alone, the women always in groups of two or more, since, unlike me, they weren't armed and wearing uniforms. The night passed and soon I wasn't seeing anyone at all. Every now and then I checked in with the dispatcher on my portable.

It was about 2 A.M. when I turned onto the bike path that runs along the river. Rounding a bend, I stopped when I saw Bert Coombs standing in front of me.

"Whew, that was close!" he said. "I was afraid you'd run right into me. Glad you looked up in time! A penny for your thoughts, Peggy O'Neill. What's going on?"

"What do you mean, what's going on?" I asked him. I unsnapped my holster. I remembered how fast he'd made knives disappear into his baggy pants in the Physics Building; he could bring them out just as fast if he wanted to.

However, he had other things on his mind. "I mean, you must be happy now, right?" he said. "Thanks to you, Nancy Drew, everybody knows Donna's sad death was of her own doing. She gave an entirely new twist to 'an apple a day,' huh?" He laughed, one of those laughs that begs you to join in. He looked like a clown in a cheap print on a motel wall.

"First she was going to kill the bad dean," he went on, "and then she got religion all of a sudden. Don't you think that's what happened, Donna got religion? Or was it depression? And she decided to kill herself instead, deeply saddened, probably, over the way her mother abandoned her, the way her father diddled bimbos, and the way Dean Strauss tricked her. Everybody tricked Donna. It was the state sport, right?"

He was talking too much and too fast. There were shadows under his eyes and his pupils were almost nonexistent. I didn't say anything, waiting for him to run down.

"I like it," he continued, "don't you? Everybody likes it now, 'cause now, at last, the campus is killer-free." He stopped, swallowed visibly, then said, "Right?"

"I don't think the campus is killer-free," I told him. "I don't think Donna meant to kill herself."

"Well, if it wasn't suicide, it's Silberman again, isn't it?" he said, rushing on. "Out to get her old nemesis, the dean. You wouldn't want to put her through that again, would you?"

"Your concern for Edith Silberman is touching," I told him, "but misplaced. There're other suspects now. And now that we know Donna had cyanide in her possession, and it's disappeared, Edith Silberman's husband having been a chemist doesn't mean as much, does it? You wouldn't know what happened to Donna's cyanide, would you, Bert?"

"Me?" He almost shouted. "Hey, no! I didn't even know she had it—how could I? Besides, Donna must've used it all up on that apple. What're you trying to say? You think I tried to kill Strauss?"

"No, you didn't try to kill him. There wouldn't have been any money in that. And you wanted money."

He widened his eyes in a parody of innocence. "Money for what?"

"For whatever it was Donna planned to spill at the banquet," I told him, "before she died. She planned to give a speech. She was going to tell everything she knew about the shady dealings of some of the administrators."

"What shady dealings?" He licked his lips. "Where would she get to know stuff like that?"

"From her father, of course. C'mon, Bert, don't play games. We both know that. He told her everything, all his sleazy little secrets. And Donna made the mistake of telling you. You wanted to use that information to blackmail somebody, but she didn't. She wanted revenge. That's what the quarrel was about between the two of you that Sumiko overheard a couple of weeks before Donna died. That was the quarrel between you and Donna in the tunnel the night of the banquet. You didn't want Donna wasting all that valuable dirt in a speech when you could get money for it by keeping it secret."

"Bull. You don't know what you're talking about. You're just guessing."

That was true enough. But what choice did I have? "Strauss just got another death threat. Is this news to you?"

Even in that light, I could see something moving in his eyes.

"Sure it is," he said. "Why shouldn't it be?"

"I just wondered," I told him. "You see, it has one of Donna's favorite accusations: 'You tricked me.' I figured that, since Donna probably didn't write it—or do you believe in ghosts, Bert?—it must've been somebody who knew her pretty well. You, for instance."

I paused, in case he wanted to say something. He didn't.

"I'm trying to figure your place in all of this. Your hanging around me, for example. I can't figure out if you're trying to scare me away or if you want to tell me something. Do you know, yourself, I wonder? And I can't figure out why you might have written those anonymous letters, the ones before the banquet, threatening to kill Strauss, and the latest one."

"I didn't write 'em!" he said, his voice breaking like an adolescent's.

I shrugged. "It's just my working hypothesis," I assured him. "Nothing for you to worry about."

"It's just your wild guess, you mean. Who says they were written by the same person?

"They were," I told him. "They were all written on one of the typewriters in the basement of the library, and the last one contained Donna's pet phrase, 'You tricked me.' In my book, that makes you Clerk Typist of the Month, Bert. Congratulations. You want to hear the rest of the hypothesis I'm working with?"

"I guess we've both got lots of time to waste tonight," he said.

"You do, anyway. I didn't call this meeting. Let's assume," I went on, "just for the sake of the argument and because we have the rest of the night to kill, you typed those letters, all of them. Why? What've you got against Strauss? Nothing. So I figure—again, on the assumption you typed them—that you typed them for somebody else." I stopped and looked at him. "Still interested?"

"Who?" he said. "And why couldn't they type their own damn letters?"

"Those were my next questions," I told him. "And the theory that came to mind has the advantage of answering both of them—partially, at least: It was someone too well known to do it himself, or herself, in the case of Donna. Or take a man like Hudson Bates, for example, one of my favorite people. He might even pay somebody to type letters like that for him. I can see from the expression on your face that you know him," I added. "Is he a favorite of yours, too? I've heard he was a favorite of Donna's—at least, when they're alone in elevators."

"I don't know what the hell you're talkin' about," Bert said. "Go on with your story; it's startin' to put me to sleep." He didn't look sleepy to me.

"Too bad you don't have your juggling stuff with you," I said. "You could provide some visual excitement while I'm talking. But not the balls, of course. You're missing a couple of those, aren't you? Maybe the clubs. I liked those."

"I said, get on with it!"

"Well, as I was saying, a memorable guy like Hudson Bates couldn't use those rental typewriters. They're too public. Somebody might see him and wonder what a guy like Bates is doing, typing letters down where the students go who can't afford typewriters and word processors. And he doesn't dare use his own typewriter, of course, for fear the police might check the typeface."

Bert's laugh was like gears grinding. "You're saying a guy like Bates hires me to do his typing for him, right? His death threats?"

"Bates was just an example," I told him. "You could also be working for Donald Trask."

"Trask! You're saying he killed his own . . ."

He stopped, stared at me in horror.

"By accident, of course," I assured him. "He didn't have to know what Donna planned to do at the banquet."

"You can't think that, Peggy O'Neill. That's really sick, you know."

"I'm capable of thinking lots of things. But one thing I'm pretty sure of is, you typed those letters, and you didn't do it for your own amusement. I'd like to know who's behind you. Whoever's using you must have good reason to think you won't talk."

"Using me?" he exclaimed. "That's a laugh."

"Is it? What's so funny about it?"

He pulled himself up straight. "Nobody uses me," he said. The words hung in the night air like a child's cry for help. Bert must have thought so, too, because he added suddenly, "You'll see."

"When, Bert? How? Are you telling me I'm right?"

"You going to the groundbreaking for the new conference center Saturday, Peggy—the 'Wolf' Center?" he asked.

The apparent change of subject was startling. "No, why?"

"Too bad. It might get interesting. Everybody who's anybody'll be there."

My skin started to prickle. "I think that must've been what Donna said to you," I told him, "the day of Strauss's banquet. I think you're quoting her."

"I'm not afraid of ghosts," he said. A small cloud moved in front of the moon, and Bert turned slate-gray.

"How could it get interesting, Bert?"

"Come and see!"

"You're going to give a speech, the speech Donna was planning to give."

"Maybe. Depends."

"You think you are. You'd better be careful. Look what happened to her."

"I don't plan on eating nothing at the groundbreaking. That was the mistake she made. Besides," he added, shrugging, trying to break the spell, "maybe it won't happen, maybe I'm just makin' all this up."

"Maybe it won't happen because you'll get what you've wanted all along—the money Donna didn't want."

"Yeah, maybe." His grin flickered on and off like a candle guttering.

I moved closer to him, my hand on my pistol butt. He took a couple of steps back, looked at me uncertainly. "Hey," he said, "what's the matter?"

"It's spooky," I said, "talking to a man who knows a killer and thinks he can handle him. I don't think you can. Maybe you'll get the money you want, but more likely you're going to get killed instead. Why don't you quit now, Bert? Go to the cops. Or tell me, tell me who you're working for."

"Maybe I will, someday. And maybe I'll finish what Donna started. It depends. Why don't you come along and see? You're clever enough, Peggy, you could find a way into the groundbreaking. Or you could go over and watch it from my apartment window. In style."

"This is about your brother, isn't it?" I said. "He's in the hospital, sick. He's dying. I have a brother, too," I added, "somewhere in the world. He could be dead, or a man like you, for all I know." And that's true.

He jumped at me. I was prepared. I shoved him back, hard.

"You've got a cop for a friend, too," he shouted. "I almost forgot that. He told you about Andy, didn't he? Well, Andy isn't dying, that's for sure, he just don't have the money to get well." He ran a few steps down the bike path. "You don't have to feel sorry for me!"

"Who, then?"

He turned away and started running again.

Twenty-Five

I called Buck as soon as I got off duty, and told him about my meeting with Bert, and that I was sure he'd sent the threatening letters. I added that Bert had practically admitted he knew who'd poisoned the apple that had killed Donna Trask.

"I'll talk to him," Buck said, without much enthusiasm. "But I doubt it'll do any good. It'll be his word against yours.".

The next evening, Thursday, as I was leaving for work, Buck phoned to tell me they hadn't been able to find Bert. His roommate Omaha said Bert hadn't been staying at their apartment for over a week. Buck added that Andy, Bert's brother, had gone into a coma the night before and wasn't expected to come out of it.

"You don't think you should be concerned about his whereabouts?" I asked him. "He's planning something for the conference center dedication.".

There was an edge to Buck's voice as he reminded me that Bert hadn't done anything to justify issuing an arrest warrant for him. "You think we should start picking people up and holding them 'on spec'?" Buck demanded.

I agreed that wouldn't be a good idea, although I seemed to recall that it had been done.

* * *

That was Thursday evening. Buck and I spent all Friday afternoon sailing, and I got a slight sunburn on my face and arms. I never tan, just burn a little if I'm not careful, then peel and fade. The cold wind and spray lulled me into thinking the sun wasn't that hot.

Later, after we'd pulled the catamaran up onto his trailer, we went our separate ways. Buck had something else to do that evening, probably cook a gourmet meal for somebody who'd appreciate it. I told him to call me when he got back from Boston.

Since I didn't have anything else to do, I went home and made popcorn and watched *The Third Man*, which I have on tape. It's one of my favorite movies, a dark comic sendup of the myth that a cowboy can stroll into a corrupt town, clean it up, and win the girl. It was just about over when the phone rang.

I froze the movie. Orson Welles, his pretty baby's face etched in black and white, was giving me a look that said, "Trust me. Or, if that's asking too much, love me." He was trying to climb out of a sewer. Something about the image reminded me of the University approaching the legislature for money.

Sumiko Sato was on the phone.

"I wonder if you are still interested in Donna Trask," she said. She was speaking so softly, I had to strain to hear her. "Donna's boyfriend, Bert, that man who juggles, is living in her apartment. You remember him?"

"How long's this been going on?" I found myself whispering, too.

"A week, almost. Longer, maybe. I don't know for sure. The first time I noticed he was there was last week. He climbs in through a window. But when he leaves, he goes out through the door, I think. I saw him once, as I was about to leave my apartment. I have considered telling the manager, but she is never here and does not answer her phone."

"Have you talked to him?"

"No!" She sounded appalled at the idea. "I never liked him that much."

"Haven't they tried to rent the apartment yet?" I asked her.

"There is a 'For Rent' sign out now, but it is hard to rent here when the school year is almost over. And nobody has come even to take Donna's belongings away."

She'd died, and now everybody seemed to be trying to forget her, except me and Bert Coombs.

"Is he there now?"

"I don't think so. He had company, somebody who came in through the door. I could hear them talking. Then I heard the door open and close a few minutes ago. There have been no other sounds from there since."

"You don't have any idea how I might get into the apartment, do you?" I asked her.

"You mean now?"

"Yes."

There was a brief pause. "I have a key," she said finally. "Donna was always very forgetful of her key, so she suggested we exchange them, in case either of us locked ourselves out of our apartments. She assumed that I would be forgetful, too, since I was her 'shadow.' She never took her key back."

"Didn't Bert have one, too?"

"Are you kidding? She would never let Bert into her apartment unless she was there, too. She did not trust him."

"Can I borrow your key?"

She considered it a few moments, then said, "It's very irregular, I suppose, but Bert's living in her apartment is very irregular, too, isn't it? Are you going to come here now?"

I looked at my watch. It was 8:50. "Yes," I told her, "if that's okay."

That was okay. I called Buck, let the phone ring ten times, noticed that my mood lightened with every ring that went unanswered, and then hung up. I was glad he wasn't home and glad I'd made the effort.

On my way out, I picked up my photograph of Hudson Bates. I was curious to know if Sumiko had ever seen Bates and Donna together.

I had no idea what I was going to find in Donna's apartment, but it seemed too good an opportunity to pass up, a chance to look through both Donna's and Bert's stuff. The police had probably gone through her things, looking for a suicide note, but they wouldn't have searched for papers she might have hidden, a copy of the speech I was sure she'd planned to give at Adamson Hall, for instance. You don't hide your suicide note.

I found a parking place down the street from Sumiko's building. The security door was still out of order. I walked up to the second floor and knocked on Sumiko's door.

When she'd let me into her apartment, I asked Sumiko if Bert had come back.

"No," she said, handing me the key. "It is still quiet in there."

"Show me how he gets in."

She took me over to a set of French doors that opened onto a small balcony, and we went outside. The balcony provided a view of the alley behind the building and, across it, the backs of old houses broken up into cheap student rooms. Sumiko said that, several times in the past week, she'd seen Bert come down the alley toward the apartment building from her kitchen window.

"He always comes here after dark, but he is very easy to recognize," she said, "because of his bowed legs and his funny clothes. I wondered what he was doing around here, so the next time I saw him coming, I looked out my balcony door to see where he went. That was when I saw him climb the side of the building, down there at the end. He's good. He uses the bricks at the corner, sticking his fingers and toes into the gaps between them, and reaches

Donna's bedroom window that way. He always leaves through the front door."

I brought out the picture of Hudson Bates and put it on Sumiko's kitchen table, asked her if she'd ever seen him before. She looked at the picture for a few seconds, and then nodded. "Who is he?" she asked.

I told her.

"That isn't the name he gave me, I think," she said. "A few days after Donna was killed, he came to my door. He seemed very nervous. He told me that he was one of Donna's teachers and she had something of his that he had loaned her—a book. He wondered if I had a key and would let him in."

"Did you?"

Sumiko smiled faintly. "I asked him why he thought I would have a key to her apartment. He said Donna had mentioned that we were friends. I kept the chain on my door while I talked to him. I told him I did not have a key and that he should talk to the manager—or the police. I made it clear to him that I thought his request was very inappropriate. He went away," she concluded with a pleased toss of her short, black hair. She handed me her key to Donna's apartment. "I hope you do not expect me to come in with you."

"I'm hoping you'll watch from your kitchen window, to see if Bert comes back down the alley. I'd hate to be surprised by him."

The key turned easily in the almost-new lock, and I opened Donna's door a crack, being quiet about it, in case Sumiko had been mistaken about having heard Bert leave. I wasn't too worried about finding him there; he had no more right being in there than I did. The apartment was dark, the drapes drawn, but I'd brought a flashlight. There was no one in the living room. In the beam of the flashlight, it was a completely impersonal room with a couch and a matching overstuffed chair and not much else. The walls were bare. The other end of the room, next to the balcony door, contained a small dining room separated from an even smaller kitchen by a room divider.

I stepped into the apartment, closed the door, and heard the lock click behind me. The living room was littered with books and pillows, the pillows slashed, foam filling oozing out of the cuts. I crossed quietly to the kitchen. The cupboards had all been emptied, their few contents placed on the counter and stove, as if somebody had started the process of moving Donna's belongings out.

Donna had used her dining area as a study. A low bookcase took up most of one wall, but the books had mostly been pulled out and were stacked in careless piles in front of it. Papers were spread across the dining room table and an electronic typewriter sat in the middle of the mess. I went back into the living room.

The entry closet next to the front door was open, its contents spilling out onto the floor in front of it. I aimed my flashlight at the couch: Photographs that had once been on the walls lay on it, the glass and frames pulled apart. One of the photographs was of Donna and her father, both wearing dark sunglasses, staring at me, unsmiling, from some brilliantly sunny place.

I walked over the beige carpeting to the bedroom door and pushed it open. It wasn't necessary to use my flashlight. The drapes were open in front of the single window, and moonlight gave the room a pale yellow glow.

Bert was there. He was sprawled on the floor, his face resting on the carpet. The handle of a knife was sticking up from his back, dark blood soaking the yellow shirt around it. Juggling equipment was scattered on the carpet around him. It looked as though some giant puppeteer had grown tired of playing with him, dropped him, and let everything he was keeping suspended in the air rain down around him. A red rubber ball, the last of the set, lay on the carpet just beyond his outstretched hand.

I turned on the light, stepped through the doorway. The room was a mess. The futon was slashed. In this room, too, the pillows had been gutted.

Although I didn't expect to find the killer hiding in the closet, bathroom, or under the bed, I checked to be sure. Some of Donna's clothes were lying on the floor, and in the bathroom, the contents of the medicine chest was in the sink, the shelf paper torn up from the shelves.

I returned to Bert and checked to be sure, but there was no life in him. I straightened up and backed away, unable to take my eyes off his body.

His death bothered me for a confusion of reasons. He'd gotten himself involved in a game for which he wasn't suited—a killing game—and he didn't know how to get out. I'd disliked him and yet found him funny and, somehow, touching—as if, with time, something might have become of him, of his nervous energy, and vitality. I thought of the craft he'd learned, juggling, and the transient magic he could create in air. I felt the loss of that now, as I stared down at his sprawled, inert body.

He wasn't a killer. He'd tried to scare me away, when he surely could have killed me instead. He wasn't a killer, but he'd known one.

His billfold was lying next to him on the carpet, old and worn. I stooped to look at it. His killer had emptied it. A few dollar bills and some papers were scattered around it, nothing that appeared significant to me. A student ID showed him flashing a taunting grin at the camera. Next to it on the carpet was a snapshot of a kid who looked a lot like Bert, but younger and with a sweeter smile. His kid brother wasn't dying, Bert had told me, he just needed better treatment. Hope's a kind of juggling act, too. And when all hope is gone, what does somebody like Bert do? His killer didn't wait to find out.

I stood up, glanced over at the telephone. There wasn't any hurry to call Homicide. Sumiko had told me on the phone that she'd heard Donna's front door close just before she called me. She'd thought it was Bert and his guest leaving together, but she'd only been half right.

She'd called me about an hour ago. A few more minutes before the police were notified wouldn't matter. Besides, if

I hadn't come in tonight, it might have been another week before Bert's body was discovered, so the police couldn't make a big deal out of it if I stole a few minutes from the days I might be giving them.

I went over to the bedroom window. It was a double-paned window that slid up and down. The latch was in the locked position, although the window was open. Using my palms to avoid leaving or obscuring fingerprints, I pushed up on the window. It rose easily. I knew this kind of window; my landlady had had them installed in my apartment just after I moved in. An extension of the handle on the top of the lower frame slides into a slot mounted on the upper window frame to lock both. Bert had somehow managed to remove the extension so that when Donna turned the handle, thinking she'd locked her window, she'd achieved nothing at all. But she would only realize that if she'd checked it by trying to open the window after she'd turned the lock.

I went back out to the living room. It would be a waste of time to search the place, since whoever had taken it apart had had plenty of time to do that. As far as I could see, nothing had been overlooked, which meant the killer probably left empty-handed.

I dialed Homicide, told the duty officer who I was, what I'd found, and where. Then I tried to call Buck at home, but there still wasn't any answer. Maybe he was pretending to be gone, so nothing could ruin his vacation.

I went next door. Sumiko let me in and I told her what I'd found. She sat down, put a hand to her mouth, and above it her eyes grew large. I asked her if she could remember the exact time she'd heard what she'd assumed was Bert leaving Donna's apartment.

"It was only the one who killed him who left," she said, "wasn't it?" She nodded in answer to her own question, and tried to remember back. "It was just a little while before I called you. Five minutes? Four?"

I'd left my house at 8:57. Sumiko and I had talked for about five minutes before that, which meant that Bert's killer had left Donna's apartment at approximately 8:40. That would give the police something to go on, when they interviewed the other tenants in the building.

There was a loud knocking on Sumiko's door, the kind people make when they are on some official errand. I went out to direct the cops to Donna's apartment.

Twenty-Six

Anne Meredith, a Homicide lieutenant like Buck, is close to six feet tall, lean, with short blonde hair and a few light freckles running from cheek to cheek across her nose. She pulled a straight-backed chair up to the coffee table and leaned across it toward Sumiko and me, both of us on the couch. Meredith has green eyes, as I do, but I don't know if mine could ever be as cold as hers when she's contemplating a corpse and the people found in its proximity. Charlie Burke, another Homicide cop I'd met before, sat in another chair at the end of the coffee table, a notebook in his hands, taking down what we said.

I'd already given Meredith the times I'd worked out with Sumiko, and cops were interviewing tenants in this and the adjacent buildings. She wanted to know why I'd come there in the first place.

I told her that I wasn't happy with the suicide theory to explain Donna Trask's death. I thought Bert was involved and I wanted to snoop around in Donna's apartment, once I'd learned that he'd been living there on the sly.

Meredith could have gone all cop on me and asked me if I didn't think I should have left that to the police, but she wasn't a time-waster. She just nodded and asked me how long I'd been in the apartment before calling Homicide. I told her the truth.

"And during your search, what did you find that we

might overlook?" she asked me, her frosty eyes staring straight into mine.

I told her about the lock on the bedroom window. She nodded. "We noticed that," she said dryly. "It might, however, have taken us a little longer, and we might not have known what it meant, if Miss Sato hadn't told us how Bert gained entrance to the apartment."

It might have taken them a little longer to find Bert, too—weeks, maybe—if I hadn't gone into Donna's apartment when I did. It suddenly occurred to me that Bert's killer might be counting on the likelihood of Bert's body not being discovered anytime soon.

I said, meaning nothing by it, that Bert must have tampered with the latch sometime before Donna died.

"Why?" Meredith asked me.

"Because," I said, "he didn't have a key to her apartment, or he would have entered it that way."

"I realize that," Meredith said slowly, as if speaking to an imbecile. "But *why* did he prepare an entrance through the window *before* her death? To insure that he'd get a couple of weeks of rent-free living afterward? That would mean he had advance notice of her death, wouldn't it?"

"Yes," I said, light suddenly beginning to dawn, "he did. He must have." Things that had only been clutter began to fall into order. "He must have tampered with the lock because there was something in there he wanted while she was alive, something she wouldn't let him have."

"Drugs?"

"No, cyanide! The cyanide that killed her and that she'd stolen from her mother a couple of weeks before. He fixed the lock so he could get into her place when she wasn't around and, after her death, he used her apartment, probably to meet the person he was working for, the one who killed him."

I was going much too fast for Meredith. I was going too fast for me, for that matter. I needed time to think it all through. I kept thinking that Bert's killer was somewhere out there in the night, unconcernedly going about his business.

"You're trying to tell me," Meredith said, "that Coombs stole the cyanide from Donna's apartment without her knowledge, and then used it to poison the apple that was meant for Strauss?"

"You're close," I said. I remembered what Curtiss Naylor had said about asking the wrong questions. 'You always get the wrong answers that way.' Or no answers at all.

Meredith looked at me thoughtfully, probably running through in her mind what she knew of Donna Trask's death. It wasn't her case, it was Buck's. Clearly I was wasting her time. She was wasting mine, too.

"But Coombs has been involved in drugs, hasn't he?" she persisted. Buck must have told her that.

"Yes, sure." I was impatient to get out of there.

She got up. "Tell Buck your theory when he gets back," she said. "It'll interest him." She didn't sound as if she believed that. At the door, she turned and asked, "Do you also have a theory about what Bert Coombs's killer was after in Donna Trask's apartment tonight? He didn't just come to talk, did he?"

"That's probably what Bert thought he came for. He was after whatever Bert was holding over his head."

"And what do you think that was?" she asked politely.

"The details of the speech Donna Trask had planned to give at the banquet in Adamson Hall before she died," I said.

"She was planning to give a speech?" Meredith looked puzzled.

"Yes," I snapped. I hate it when I can't get through to people.

She shrugged, smiled thinly at my frustration. "Never mind," she went on, "I hadn't heard about the speech. But why now?" she asked. "I mean, why did he kill Bert Coombs tonight—especially before he'd gotten what he came for?"

"Because he couldn't keep Bert quiet any longer, and he knew it. Bert was planning to interrupt the groundbreaking ceremony tomorrow and spill all the dirt Donna had gathered on some of the University's bigwigs. The killer must have been desperate. More desperate than Bert realized." I must have been, too, to use a work like "bigwigs." But I was angry and frustrated and in a hurry.

"A University bigwig killed Bert Coombs?" Meredith asked skeptically.

"Yes," I told her, and began counting to ten. It helps, sometimes.

Finally, she said again, "Tell Buck about it. But I think it's more likely that this was a simple drug killing, or a killing related to something else boys fight and die for. That theory also explains why the apartment was searched, without turning Donna Trask's suicide back into murder. But maybe Buck'll see something more in it than that."

I wanted to know one thing from Meredith before she left. "Did the killer enter the building through the back door?"

She gave me a surprised look. "Why?"

I don't answer 'why questions.' "Just curious."

"The lock was broken. It wasn't a very strong one to begin with. But it didn't have to be the killer who forced it. One of the tenants could've done it. We'll find out."

"The last time I was here," I told her, "three weeks ago, there wasn't anything wrong with that door."

Bert's killer's chances of not being seen were much greater if he'd come and gone through that door and used the stairs at the end of the hall, even though it meant forcing the lock.

Meredith looked at me closely. "You're not holding anything back, are you?"

"No." Just a hunch growing toward a certainty I wasn't sure I'd ever be able to prove.

* * *

I tried to reassure Sumiko that there'd be cops in the building the rest of the night, but she wasn't convinced. She asked me to drive her to some friends' house. After she'd called them, I drove her the ten or so blocks to where they lived, and dropped her off. I waited until a porch light went on and the door opened, then made a U-turn on the empty street and headed for home.

It was 10:30. I was feeling the effects of a day spent sailing, stumbling upon a corpse, then having my ideas treated like those of an overly imaginative child.

The freeway would have been quicker, but I didn't want to pit my dulled instincts against those of drunken drivers, so I stayed on the side roads. I crossed the river, skirting the edge of the New Campus. On my right was the land Harold McCord had cleared for the new conference center, waiting for tomorrow's groundbreaking ceremony. A grandstand, complete with podium, stood where the ceremony was going to take place. Bert had threatened to put in an appearance, to complete what Donna had begun a month before, if he didn't get what he wanted. He hadn't got what he wanted, but he wasn't going to make good on his threat either.

The grandstand was deserted now, some of its distinguished occupants-to-be at President Wolf's mansion, celebrating. I wondered if Bert's killer was there, too. And Donna's.

Bert lived nearby, I remembered. He'd offered to let me watch the ceremony from his apartment window. I wondered why he'd been staying at Donna's place. Maybe he didn't like the dust and noise of the heavy machinery demolishing his neighborhood. Maybe he'd had some kind of falling out with Omaha, who was soon going to be meeting Lt. Anne Meredith and trying to answer a lot of questions about his whereabouts that night.

Most likely, though, Bert had felt safer staying at Donna's place while he waited for whatever he hoped to get from the man he was working for. At least he'd been tell-

ing the truth when he said that he wasn't afraid of Donna
Trask's ghost. If my theory was correct, however, there
was only one other person who had more reason to fear
her ghost than Bert.

I saw the murder scene in Donna's apartment, Bert's
body sprawled on the floor. He was too thin for the colorful clothes he wore, and he was surrounded by the tools of
his juggler's trade, the battered old equipment case open
and empty. I thought of the first time I'd talked to him,
when I'd acted as his assistant as he juggled on the Mall,
emptied the money he'd earned from his cap into that
case. I saw him juggling those clubs that looked so heavy
but turned out to be hollow plastic bottles wrapped with
tape. One had gotten away from him, I remembered, and
had hit the ground next to me. It'd bounced, ended up in
my lap. Bert had swooped down, taken it from me, shot
me a grin.

I hadn't seen the clubs around Bert's body. I couldn't remember seeing them anywhere else in Donna's apartment,
either.

I made a U-turn on the empty street and headed back
the way I'd come, toward the New Campus. I parked in
front of Bert's apartment building and studied the house,
my tiredness forgotten for the moment. The windows in
the front room on the second floor—Bert's and Omaha's
apartment—were the only ones lit.

As on my first visit, the door wasn't locked, not even
closed properly. The stairs going up to the second floor
were old, and made a lot of noise, no matter how quiet I
tried to be. The hallway up there was dark, too, but I could
see that the doors to a couple of the apartments were
open, as if whoever had left couldn't be bothered to close
them. The door to the apartment I wanted, however, was
closed, and light seeped into the hallway from under it.

Last time, I'd interrupted Omaha in his lovemaking.

I'd brought my flashlight with me, not so much because
I expected to use it for its designated purpose, but because

it was possible that whoever had killed Bert had come here looking for what I was looking for now.

I knocked. There wasn't any answer. I waited a moment, then knocked again. This time, I heard footsteps coming hesitantly to the door.

"Who is it?" Omaha's voice was cautious.

"Peggy O'Neill," I said. "I came looking for Bert one day a couple of weeks ago, remember?"

Silence. Then, "He's not here."

"I know that," I said. "I need to talk to you, it's important. Open up."

The door opened as far as it could on the chain. A slice of Omaha's face showed in the room's dim yellow light.

"What d'you wanna talk about?" A faint smell of marijuana drifted out with the question.

"Has anybody been here before me?"

"Why d'you wanna know?"

"I'm a cop," I said. I dangled my shield in the narrow door opening. "Open the door. I'm not interested in what you're smoking."

His eyes flickered from me to the badge and back to me, then he closed the door, removed the chain, opened the door to let me in.

A table lamp on the floor by Omaha's sofa bed threw enough light onto bare wood to illuminate the room. It had been ransacked like Donna's apartment.

"What happened?" I asked.

"How the hell should I know?" He sounded annoyed as well as scared. "Somebody clobbered me. Look." He bent down and showed me the back of his head, like a child who wants his mother to kiss it better. Whatever he'd been hit with had broken the skin, and blood matted his hair. When I touched the spot, Omaha flinched.

"I went to the bathroom," he said, "down at the end of the hall. I come back to the room, the door's open just the way I left it. I come inside, and boom! The next thing I know is, I'm trying to get up off the floor and my head aches like a bitch."

He went over to his bed, sat down, and gingerly fell back onto it. A miniscule roach was balanced on a black plastic ashtray, pinched into a paper clip. He picked it up carefully and struck a match to it. Miraculously, he didn't scorch his lips. Or maybe they were used to it.

"Did you see who it was?" I asked him.

"No way," he managed to say while inhaling the smoke. "It could've been you." His eyes narrowed on the flashlight I was holding in my hand. "My head still hurts," he said, exhaling nothing but air. It's magic, how they do it.

He didn't know how lucky he was, still able to feel an aching head and suck dope. I asked him how long ago it had happened.

"You think I looked at my watch? For one thing, I don't have one that works anymore. What time's it now?"

It was ten to eleven.

He shrugged, looked at the little brown roach, slid it from the paper clip, and dropped it reluctantly into the ashtray, where it disappeared in the ash. "I been sitting here, wondering if maybe I ought to see a doctor— concussion, right?—for maybe half an hour, maybe longer, I don't know—but I don't know any doctors. And I don't know how long I was out before that, either. I was just lying here getting high and thinking about stuff until I had to go to the bathroom."

I left him where he was and started over toward Bert's area. I stopped when I got to the old table in the dining room. It was cluttered with parts of bleach bottles and colored tape. A single juggling club lay smashed open like an egg.

"What's this for?" I asked Omaha, although I already knew.

He glanced indifferently over at me. "They're bottles. I'm makin' new clubs—for juggling, you know? You take plastic bottles and you cut 'em up and glue the parts together so they're longer than just the bottles are, and then you wrap 'em in tape. Bert taught me how to make 'em that way. The real things cost too much; me and Bert couldn't afford 'em."

"None of this is Bert's stuff, is it?" I asked him.

"I told you, it's mine. I'm making new clubs for our act. Hey!" He'd come over to see what it was that interested me. "The son of a bitch broke it!" He picked up the smashed club and looked at it, shaking his head. "You know what this is all about?" he asked me.

Yeah, I did. Less than two hours ago, Bert's killer had stood where I was now, looking down at this table. And he'd realized the significance of the bleach bottles. He'd smashed the club to see what was inside it.

Had he then remembered that Bert's colorful clubs hadn't been in Donna's apartment?

I checked out the rest of the apartment. The blanket that had been stretched across half the room to separate Bert's space from Omaha's had been pulled down, and it looked as though somebody had mindlessly kicked his things around in frustration. There weren't many places to hide things. In the kitchen, a window at the back was open. An old wooden landing, most of the paint gone, ran the length of the building beneath it, ending in a steep flight of steps down to the ground. The person who'd attacked Omaha must have come into the apartment that way.

There hadn't been much for the killer to ransack in the kitchen either. I went back out to the living room and asked Omaha if Bert had some other place in the building where he kept his stuff. He said there wasn't any other place and besides, Bert didn't have much. "He hasn't been staying here lately," he added. "Some cops were asking about him a couple days ago, too. I told 'em I think he's been staying at the hospital, or something, with his brother. But he wouldn't have come back here and hit me and messed the place up like this."

"It doesn't sound as though you guys communicate much," I said.

"We aren't friends, if that's what you mean," Omaha said. "We just room together to save money. We met on the Mall last year, at the U, both of us was juggling. He said he could get me a job in the carnival this summer, but whenever I remind him of it, he acts like he doesn't remember."

"Do you know where his clubs are?" I asked him.

"His juggling clubs?" Omaha looked at the bleach bottles on the table and back to me, puzzled. "They're wherever he is, I suppose, with all his other juggling stuff. Why? What's so special about clubs all of a sudden?" Before I could tell him, another thought occurred to him, one he might have had sooner if he hadn't had such an aching head. His large eyes narrowed into slits. "What's this all about anyway? Why're you asking so many questions about Bert? Where is he?"

"He's dead," I told him.

"Dead!" Omaha's eyes opened wide. "How'd he die?"

"Somebody murdered him."

"Oh God," he said. "I'm in deep trouble, right? I mean, the cops are going to think I did it. I gotta get out of here."

I told him to take it easy, that unless he'd killed Bert, he didn't have anything to worry about. He didn't look as though he believed me. "Somebody murdered him for his clubs?" He laughed crazily at that. "What's so special about them? Somebody think they're full of drugs or something?" Then, considering the possibility, he asked, "Are they?"

"Something like that," I replied. "I think Bert had something hidden in one of them, something he thought would keep him alive."

There were noisy footsteps on the stairs, an officious knocking on the door. As I went to open it, Omaha called after me, "Something that would keep him alive, in a bleach bottle? And he was always telling me I was dumb!"

It was Anne Meredith and her merry men, looking none too merry when they saw me again.

I managed to get out of there after only about fifteen minutes, although Meredith's attitude implied that I hadn't heard the last of this. That was okay with me. I was still on my way home. I wanted to talk to Buck, tell him everything I'd discovered and what I was beginning to make of it. Maybe he'd have some ideas about how to go about proving it.

As I was leaving Omaha's apartment, I thought of something else. Instead of going down the stairs to the first floor, I turned left and went down the hall to the bathroom, retracing Omaha's steps before he'd gotten knocked out.

I could smell the bleach even before I opened the bathroom door, and I laughed when I saw the plastic bottle on the floor inside. Someone had smashed the bottle hard against the sink, someone obviously too frustrated to think clearly. It had burst, and the acrid smell of bleach was overpowering in the small space, burning my eyes and forcing me to hold my nose. Bleach was puddled on the floor and soaked into the peeling wallpaper.

Whoever had done this must have splashed bleach on his clothes; he couldn't have avoided it. Whoever had done this was nearing the end of his rope, too.

I thought of going back and telling Meredith about the exploded bottle and its meaning, but decided she'd just dismiss it as evidence that the killer had been looking for hidden drugs "or the other things boys fight and die for." She'd tell me to save it for Buck, bore him with it when he came back from Boston next week.

Oh, I'd bore him with it, all right, but I wasn't going to wait a week. Something told me he was going to have to postpone his vacation. Poor man! I just hoped he'd be home when I called.

It was 11:20 when I got back to my car. As I drove away from the curb, I asked myself where Bert could have hidden the details of Donna's speech. He'd had all the time he needed since Donna's death to find a place to hide them in her apartment, but it couldn't have been there.

Maybe he'd hidden it somewhere else in his own apartment building. I glanced at the old building, standing almost alone in the moonlight, growing smaller in my rearview mirror. It resembled one of the last teeth in an old mouth. It didn't seem likely he'd hide what he thought would keep him alive in a building he didn't spend much time in anymore. Maybe he'd hidden the information somewhere in Donna's building.

In my mind's eye, I walked down the hall from Sumiko's apartment and went past Donna's, just as I'd done the first time I talked to Sumiko. She and Donna had met while standing in front of their doors. Later they'd exchanged keys, because Donna was always locking herself out, and she assumed that Sumiko—her "shadow"—would be absent-minded in the same way.

They'd exchanged keys. Sumiko had Donna's key, and Donna had Sumiko's.

Which meant, of course, that Bert had had access to the key to Sumiko's apartment ever since Donna's death. And it was likely that Bert's killer had that key now.

The thought frightened me, until I remembered that Sumiko was in no danger—at least, not tonight—since she wasn't in her apartment and the building would still be swarming with cops.

For the moment, Donna's and Bert's killer was powerless. There wouldn't be a better time to try to make that condition permanent. It occurred to me that there might not be any other time at all.

I pulled into an all-night gas station and used the pay phone to call Buck. The phone rang a long time with no answer, only this time my heart didn't lighten with every unanswered ring. What if he'd already left? I gave it my usual ten rings, and was about to hang up, when he answered. He sounded as if he'd just come in the door and had hurried to get the phone.

I told him what had happened since we'd gone our separate ways that evening, which seemed so long ago. I told him what I wanted to do now, and why I thought it was the only chance we had to catch a killer.

"We could both lose our jobs tonight, Peggy," he said.

"I know that."

"You're going to have to stall him," he told me, "and even so, I'm not sure I can do it. Search warrants aren't as easy to get in reality as they are on television."

"I don't watch much television," I told him. "Maybe you'll get lucky and find a judge who does. I'll stall him," I assured Buck, "if he's there. It's possible he didn't go to Wolf's party, of course. He's had a busy night."

"In that case, you'll be off the hook. I won't be." He hung up.

I wished I felt as confident as I sounded on the phone, as I watched the red chili burrito heat up in the gas station's microwave oven. I took it out to my car to eat, tossing it back and forth between my hands on account of the heat. My breath was going to be hideous, but that was the least of my worries.

Twenty-Seven

I parked on the street, next to a fire hydrant and under a sign that said "No Parking Anytime." It was a few minutes after midnight. I looked up at the mansion the University gives its president to use. All the downstairs windows were ablaze with light. It looked like a cruise ship as viewed by a shark, or a minnow.

A white limousine was pulling away from the front steps on the curved driveway. President Wolf was standing at the curb watching it go, his vice president, Bennett Hightower, one step behind him, rubbing his hands the way butlers do. The rumor mill was already at work, speculating that Hightower was going to succeed Wolf as president. As the limousine passed me, I glanced in the open back window to see who was leaving. It was Harold McCord. I took it as a good sign: Rats know when ships are about to sink.

My skin felt hot and itchy on account of the sunburn. I was in jeans and a T-shirt and my fingers reeked of burrito. I waited until Wolf and Hightower had disappeared into the house, chatting peaceably. I went up to the front door and knocked. A liveried man with a measured smile opened the door for me. The smile disappeared when he saw how I was dressed. I showed him my shield and told him I had to talk to one of the other campus cops, on business. A city copy materialized from nowhere, looked at the shield and me, and let me past. He was whispering into a walkie-talkie as I left the entryway.

The living room was empty; it looked as if it hadn't been used in years. It was two stories tall, with open corridors running the length of the second floor on both sides of the stairs. Something moved in the shadows up there. I half-expected to see Bert Coombs, in green and yellow, leap up onto the balustrade from the shadows and start juggling, using his clubs with the dark secret that hadn't saved his life, but it was just a security guard.

I passed through the living room and entered the dining room, following the low buzz of conversation, the clink of glasses, and a high-pitched, humorless laugh that went on and on. Because the night was so warm, the French doors on the far wall were open onto a large terrace. Uniformed bartenders at both ends of the room dispensed drinks from portable bars, and pretty young women wearing fixed smiles and pinafores circulated with trays from which guests snatched little canapés. Japanese lanterns hung like moons from wires across the terrace, beyond which Glen Lake stretched away from the house like lead.

A couple of guests looked uncomfortable and out of their element, as if they might be city cops, and they probably were. Security wasn't being left solely to the campus cops this time.

"What in the world are you doing here, Peggy?" It was Paula, looking as stunning as she had a month before at the banquet. She'd somehow snuck up behind me. I noticed she was wearing the silver bracelet I'd made famous.

"I'm here to catch a murderer," I told her, my eyes searching the dining room and terrace to see if my killer was there. "That's not the same outfit you had on at Strauss's banquet, is it?"

"Have you been drinking? Bixler's here, too!"

"Of course he is. Where's Lawrence?"

"Out on the grounds somewhere, wandering around. Peggy, you've got to get out of here!"

"No, I don't."

Coming away from one of the bars was Donald Trask, carefully balancing a full glass. He was showing more concentration on his face than I'd ever seen on Bert's when he had a variety of odd things moving through the air around him. He disappeared onto the terrace.

"What the hell you doing here, O'Neill?"

That, of course, was Bixler, and he couldn't believe his eyes. I couldn't believe them either, since they were popping out of his head.

"I'm going to catch a killer," I said, flinching from his meaty fingers grabbing at me.

"What was that you said, Officer O'Neill?"

It was President Wolf, who'd come up behind Bixler.

"She's suspended, sir," Bixler rushed to tell him, "as of right now! She's here entirely on her own providence." He meant provenance, but he was right anyway.

"Well, then," Wolf said, trying to control his impatience, "I'll have to rephrase the question, won't I? What was that you said, Ms. O'Neill?"

Before I could reply, Jeremiah Strauss entered the dining room from the terrace. When he saw us, he stopped in his tracks and stared. Then he started over toward us, immense in a dark suit some thirty years out of date. His craggy mouth was slightly open, his eyes small and intent. He was trailed by Donald Trask, who was finding it easier to carry his drink now that the level of liquid had dropped.

I supposed Strauss was about to grumble "What are you doing here?" too, but, before he could, Hudson Bates, arriving suddenly from another direction, did it for him.

Bates, as usual, was mostly expensive clothes and mousse.

"Excuse me, President Wolf," he said, inserting himself deferentially among the men, "why don't you let me take charge of this?"

Donald Trask snickered.

"Young lady," Bates said, ignoring Trask and reaching an arm out to stop one of the women in pinafores pushing canapés. "Find one of the policemen—a real policeman, I mean—and do it discreetly. Tell him we have a trespasser, and that we want her expelled at once."

To Bixler, standing there with an appalled look on his face, he said, "The campus police force seems to be no better able to handle the situation here than a month ago in Adamson Hall."

Even I felt that that was being unfair to Bixler, who started to protest, but nothing came out. The serving wench, or whatever she was, looked at President Wolf for confirmation of Bates's order.

Wolf looked at me for a long moment. "You're here to catch a killer," he said. "Donna Trask's?"

He didn't seem fixated on the idea that she'd committed suicide. "Yes," I told him, "and Bert Coombs's. Coombs was murdered earlier this evening."

"I don't think I know that name," Wolf said.

"He was the juggler arrested at Donna's funeral, her boyfriend."

"Let Bates call in the police," Strauss said to Wolf. It was a growled order.

Wolf glanced at him quickly, then looked back at me. "You've been snooping around in this matter a long time, haven't you?"

"Yes," I said.

"You believe you can prove what you say?"

"Yes."

"You know who the killer is?"

"Yes. He's one of you."

"One of us?" That was Bates, speaking in a tone of exaggerated disbelief.

"You're making a mockery of my daughter's death," Donald Trask interjected. To Wolf he said, "This woman came to my home and pretended to be Donna's friend. You saw her. She's crazy."

Wolf's face was impassive. "Do you mean that he's one of us four, or somebody in this house?"

"One of you four," I said. I like playing twenty questions. It was using up time, and that was important.

"Who?" he asked.

"Crowds make me nervous," I answered, looking at the people in the room behind him and out on the terrace. It was a funny place to be clearing up a murder: Four well-dressed men—not counting Bixler—and one gorgeously and one tackily dressed woman, against a backdrop of beautiful people, some of whom were clustered in little groups, their heads together, wondering in whispers what was going on. There should have been music.

"Let's go into my study," Wolf said. "Do we need Lt. Bixler?"

"I don't think so," I said.

We followed Wolf. Bixler stared after us, his mouth hanging open. I caught Paula's eye behind him, gave her a wink and a smile that tried to look brave, and then the door shut behind us.

A wall switch controlled a floor lamp over by the couch. Wolf turned on a gooseneck lamp on his desk. Its circle of light illuminated an Agatha Christie mystery sprawled open on its face on his blotter and a travel alarm clock.

"Make yourselves comfortable," Wolf said dryly and added, "if you can. Ms. O'Neill doesn't strike me as stupid. She did, after all, discover that Donna Trask had access to cyanide, helping clear Edith Silberman's name. We owe her our attention for that." I glanced over at Jeremiah Strauss. His fat lips thinned at the mention of Edith.

"For her sake," Wolf continued, "I hope she has come here tonight with something to say. For our sake, and our University's, though, I hope she is wrong." He looked at me, his large eyes cold with the threat of what my being wrong would entail for me.

Hudson Bates couldn't believe what he was hearing but, simultaneously, he was trying to absorb Wolf's words, cadences, and gestures, in anticipation of the day when he would possess a study like this one and would have to deal decisively with the unexpected.

Donald Trask gingerly felt his way onto a sofa beneath

a wall of books, his glass trembling slightly. He hadn't drunk from it since he'd heard me say that his daughter's killer was one of them.

Strauss settled with a grunt into a dark leather armchair and Wolf took the swivel chair at his desk. Bates looked around. There was no place where he could sit alone. He reluctantly sat on the sofa, but as far from Trask as possible.

"Well, Ms. O'Neill," Strauss said, "get on with it."

"There's nobody in this room who didn't have a motive for wanting you dead, Dean Strauss," I told him, "as I'm sure you know."

"Me, Officer O'Neill?" President Wolf asked. That grin again. He couldn't help it.

"Yes, of course, you, too. Strauss knows a lot about you, and he's used that knowledge to get things he's wanted—the University Scholarship, for example. You weren't president, of course, when he took a huge bribe to expand the University onto the other side of the river, but you must have heard the rumors about it. In spite of that, you made him chair of the conference center committee last year. You gave in to pressure from him to do that."

"These words are slanderous," Strauss said.

Wolf wasn't particularly put out by what he'd heard. He said, "But exactly what is it Jerry has that he's holding over me that would compel me do his bidding?"

"Probably more than one thing," I told him. "However, shortly after you arrived here as president, you bought a piece of land from the University, you and Donald Trask. That transaction was probably illegal. You might have been able to explain it as a 'perk,' the kind that top executives of every big corporation are expected to get now and then. But you promptly turned around and sold that land to a developer, making a big profit. That's not a very appropriate thing for a University president to do, especially not with property that belongs to the taxpayers. Jeremiah Strauss must know the whole story, after all, Donald

Trask doesn't seem to keep anything from his good friend Jerry.

"The thought occasionally must have occurred to you, President Wolf," I went on, "how much more pleasant life would be without Jerry Strauss and the little things, such as the University Scholarship, he asks you for and you don't have the guts to refuse him. So there's your motive for murder: removing a man who knows too much about you for your own comfort and for your sense of who you are—and who knows how to play on your fear of scandal."

Wolf looked concerned, but not on his behalf, on mine. "This is very disappointing, Ms. O'Neill," he said. "You don't expect to convince anybody I tried to murder Jerry Strauss on the basis of what you've just said, do you, even if you had proof?"

"After tonight," I assured him, "I think I'll have enough proof to put Donna Trask's and Bert Coombs's killer in prison for life."

I turned to Trask. "You were the go-between between Strauss and Harold McCord fifteen years ago, at the time the University was expanding across the river. You were McCord's emissary, and it was you who funneled McCord's payments to Strauss."

"That's a lie!" he croaked.

"But even if it were true, so what?" Wolf asked.

"Your friend Jerry," I told Trask, "dealt you out of his latest scheme—getting the University to sell Harold McCord the land for the new conference center. This time, the University already *owned* the land. It owned the land thanks in part to your efforts fifteen years ago. You thought you should get something for that, for your valuable service back then, but Strauss didn't agree. So you've got good reason to hate Strauss and to want him dead."

Trask's eyes were awful as they tried to meet mine. "You think," he stammered, "you think I'd sit there . . . at the banquet . . . and watch my daughter . . . my princess . . . take poison I'd meant for Jerry Strauss?"

"You would if you didn't know what she was going to do when she got up there," I answered him. "After she got to the podium, it all happened too fast for your drunken brain to process in time to do anything about it. I was there, I watched you struggle out of your chair and fall back into it."

"If I'd killed Donna," he said, "I'd have killed myself by now."

Strauss made a disgusted noise. Trask turned and glared at him.

"But you *did* kill her," I told him. "You 'shared' everything with her. Not just your sex life, but everything else, including your shady business dealings with Strauss, McCord, and Wolf. You gave her all the ammunition she needed to damage all of them at the banquet, if she'd had the time. You weren't just a conduit for your friend Jerry, feeding him all the corruption you were involved in; you were a conduit for your daughter as well. And you also passed on to Donna the contents of Strauss's speech, and how he planned to use the apple. You set her up to die."

He tried to say something. Nothing came out.

I looked at the clock on Wolf's desk. I was talking too fast. Buck needed more time.

I turned to Hudson Bates. His large brown eyes met mine without blinking, innocent but wary, a look of studied amusement on his face. "You've done Dean Strauss's dirty work for him for what—almost five years? You've seen all the favors he's done for people in power, people who could be of help to him. But when you asked him to use his influence to get a position for your wife at the U, he turned you down. That must have rankled, Bates."

"Of course it rankled," he said, "I admit that. But surely you don't expect me to break down and confess that I tried to murder him." He tried to catch Wolf's eye, to share the joke with him.

"No," I agreed, "you didn't try to murder Jeremiah Strauss." I looked around the room and said, "Nobody tried to murder Strauss."

"What the hell's that supposed to mean?" Donald Trask demanded.

"It means that Donna was the intended victim all along."

Twenty-Eight

"Why do you say that, Officer O'Neill?" Wolf asked me, breaking the silence that followed.

"Three weeks before the banquet in Adamson," I said, "Donna stole cyanide from her mother. She couldn't have known about Strauss's speech then, or about how he intended to use the apple, because that was two weeks before he started boasting about his speech to his colleagues.

"It wasn't just a coincidence that Donna stole cyanide from her mother and, three weeks later, was killed by an apple laced with the stuff. Unless you believe in coincidences like that, the two things must be connected: The murderer had to know Donna possessed cyanide before plotting his crime. Who could have known that?"

"My daughter knew it," Trask broke in roughly. "She poisoned the apple herself. Maybe she intended to let Jerry eat it—she was a very disturbed child—but she changed her mind and ate it herself."

"No, she didn't," I said. "That's a tidy theory, but it's not going to hold up. For one thing, it doesn't account for the fact that Bert Coombs tampered with the lock on Donna's bedroom window before she died. He wanted something from her apartment while she was still living in it. I can think of only one thing he wanted—the cyanide. And he got it."

"Why?" President Wolf asked. "You don't think he poisoned the apple?"

"No. The only other person who might have known she had cyanide was her—"

"I didn't know about it!" Donald Trask interrupted loudly.

"Probably not," I agreed.

"Why'd she steal the cyanide in the first place," Strauss suddenly wanted to know, "if she didn't plan to kill herself with it? Or me?"

"I think it's possible she did think of committing suicide. How seriously, we'll never know. But she didn't intend to commit suicide the night of your banquet. She had something she wanted to do first."

"What?" That was Wolf.

"She wanted to ruin all of you," I said.

"Me, Miss O'Neill," Hudson Bates asked. "What could Donna Trask have said at the banquet that would have ruined me? I did all I could to help her, I gave her as much time as I could possibly spare."

"You gave her too much of your time," I told him, "some of it after hours. I can produce two witnesses to that. One will testify that he saw the two of you kissing, the other that you came to her door, a week after Donna died, and asked if she could help you get into Donna's apartment, to retrieve something you'd lent her."

"She framed me!" Bates hollered, looking wildly around the room for help. "She waited until there was a witness, and then she kissed me—in public! She was trying to make me look bad."

"What was it you wanted from her apartment, Bates?" Donald Trask asked him, his voice dangerously soft.

"Nothing! They won't be able to prove anything."

"Whatever it was," I told him, "the police are going to be looking for it now. They'll find it, if it's there."

Bates slumped down on the couch. "It was a book. It had my nameplate in it. She took it from my apartment.

She was planning to frame me. But nothing happened between us, really!"

"You sleazy little turd," Trask said, and put his drink down on the floor.

"The truth doesn't matter," I said to Bates. "What matters is that Donna Trask could have ruined you by making her story public. It looks to me as though she had enough on you to do the job."

Donald Trask tried to grab Bates. "It's not true!" Bates said, getting up and darting to the door. "No matter how bad it looks, Donna was only in my apartment for a few moments. I wanted to talk her into giving up on the Humanities graduate program!"

"Stop it, Don!" Wolf said in a voice of quiet steel. "Sit down, both of you." Trask froze in mid-stride. He stared at Bates, his lips trembling, and went back to the couch. Bates stayed where he was, by the door.

"Are you saying Bates murdered Donna?" Wolf asked me.

"No," I replied. "I was just answering his question about what Donna had on him. As I've said, she had something on each one of you, and Bert Coombs knew it. Bert also knew that Donna planned to get up at the banquet in Adamson Hall and tell everything she knew. He thought the information she had was worth a lot of money. He needed money badly, a lot of money, to try to buy medical treatment for his brother, who's dying. But if he wanted to get money for the dirt Donna possessed, he had to stop her from giving it away at the banquet—and the only way to do that was to kill her. He didn't have the guts to do that himself, however. Besides, if he did kill her and then tried his blackmail scheme, he'd be in serious trouble if whoever he was blackmailing decided not to pay up, but went to the police instead. That's always a possibility, even among men like you," I added, favoring them with a little, mean smile, not unlike Donna's last one.

"Wait a minute," Donald Trask said. I stopped and looked at him. We all did, waiting for him to gather his thoughts. "You talk as if it were a . . . a given . . . that my daughter planned to expose Jerry," he said, "and maybe President Wolf, and Bates. But she wouldn't have done that, you see."

"Why not?" I asked him.

"Because—" He was straining his mind, working this one out. His hair spilled over his forehead, down into his angry, bloodshot eyes. "Because—*that would have meant ruining me as well!*"

It came out in a rush. Then he fell back into the sofa, exhausted with the effort of having delivered this telling blow. His eyes stayed on mine, daring me to find a response to that.

I didn't say anything, just let his words hang there in the room. The silence dragged out. Then an eerie noise erupted in the room, and all of us turned our eyes to its source.

" 'That would have meant ruining me!' " Strauss said. The noise started up again. He probably hadn't laughed in years, and this was the best he could do without practice. "Donny-boy," he went on, "I'll bet that was the last thing she had on her mind!"

Trask was up off the couch before Strauss finished the sentence, lunging at him. Strauss's long arm moved through the air faster than I would have believed possible, and his heavy, open hand hit Trask on the side of the face, batting him away as if he were a fly. The noise made me flinch.

Strauss, his eyes like slate, stared down at Trask on the dark carpet. "It was you she wanted to ruin, Trask. She just didn't have the guts to admit it. So she went about it indirectly, pretending it was the University, me, us, she was out to get!" He looked around at the faces of the other men there, glistening in the yellow light.

After several tries, Trask managed to get to his feet, and stood just out of Strauss's reach, rubbing his swelling cheek, debating whether or not to make another kamikaze run. A thin trickle of blood dribbled from the corner of his mouth. He decided against it, went back to the couch, and put his face in his hands. His glass was on the floor next to his feet, its contents staining the rug.

"All right, Ms. O'Neill," Wolf said. "Who is your killer?"

I looked at the clock. I'd forgotten when I started and how much time I'd used up, but I couldn't put it off any longer. *Please, Buck, hurry up!* "Do you want to tell them, or shall I?" I asked Strauss.

"You tell them," he said. "It's your story."

"No," I said, "it's yours. It's been yours all along. I'm only trying to figure it out."

"What's that supposed to mean?" Hudson Bates asked, staring from one of us to the other. "What story?"

"Strauss killed Donna," I said. "When Donna wouldn't agree to use her information to blackmail Strauss, Bert went to him and told him what Donna planned to do with the apple. It was the only chance he had to get any money out of the deal. I don't know if Bert fully realized that it would result in Donna's murder or not. My guess is that Strauss had to convince Bert that the only way they could stop Donna was to kill her. In any case, Bert also told Strauss about the cyanide, and said he could steal it from her.

"It must have seemed like the perfect crime to Strauss: The banquet was supposed to be the triumphant moment of his life. Nobody would dream that he would deliberately pull it down around his own head, that he would make himself look like a fool—not Jeremiah Strauss, the biggest egotist on campus. But you've never done what people expected of you, have you?" I asked him. "You let people think you'd suffered a big defeat in the case of the new conference center, too, when in reality you—and McCord, of course—were the only people who came out ahead."

He didn't reply, just stared at me, a strange look of contentment on his face. It's not pleasant, being stared at by a seemingly contented man who's killed twice, once only hours before.

Wolf said, "If I understand you correctly, you believe Donna Trask knew that Jerry was going to give a speech involving an apple. Bert Coombs went to Strauss with that knowledge and the knowledge of the cyanide, and together they concocted the scheme to poison the apple. Right?"

"Right."

"Why couldn't this Coombs have gone to someone else—to Bates, for example, or even to me? Why did it have to be Strauss?"

I looked at Strauss to see how much he enjoyed that question. His face showed only interest in how I'd handle it.

"The apple," I said, "was a weapon. Somebody had to trigger it at the right moment. If it went off at the wrong moment, it wouldn't do any good at all. You see, Donna planned to give her speech before eating the apple. Just as taking a bite of the apple was to be the climax of Strauss's speech, so it was also going to be the climax of hers. But if she'd been allowed to give her speech, her death at the climax wouldn't have accomplished anything for Strauss—or any of you. So she had to die before giving her speech, obviously.

"Remember what happened immediately after Donna went up to the podium and turned on the microphone? Only Strauss did anything that could be called triggering the apple. It's captured quite clearly in the photograph that appeared in the newspaper the next day. It's really a beautiful photograph of Strauss murdering her."

"He got up from his chair," Wolf said, "and started toward her."

"Yes, and he was moving fast. And if he'd got the apple away from her without her eating it, the evening would have gone on as planned—except, of course, that Strauss wouldn't have taken a bite out of it himself; he'd have held it up at the climax of his speech, and disposed of it safely later. Of course, there would have been Donna's unfortunate interruption of the festivities, which we—the campus cops—would have handled by taking her away with as little fuss as possible. That would have been embarrassing, but not much more than that.

"So Strauss had nothing to lose by rising from his chair and starting for Donna. You might also recall that when Donna reached over Strauss's shoulder to get the apple, he seemed to make an attempt to prevent her. His reflexes were remarkably slow. You saw how fast he was, President Wolf, at the funeral, when he prevented Trask from falling into his daughter's grave. And you saw how fast he was a moment ago, when he slapped Trask down." I turned to Strauss. "And Theresa Durr told me how quick you were when you played jacks with Donna when she was a child."

I watched him as I reminded him of that, saw a shadow move in his eyes and quickly disappear.

"Donna saw him coming toward her," I went on, "and she realized he was going to take the apple away from her. So she decided to speak her climactic line then and eat the apple—an act which she knew would make a fool of him and a mockery of his speech. She didn't know that was exactly what he wanted her to do.

"She thought she could go on with her plan to expose all of you at some later time—any time she felt like it, really—probably by taking her evidence to the student newspaper, which would have had a field day with it."

"None of the rest of us made any attempt to stop her," Wolf said.

"That's right. You actually sat back down when she went to the podium. Bates never stirred from his chair. So none of you could've known what she was going to do, or that the apple was poisoned."

"And the death threats," Wolf said. "You sent those to yourself, of course, didn't you, Jerry?"

Strauss just stared at him. He was still looking relaxed.

I said, "They were typed by Bert Coombs. Strauss couldn't have done it without being recognized. The most recent one Coombs sent on his own, his last threat to Strauss to come through with money to save his brother."

"What proof did she have against us?" Wolf asked me. "Just the sort of rumors that fly around this place wouldn't have been enough."

"You must know," I said, turning to Donna's father.

He was sober now. He stared unblinkingly at Strauss. "Bank records," he answered, "from fifteen years ago, and later, too. Harold McCord's payments to me, and records of my payments to Jerry. I told Donna everything. I loved her, you see, I wanted to share my life with her! But then, one night, I discovered that she'd gone through my files and taken the records. I begged her to give them back. She laughed at me, said she only wanted the information for her own amusement."

Maybe that's what she'd wanted the cyanide for, I thought.

Trask suddenly looked at Jeremiah Strauss. "You killed her, Jerry? You killed my daughter?"

Strauss used his arms and legs to lift himself out of his chair, all in one smooth, quick gesture, just as he'd done at the banquet, and stood towering over all of us. I didn't back away, because I knew how fast and how strong he was, and the room was too crowded to allow for much in the way of maneuvering. His gaze raked the other men, as if looking for something in one of them, somewhere, that wasn't sickening to him and that he could use. He gave it up and looked at me. "You'll be hearing from my lawyer," he said. "I advise you to get one for yourself."

He turned and went to the door, opened it, and started out of the room. Buck Hansen stood in his way, holding a bleach bottle in his hand. He'd been about to knock on the door. Behind Buck, Bennett Hightower, the vice president, swayed like a tree in an uncertain wind.

"You were looking for this earlier tonight, I think," Buck said to Strauss in a voice he reserves for killers. "It was in the apartment next door to Donna Trask's."

Buck flipped it at Strauss, who let it fall at his feet, where it bounced, as once it had done at mine.

"Send the guests home," Wolf called out to Hightower. "Tell them the party's over. Oh, and Bennett, see about canceling tomorrow's groundbreaking ceremony, too, will you? I'll have a statement for the press in the morning."

The University's next president showed no surprise, just vanished, as good butlers do. In the study behind us, I guessed that Hudson Bates was making notes on how a man like Wolf deals with a crisis of this magnitude.

Twenty-nine

I got a good night's sleep. The next afternoon, I drove down to Buck's office. It was too nice a day to spend indoors, so we went out and sat on the edge of the fountain on the plaza in front of the Justice Building. The fountain had only just been turned on, and sunbeams danced in the jets of water. It was summer weather in the middle of May.

Buck didn't look like he'd slept at all. This was the first time I'd ever seen him in need of a shave, and his hair was uncombed. He didn't look like a man about to embark on a vacation. There was a good reason for that.

"If we hadn't found the clothes Strauss wore the night he killed Bert Coombs," he said, "we wouldn't have much chance of convincing a jury that he killed anybody." I was eating a sub I'd bought on the way over. Buck was drinking coffee from his thermos cup. "A good lawyer would make minced meat out of those arguments of yours. And if you hadn't guessed correctly that Bert's clubs were hidden in Sumiko's apartment, we wouldn't have had enough evidence to get a warrant to search his house."

After leaving Omaha's apartment, Strauss had gone home and changed into a suit. He'd arrived at Wolf's party, according to witnesses, about an hour before me. He hadn't bothered to burn or otherwise get rid of the clothing he'd worn at Omaha's, so when the Homicide squad found them, on the floor of his bedroom closet, the bleach from the broken bottle in Omaha's bathroom had done its work. Buck's men also found the key to Sumiko's apartment on Strauss's bureau.

"He obviously didn't expect anybody to find Bert's body anytime soon," Buck said, "and he had no reason to think he'd be suspected even if it were found, so he wasn't in any hurry to destroy the evidence."

That's why I'd called Buck last night. I knew we had to hurry if we were going to get the evidence.

Apparently Strauss hadn't known of Sumiko's connection to Donna, but he might eventually have decided to see if the key fit any of the apartments in Donna's building, once the fuss over Bert's murder had died down. I shuddered at what that might have meant for Sumiko.

The plastic bottles, stripped of their colorful tape, had been hidden among Sumiko's cleaning supplies, beneath her sink. One of them contained not only copies of the records Donna had stolen from her father, and notes Bert had made of what Donna knew of Wolf's and Strauss's business dealings, but also Bert's confession implicating Strauss.

The bleach-stained clothing and whatever else the crime lab people found to prove Strauss had been in Donna's apartment were probably enough to convict Strauss, but you never knew. As Edith Silberman had said, justice is usually just what you can afford in the way of an actor who's studied the law. Strauss would be able to afford a good one. And, after all, he was a University Scholar, he'd been a dean at a major university. People like that don't kill, do they?

Buck said, "I suppose you have an explanation for why Bert let Strauss into Donna's apartment?"

"Sure, for what it's worth. I don't think Bert believed Strauss would kill him before he'd gotten hold of the evidence Donna was going to reveal at the banquet. He didn't realize how desperate Strauss was, or how arrogant and self-assured. Strauss took a big risk, too, coming to

Donna's apartment, even though he used the back stairs. But he must have figured that even if somebody did see him, they would probably have forgotten by the time Bert's body was discovered.

"Bert wasn't meant for this kind of game," I went on. "He didn't really want Donna to die—that's what he was doing in the tunnel before the banquet, trying to save her, to talk her out of going through with her plan—but he'd let Strauss convince him that that was the only way he'd be able to get the money he needed to save his brother's life. Strauss knew that once Bert realized his brother was going to die, he'd confess—or, as Bert told me, finish the speech Donna wasn't able to."

"There's another thing that bothers me," Buck said. "Why Jeremiah Strauss got involved with Harold McCord in his shady dealings. He didn't need the money. From all I've heard, he was quite well off."

I smiled. "His inheritance, you mean, the one he got just at the time he influenced the University to expand over onto the New Campus side of the river? I'm sure you'll know all about his financial affairs soon, but one thing I can tell you now is, there wasn't any inheritance. That was just the story he told to explain the money he got from Harold McCord fifteen years ago."

"How do you know that?"

"A funny old guy I know found out. He called me just before I came over. His name's Curtiss Naylor, a long-time acquaintance and adversary of Strauss's. He thinks Strauss made a chump out of him fifteen years ago, and again last year, and he doesn't like that. A week or so ago, he and I were wondering about Strauss's inheritance, so he took it into his head to try to find out something about it."

"How'd he do that?"

"Well, Strauss never put down in his biography where he got his B.A. degree. That seemed a little odd, so Naylor called the university where Strauss did his graduate work, and asked them. They looked it up for him. It was a small teacher's college in Ohio—kind of an odd place for a rich kid to go to school. So Naylor called there and they searched their files and found the name of Strauss's high school."

"Maybe we ought to hire this Naylor," Buck said. "He seems persistent."

"The person Naylor talked to at the high school knew Strauss's story without having to look it up," I said. "Somebody had been there before Naylor, asking the same questions about Strauss."

Buck swallowed some coffee. "Donna Trask."

"Yes. Strauss had been given a hardship scholarship to college from his high school, thanks to his mother, who taught there."

"And what did his father do?"

"Died before Strauss was born," I told Buck. "Leaving no savings and no insurance. The mother raised and educated her son Jerry on her schoolteacher's salary."

"No big inheritance."

"None," I said. "But according to Curtiss Naylor, when the principal of Strauss's high school heard what a distinguished man he'd become, he suggested they could have a day in his honor, if Strauss would be willing to return and give a speech."

"I'll see that he gets the word," Buck said.

A shadow fell across us and we looked up. A uniformed cop was standing there. He bent down and whispered something in Buck's ear that I couldn't hear, and then turned and walked away toward the row of squad cars parked at the curb.

Buck got up quickly. "Back to work," he said.

I scrambled to my feet. "What was that about?" He was walking faster than usual, back toward his office. I had to skip a few steps to catch up.

"Strauss posted bail a little while ago," he replied, staring straight ahead. People on the plaza got out of his way.

"So what? Now he'll know what it felt like for Edith Silberman, waiting for justice's wheels to turn. What's the hurry, Buck?"

"I guess justice's wheels have already turned," he said, "if that's your concept of justice. Strauss had something waiting for him outside the courthouse that Edith Silberman didn't."

"What?"

"Donald Trask."